GUAVA *and* GRUDGES

GUAVA *and* GRUDGES

Alexis Castellanos

BLOOMSBURY

NEW YORK LONDON OXFORD NEW DELHI SYDNEY

BLOOMSBURY YA
Bloomsbury Publishing Inc., part of Bloomsbury Publishing Plc
1385 Broadway, New York, NY 10018

BLOOMSBURY and the Diana logo are trademarks of Bloomsbury Publishing Plc

First published in the United States of America in September 2024 by Bloomsbury YA

Bloomsbury books may be purchased for business or promotional use. For information on bulk
purchases please contact Macmillan Corporate and Premium Sales Department at
specialmarkets@macmillan.com

Library of Congress Cataloging-in-Publication Data
available upon request
ISBN 978-1-5476-1371-7 (hardcover) • ISBN 978-1-5476-1372-4 (e-book)

Book design by John Candell
Typeset by Westchester Publishing Services
Printed and bound in the U.S.A.
2 4 6 8 10 9 7 5 3 1

To find out more about our authors and books visit www.bloomsbury.com
and sign up for our newsletters.

This book is for Belle, who was with me for the first page and gone by the last. I miss you.

GUAVA and GRUDGES

CHAPTER ONE

There are probably better ways to spend the first night of summer than breaking into a bakery. Like going to a bonfire or setting off on a vacation or heading to the party my best friend, Rose, keeps texting me from. But instead I'm creeping through a dark alley hoping no one spots me.

Okay, so the bakery *is* owned by my family and I *do* have the keys, so it's not exactly breaking in, but it is well after business hours and my parents technically aren't aware that I'm here—for all they know, I'm still at home in bed. My dad can probably tell that I use the kitchen when he's not around, but he's never said anything about it. Maybe he thinks I'm in here perfecting my Cuban baking skills, cooking pastelitos de guayaba until they taste just like his. I'm the heir to his kingdom, after all.

I wonder what he'd do if he knew I was making my own creations, deviating from the family-approved recipes. He'd probably be more upset with *that* than my sneaking out.

Good thing he isn't here.

Once inside, I flip on the lights and begin setting up my station. My phone buzzes in my back pocket, likely another text from Rose with another reason to join her at Devin's party tonight. But I'm on a strict schedule this summer, and I need all the time I can get to perfect my recipes. I pull on my apron, embroidered with my name by my abuela, and wash my hands. Last night I worked on my new croissant recipe, and when I ran out of time, I opted to do the second proof in the fridge.

But when I open the fridge tonight, the croissants aren't in the same spot I had left them. I look around the shelves, growing a little frantic until I see the plastic container shoved into the back of the top shelf. Someone must have crammed the three gallons of whole milk on the shelf so hard that it knocked the lid off the container.

"No, no, no," I say, pulling out the milks so I can reach my croissants. "No!" I cry out again as I pull aside the lid and hope they're still usable. But the damage has been done. The croissants have dried out entirely, turning my beautiful, layered dough into a crusty mess. There is no saving them. And to add insult to injury, I buy all my own ingredients for my experiments, so this means thirty-six dollars of my hard-earned cash has been wasted.

"Stupid milks," I mutter, dropping down to the floor with the desiccated croissants in my hands. They look so shriveled and sad. Is there a market for croissant raisins?

Normally a setback like this wouldn't bother me so much—trial and error are a normal part of recipe testing, after all—but the stakes feel so much higher these days. So far, the summer before senior year hasn't felt as carefree as the ones before. My future looms just on the other side of August, and both of my parents have already made it very clear what their expectations are. Unfortunately, they have very different visions in mind. Even more unfortunate is neither of their visions align with mine.

I pull out my phone, ignoring the red bubble of my unread texts and navigating instead to *La Mesa*'s website. The banner on their homepage is familiar to me now: TENTH ANNUAL SCHOLARSHIP COMPETITION. I click on the link for the millionth time and read the description again.

For Latin American students interested in furthering their food-related education, our scholarship awards $10,000 and a special feature in our September issue to one talented applicant. Two runners-up are awarded $5,000 each in addition to having their recipes published in La Mesa's *magazine. To apply, please submit an original recipe, a process video no longer than a minute showing how to make your recipe from start to finish to be posted on social media, an essay telling the story behind your recipe, and a completed application. Applications are due July 18. Eight finalists will be chosen by our judging committee and announced August 8. On August 22 the* La Mesa *chefs will be announcing the winners on an hour-long live stream, where they will cook all eight recipes.*

Winning this competition is the key to my future. That money would get me one step closer to my dream of going to culinary school in Paris. After that is probably years of grueling away in kitchens around the world until I finally become a head pastry chef with my own kitchen, serving up my take on Cuban American desserts. But first, I need a winning recipe.

I have just under four weeks to develop the perfect recipe, and I'm off to a terrible start. I put down my phone and stare at my crusty croissants. If I don't figure out an award-winning recipe soon, I'll spend the rest of my days wasting away at the family bakery, baking the same things we've baked since 1987.

My phone buzzes again. And again. Rose is sending me a flurry of texts.

I'm bored.

Come save me

Catherine has been bragging to me nonstop about her PSAT score

Lor is here come be my wingwoman I need you

My croissant failure hasn't exactly put me in a partying mood, but I don't have nearly enough ingredients left over to try making them again tonight, either. I open the calendar in my phone and look over my timeline.

If I go to the grocery store for ingredients tomorrow and pull an all-nighter next week I can get back on track. I'll have to pick up more shifts at the shop to account for the lost ingredients, but since my mom is the scheduler, I don't think I'll have a problem.

My phone begins to vibrate again, a phone call this time.

"Amy!!!" Rose cries into the phone. "Ammmyyyyyyy!"

"Yes, you've reached Amy, what is it?" I ask, deadpan.

"Get your cute little butt on that bike of yours and COME HERE. I'm dying without you. I put on One Direction, and Devin snatched the speaker from me and insisted that they were not 'the vibe of the night' or whatever."

"I don't know, Rose. My croissants are a total bust and now I've lost all this time . . . I'm not exactly fun to be around right now," I tell her as I walk out to the back dumpster and throw my dead croissants in. "I'm just going to go back home and sleep."

"You know, I saw Sofía talking to Peacoat Kid," she tells me. That catches my attention.

"Class Dealer Peacoat Kid?" I confirm. My sister *loves* rebellion. Anything that our family does not approve of, she does with gusto. And because she is the beloved youngest child, she never gets in trouble for it. It also helps that I make sure she never gets too deep into whatever rebellious urges she has.

"Yep, Port Murphy High's number-one source for pills. You should come here and save her!"

Even if Rose is lying to get me to go to the party, I won't take that chance. Sofía should be nowhere near Peacoat Kid.

"I'll be there in fifteen."

Rose squeals in delight, and I'm almost positive now that she's lying about Peacoat Kid.

I rush and clean the dirty container and set the kitchen back up the way my dad left it. While I lock up Rose sends me three more texts that I don't look at. I hop on my bike and head off down Main Street toward Devin's house.

At this time of night, most of the businesses are closed except for the bar at the far end, where only a handful of locals can be found. The main drag is quiet and deserted, but even in the dark it holds on to its small-town charm: lampposts decorated with bright perennials and building facades from the 1800s that carry the vestiges of the past. The local co-op still has the original sign for the Port Murphy General Store, and the antique store on the corner still has the name Richmond Mills painted in white on the brick exterior.

As I make my way down Main Street, my eye catches on the community board in front of the town square. With the school year recently ending and summer in full swing, the board is full of flyers.

The tires of my bike squeal as I come to an abrupt stop in front of the square. A little detour won't take up too much time, I tell myself as I walk my bike up to the board.

There's a poster advertising the city's fireworks show, which is always lackluster and has historically low attendance. Someone is starting up a yoga in the park series and someone else is advertising their work as a dog walker. But they're not what I'm looking for.

I zero in on the poster promoting Morales Bakery's Fourth of July special and tear it down.

Morales Bakery is the *other* Cuban spot in our small town, and the biggest competition for Café y Más, our family shop. You'd think after three decades of existing across the street from each other the two bakeries would have come to some kind of truce, but the animosity runs deep. The Morales family isn't just the family that runs the rival bakery across the street. They're the family that undermined my abuelo at every turn when he worked for them before ultimately betraying him.

The way my abuelo told it, at first the Ybarras, my family, and the Moraleses were the best of friends back in Cuba. After Castro's revolution, the Moraleses fled to Miami in the sixties and lived there for a few years before relocating to Seattle, so Blanca Morales could attend nursing school. Andres Morales and his wife ended up settling down in Port Murphy, where they started a family and opened a bakery.

My abuelos, Felipe and Josefina, and their children (including my dad) fled Cuba in the late seventies and settled in Miami, like many exiles before them. They had no money and no close relatives to help them out in the States, and according to the brief stories I've gotten from my dad, those years were difficult. Things were only made worse when my abuela was diagnosed with breast cancer a few years later. Battling her cancer drained them of most of their savings, and the Ybarras were struggling. And so they reached out to old friends from Cuba.

The Moraleses were happy to help my family back then. Blanca Morales was now a nurse at a hospital in Seattle and was able to get my abuela a good doctor, and Andres had a job for my abuelo at his bakery. Together my abuelo and Andres built up Morales Bakery, adding new things to the menu and drawing in loads of new customers. The bakery became a local favorite despite folks not having known anything about Cuban food or culture before the bakery popped up in their town.

My abuela's treatment went well, and the American dream was finally coming true for my family. Until the Moraleses betrayed us. Their shop had been doing okay before my family showed up, but as soon as Morales Bakery started using my abuelo's recipes their shop blew up. And when my abuelo asked to be fairly compensated for the work he had done for Morales Bakery, Andres said no. So my abuelo took what meager savings he had and opened up his own shop, where he had complete ownership over *his* recipes.

That all went down almost twenty years before I was born,

but I was raised with the memory of that betrayal in me—it is practically part of the Ybarra DNA at this point. Which is why I crumple up the Morales poster in my hands and glance over my shoulder to check for witnesses before shoving it in my backpack to be disposed of later.

With that detour out of the way, I hop back on my bike and head down to Bayview Road. This is where all the rich kids from school live. The houses are all waterfront with docks and boats in the back, pristine manicured gardens, and at least one luxury car in the driveway. Most are owned by people made wealthy by one of the many tech giants in Seattle.

Devin's father mostly works as a consultant, I think, and her parents travel a lot, mostly without their kids. Devin takes advantage of their frequent absences, large liquor collection, and general negligence to throw ragers every summer. She also guilts them into one lavish Europe trip every year. I couldn't come up with anyone with a life more opposite to mine, but Devin is nice enough.

As I roll down the long driveway through pine trees and blooming rhododendrons, I can already hear the party. Some of it has spilled out to the front lawn and porch, where my peers have perched themselves on the railings as they pass around a joint.

I drop my bike down on the damp grass next to the driveway and stroll up to the house.

"Amy!" I hear someone say in surprise before coughing on the hit he just took. James Locicero—nephew of the owner of Locicero's, the only decent sit-down restaurant in town—is gaping at me in surprise. "I never see you at these things!"

It's true that I usually skip Devin's parties, but not always because I *want* to. Most summers I'm balancing two jobs and am too tired to do anything other than flop down on my bed at the end of the night.

Unloading all that on James seems like a bad move, though. I'm saved from having to formulate a response when I hear someone else cry out, "Amy!"

Rose barrels out of the front door, Smirnoff Ice in hand, and shrieks with glee when she sees me.

"Amy!"

"Yes, yes, you got what you wanted," I tell her as she tries to tackle me with a hug. I'm nearly half a foot taller than she is and heavier, so she doesn't even come close to making me lose my footing. I hug her back regardless.

"I lied about Peacoat Kid," she mumbles into my chest, her ice-cold drink burning my lower back where my shirt has ridden up.

"I figured," I say, and I can't say I'm mad at her. After the croissant failure, I might as well hang out with Rose and hold her hair later when she pukes in some bushes.

"You need a drink," she continues, speaking directly into my cleavage.

"And you need some water," I tell her, peeling her from me and grabbing her hand.

Devin has pulled out all the stops for this party. Christmas lights have been strung up all around the house, providing just the right amount of ambient illumination to make it look like something out of an indie teen film. A seriously powerful sound system blasts dance music, and there is even a giant fold-up table full of cheese as soon as you walk into the house.

9

Goat cheese, Camembert, triple creme brie, apple cheddar, twenty-four-month aged Manchego (according to the carefully written label), and more, but Rose drags me away before I can inspect it further. At least half of Port Murphy High is at this party, in addition to kids from other nearby towns. The dining room has been turned into a flip-cup arena, where people are chanting names and shouting.

The kitchen is by far the most cramped room. Everyone has chosen to stay close to their source of alcohol, whether that be the tub of ice filled with handles of vodka and Smirnoff Ices or the keg.

"What's your poison?" Rose asks, dumping out the remainder of her drink in the sink and dropping the bottle in the recycling bin. Next to it is the compost bin, where the drunken teenagers have mindfully been throwing away their uneaten strange cheese and used napkins. Even drunk, the Earth comes first.

"Two waters," I tell her.

"Boo!" she responds immediately, bending down to pick up two Smirnoffs.

"Absolutely not," I tell her. "Those are disgusting."

Rose groans and picks up the vodka.

"Just have one drink with me, okay?" she pleads. "This is our last chance to let loose and do whatever we want! After this summer it will be college applications and SATs and then job applications and *bills* and *taxes*!"

"Okay, fine, fine," I say with a laugh. "I'll make some vodka cranberries."

Rose claps with joy and watches as I put together our drinks.

"What has Sofía been up to anyway?" I ask as I get some ice.

"Nothing terrible," Rose assures me, her voice serious. "She's been hanging out with her gaggle of friends in the backyard. Someone got the fire pit going, and she's just been roasting marshmallows, very tame stuff."

"Good," I say, reassured. Rose is an only child, but we've been best friends since the second grade. Sofía is basically her little sister, too. "Taste it," I instruct her, handing over one of the cups. It's more juice than vodka, but I doubt Rose will notice. I added a squeeze of lime juice from a lime that might have been more decoration than practical, but it served to give our drinks that pinch of zing it needed.

Rose takes a big slurp of the drink and smacks her lips in satisfaction.

"Perfect. ¡Salud!" She crashes her Solo cup against mine before putting it back to her lips and taking a deep swallow. "Now, we dance!"

Rose goes out the back door to the deck, where she seems to have commandeered her own speaker and has One Direction playing at full blast. We dance alone on the deck, screaming the lyrics as the vodka begins to make my head spin.

"One more drink?" Rose begs, and it doesn't take much convincing to go back into the kitchen and make us more. Rose stays out on the deck, where one of our classmates, Liz, has joined us in our dance party.

"Well if it isn't my big bad sister." I look up and see Sofía leaning against the doorway to the dining room, a sly grin on her face. Her wavy dark hair is loose around her head and in desperate need of a brush. She wears a pair of baggy jeans and black crop top that has a melting smiley face embroidered across the front. She manages to make the rolled-out-of-bed look very cool and unapproachable.

"I heard you've been by the fire all night, you little pyro," I tell her, pouring vodka into my cup.

"You know me, like a moth to flame." She sidles up next to me and watches as I pour cranberry juice into the cups.

"Don't stay out too long tonight, we have the Barry wedding tomorrow morning," I remind her.

"We just need to load the van, it's no big deal," she says, brushing off my warning.

"Whatever," I say, slightly annoyed. "I have to go bring this to Rose. Text me when you leave."

"Yup," she says before blowing a kiss in my direction and filling her empty cup with water from the sink. Maybe she listened to what I said after all.

When I go back out to the deck, Rose is nowhere to be found and Liz is dancing by herself.

"Where's Rose?" I ask over the music as Liz grapevines and shouts along to the song. "Liz!" I shout, waving my Solo cup in her face. She looks up at me but continues her, what appears to be choreographed, dance routine. "Where did Rose go?"

Liz shrugs and resumes her performance. The only place I can imagine Rose going to at this point is the bathroom, so I go back into the house through the open french doors that lead to the family room.

Here the vibe is very different. Some song made popular on social media is blasting from the speakers, but no one is dancing. Groups of people are hanging out in pockets around the room, Smirnoff Ices and red Solo cups in hand. I may have only been to a party here once before, but I remember where the bathroom is.

Some people catch my eye and nod hello, and I apologize to others as I have to squeeze in behind them to get through doorways. I'm in the formal living room, my attention caught by the spread of various forms of cocktail weenies, from pigs in a blanket to weenies swimming in barbecue sauce. Rose can wait a little longer for her drink. I set it down to grab a pig in a blanket, and just as I pop it in my mouth, a familiar voice—one I thought I'd never hear again—rumbles behind me.

"Ana Maria?"

CHAPTER TWO

My name isn't really Amy. My full name is Ana Maria Ybarra, named after my mother's favorite great-aunt. I *love* my name and think it sounds beautiful—but only in Spanish.

In English the cadence of my name is completely lost. Ah-NAH Ma-RIA becomes Anne-UH Mur-REE-Uh, making it sound like it reeks of disappointment. Even as a five-year-old in kindergarten I couldn't stand it.

When my teacher and classmates would say my name incorrectly I would cry in frustration and throw a fit. There were parent-teacher conferences, and Ms. Golding tried her best but it was never *right*. One day, she came up with a solution.

We could take the initials of my name, AMY, and use that as my name in class.

And so Amy Ybarra was born.

Sometimes I forget altogether that my real name is Ana Maria. My parents usually call me by terms of endearment instead of my name, and Sofía—whose name sounds great in both English and Spanish—usually calls me Amy to irritate me.

Even Rose, my closest friend, calls me Amy. Amy is the all-American girl with a stellar GPA and her nose in a book. She speaks perfect English, enjoys casseroles, and sneaks out of the house. Ana Maria is the dutiful Cuban American daughter who helps her parents at their bakery and looks after her little sister. She speaks perfect Spanish without a gringa accent, makes the best flan de coco, and listens to Buena Vista Social Club while she works.

I'm both girls, but sometimes it doesn't feel that way. Sometimes it feels like I'm not allowed to be both Amy and Ana Maria. Not until this moment, as a voice rumbles my given name in a room full of people who only know me as Amy.

"Ana Maria?" The voice says again (pronouncing it perfectly, of course), a little uncertain this time.

I cough on the pig in a blanket I had just scarfed down. Puff pastry crumbs are on my lips and fingers, and I rush to wipe them off. My fingers stain my jeans with oil as I nervously swipe them on my thighs.

When I turn around, my lips glossy from the grease of the pig in a blanket, it feels like Amy and Ana Maria have crashed into each other in a head-on collision.

Because in front of me is Miguel Fuentes, a boy that has felt like a figment of my imagination for the last six months.

"I thought that was you," Miguel says, a satisfied smirk on his face. He smiles broadly, the dimples on his cheeks appearing under his stubble.

I must be hallucinating. Or dreaming. Maybe I never woke up this morning and this is a weird dream featuring a strange mix of foods and the boy I thought I'd never see again.

For months I've been thinking back to the day I met Miguel, of how magical and surreal the whole thing had been. What was meant to be a boring college tour at UCLA had turned into a whirlwind food tour with a handsome stranger. A day that had ended with a kiss, and the brilliant idea to not exchange phone numbers or anything. In my mind, keeping in touch long distance would have cheapened the magic of that afternoon. In reality it just meant a lot of screaming into pillows with frustration and sighing dreamily. Rose has, quite rudely, pointed out that I *would* meet a random Cuban dude and fall head over heels for him. I've never dated anyone in Port Murphy before. No one has really caught my interest, and, although not an explicit rule, I know my parents would like to see me with a Cuban. And since the only Cubans in town are my cousins or Moraleses, my options here are zero.

Until right now.

Miguel looks just like he did six months ago: slightly disheveled hair, white T-shirt tucked into jeans, and a blue unbuttoned flannel. He has a camera slung over his shoulder and a gold chain around his neck with a charm for San Lazaro.

In other words, he looks unfairly good.

"This is weird," I say, the alcohol turning my brain to mush in an instant. "This is so weird," I repeat.

"Weenies!" Jordan, a dude from my algebra class, exclaims, cutting in between Miguel and me so he can ladle weenies in barbecue sauce into a used Solo cup.

I catch Miguel's eye, and we laugh as Jordan scoops up a second spoonful.

"How about we go talk on the porch," Miguel says over Jordan's mop of curls. Miraculously, Jordan has managed to cut the tension with his enthusiasm for weenies, and the buzzing in my head that started when I saw Miguel has begun to quiet.

Until he reaches for my elbow, grasping it tightly in his hand and pulling me through crowds of people. As soon as our skin touches, my stomach drops and my head rushes and I'm buzzing with excited anticipation all over again.

Definitely not a dream.

When we make it out the front door, the crowds have thinned out enough for him to drop my arm, and I physically ache when he lets go. I follow him along the wide veranda to the side of the house, away from the group I had seen earlier sharing a joint.

Miguel leans back against the railing and looks down at me with a quizzical smile, like he's also delightfully confused by our surprise reunion.

"You said you were from Seattle," he says with a playful challenge.

"Well, most people don't know where Port Murphy is. It's easier to say Seattle, it's only an hour away."

"You could say Forks," he suggests. "I hear it's quite the popular destination."

"Is that what you're out here for? A little vampire pilgrimage?"

He laughs at that, a low, deep rumble that has me gripping the cups in my hands a little harder. I swear I even hear the plastic crack a little.

"I'm working in town for the summer. My uncle got me a job out here."

"This is so weird," I say, *again*.

"It really is." He laughs. "Are both those drinks yours?" He asks, jerking his chin at the cups I have in a death clutch.

"One was supposed to be for my friend, but she disappeared somewhere. Do you want it?"

"A concoction by *the* Ana Maria Ybarra?" he says, and the way he says my full name sends shivers down my spine. I need a stable surface. I sidle up next to him against the railing and pass him Rose's drink.

"Don't judge my work by this drink alone," I warn him. "My options for mixers were limited. I wish you did have something of mine to try, but I came empty handed."

"Well, I'm here all summer," he says, taking the cup from my hand. I swear he lets our fingers touch on purpose, letting them linger for a moment before pulling away. Memories from six months ago come rolling back at the touch and I can feel myself blushing.

"Don't they have jobs in LA?" I ask, trying to banish those memories.

"It's a tough market out there, Ybarra. You can't turn down nepotism when it comes your way. Besides, you once told me the Pacific Northwest is the most beautiful place to spend a summer. I had to come see what it was all about."

"Well then, as a fellow nepo baby, cheers," I say, lifting my Solo cup to his.

"¡Salud!" he says when our cups smack together, sloshing sticky red liquid over our fingers.

We take our sips while looking at each other over the rim of our cups. He's smiling so big that his eyes are nearly slivers and his dimples are on full display. I never thought I'd see that smile again.

"The universe is up to something," he says, as though he can read my thoughts. "I stuck to our rules. I never googled you or anything, though I was tempted."

"I didn't either," I say. I don't mention all the times I almost did. And there had been many times. "You know, my mom found out I ditched the tour. I did *not* tell her I ran off with a boy I had just met, but she was pissed anyway."

"Oof," he says, knowing the wrath of a Cuban mother himself. "Was it worth it?" He wiggles his eyebrows and somehow manages to be both silly and suggestive.

"You're just fishing for compliments," I tell him, slapping him on the shoulder playfully. "It was worth it for that shawarma sandwich."

"Just the food?" he asks teasingly, his voice a little lower.

"The company was decent, but I was really in it for the food," I tell him, shooting him a playful glance.

"Well, since I gave you a food tour of my hometown, I think I deserve a tour of Port Murphy from you," he insists.

"I mean, you've already experienced the best Port Murphy has to offer at the Weenie Table," I tell him seriously. "Have you ever seen so many cocktail weenies in different forms? Have you ever seen a guy guzzle a cup full of cocktail weenies and lukewarm barbecue sauce before tonight?"

"That was a first," he says with mock solemnity. "I hope to never hear those sounds again."

"Wait until you hear Jordan after a keg stand," I tell him. "Just a symphony of gurgles and burps."

"I'd rather not experience that," Miguel says, shuddering.

"You'll be safe if we stay out here," I promise.

"No ditching this time?"

"This is Port Murphy," I say, deadpan. "This party is likely the only exciting thing happening tonight."

"We can make our own excitement, can't we?" he asks, meeting my gaze. "Why don't we sneak into your parents' bakery so I can taste test those pastelitos de guayaba that you bragged so much about?"

"That's not a half bad idea," I say. "But I don't let just anyone sneak into the bakery with me, you know." I turn to face him, resting my hip against the railing. He matches me, and his hand reaches out to my elbow.

"I promise to be good," he says. "And I'm hungry."

His hand slides down my arm, his fingers grazing against my skin until he takes my hand in his. And it's like we're back in LA, where this guy I'd just met saved me from heat stroke and a college tour I didn't want to do by taking me around to his favorite food spots near the campus. The fastest way to my heart has and always will be food, and he'd found the express route.

Now, miraculously, he's here, in my town. That same instant, electric connection when we had first met has not gone out in the months that have passed. As his thumb grazes across the back of my hand I think that the feeling is somehow stronger now.

I'm ready to pull him down toward the side steps when I hear Rose behind me letting out the most telenovela-worthy stage gasp.

"AMY!" she shouts, startling me and everyone else on the porch so badly that the crowd outside silences for a moment. "How could you *fraternize with the enemy*!!"

I turn to look at my best friend, who clearly must be losing her mind, ready to shake her until her wits return.

"Rose, what is your problem?" I ask, seriously irritated. She has just broken through the haze of this picture-perfect, absolutely fated second-chance encounter with the guy I have been crushing on for the last six months. And for what? To scream nonsense at us? Her eyes are nearly bulging out of their sockets when she turns her attention to me.

"What's *my* problem? You are committing the first cardinal sin of being an Ybarra!"

"Are you now the arbiter of Ybarra sins?" I ask. Maybe she'd had more to drink than I realized. "This is Miguel, the guy I met in LA," I explain to her slowly. "I told you about him." I would be embarrassed to admit this in front of Miguel if I weren't already so embarrassed by Rose's outburst.

"You did *not* tell me he was a Morales!"

"He's not!" I say, immediately offended. Like I'd ever do something so stupid as getting involved with a Morales. "His last name is Fuentes." I look up at him to confirm. "It's Fuentes, right?"

"Yeah . . . ," he says slowly, his wary eyes on Rose, as though expecting her to pounce on him next.

"He showed up tonight with the Morales twins," Rose hisses at him. "He's their *cousin*."

A different kind of electric shock shoots through me. That can't be. He's a Fuentes. He's *from LA*. There's no way the Morales twins are his cousins.

But he had said that his uncle got him a job here this summer.

"Where are you working this summer?" I ask him slowly, dreading his answer.

"Why does it matter?" he asks instead of answering.

"Answer the question!" Rose demands, even louder than before.

Miguel jumps and says, "Morales Bakery."

No.

My head drops into my hands. This can't be happening. The one guy I've ever liked—who I met hundreds of miles away in a completely different city—is a *Morales*.

"I have to go," I mumble, dropping my half-finished drink on a table decorated with a mosaic of a frog.

"Ana Maria," Miguel calls out, but Rose is there to block him.

My feet are picking up speed. I'm running down the veranda, past the smokers, down to the lawn where I had dropped my bike. My fingers are clumsy as I undo the buckles on my helmet, my sticky fingers unable to gain purchase on the plastic.

I growl in frustration, trying to banish the look of hurt and confusion on Miguel's face from my mind. Once the buckles are loose, I slam the helmet on and pull up my bike.

I climb on, my gut swirling with dread as my mind struggles to comprehend what has just happened.

Every family has its rules. Some are the kind you're expected to follow but the consequences of breaking them are light. Empty the dishwasher when you get home from school. Take off your shoes at the front door.

Some have more serious consequences. Like not texting my

mom to let her know where I was after going to Rose's house after school. Or bringing home a lackluster report card.

And then there are some rules that must *never* be broken.

"Ana Maria! Wait!"

I risk a look over my shoulder as I peddle down the winding driveway, and he's there, leaping off the veranda to chase me. He's gotten past linebacker Rose, but she's not far behind him.

Even from yards away I can make out the plaintive expression on his face from the hazy amber light leaking from the porch. Doesn't he know this isn't how he's supposed to act? Ybarras and Moraleses are opposing magnets, meant to repel each other at every turn.

I turn around and pedal harder, determined to be the force that repels.

Because some rules are never to be broken.

At the top of that list? Never, *ever* trust a Morales.

CHAPTER THREE

Miguel Fuentes?" Emily, the unnervingly cheery UCLA tour guide with a hand-drawn smiley face on her name tag, calls out from her list of prospective students. No one answers.

If this guy doesn't show up soon I'm going to lose my mind. The people that arrived *on time* for the campus tour are all standing in full sun in the middle of this bizarre winter heat wave Los Angeles is having. Mom dropped me off ten minutes ago, the smile on her face a clear sign that she thinks I'm going to fall in love with her alma mater on this tour. I already know I don't want to go to school here, so instead of letting her see my complete lack of interest live, I convinced her to spend the day with her sister while I sweat my way around campus.

"Miguel Fuentes?" Emily tries again, changing up her pronunciation. She wipes a hand across her brow, mopping up the river of sweat that has started to accumulate. "Miguel?"

Everyone's heads swivel around as they try to find the missing Miguel.

"No Miguel?" Emily tries one last time.

"Here!" An out-of-breath voice calls out from behind me, followed by the sound of sneakers slapping against the concrete as Miguel finally appears.

Looking at him, you wouldn't know there was a heat wave in Los Angeles this weekend. He's in a black shirt and jeans with a backpack slung over one shoulder. Instead of looking disheveled and gross—which is how I and most of the group looks at the moment due to the sweltering heat—he looks laid back and comfortable. His dark hair is a little overgrown, an errant lock falling over his eyebrows, and his skin is the golden tan of someone who lives somewhere sunny.

"Miguel Fuentes?" Emily confirms.

"Miguel Fuentes," he repeats, shooting our tour guide a smile that shows off his unexpected dimples.

Emily nods and continues down the list, but instead of following along to see who raises their hands to what names, my eyes stay on Miguel. I'm not sure *why*. He's certainly attractive, but LA is overrun with attractive people. I can go for a walk around the block in my tia's neighborhood and bump into at least ten people who are probably models or actors or influencers.

Maybe it's because he's the only other person in our tour group who's here solo, but unlike me, he doesn't look uncomfortable at all. That's probably it.

I'm still admiring his profile when I suddenly sense eyes on me. Then *Miguel* turns his eyes on me and catches me staring. I jump like I've been shocked and turn to see that the entire group, in fact, has their eyes on me. Emily is staring me down, irritation creeping into her cheerful mask.

"Ana Maria Ybarra?" She says in the most grating American accent. This is clearly not the first time she's called out my name. My mom signed me up under my full name and not my nickname, which is why I hadn't caught it.

Not because I was distracted by some stranger.

"Call me Amy," I reply as I raise my hand in acknowledgment. Emily gives me a weak smile and makes a note.

"All right, that's everyone! Let's get this thing started."

Emily begins her tour with a perfectly practiced speech. There is no room for questions or interruptions in her monologue, and even if there were, I don't think anyone would take her up on it. We follow in stoic silence, using brochures as fans to try and cool down. It's not long before my head begins to pound from the sun and heat, and I can't focus on anything Emily is saying. After my embarrassing moment with the group, I opt to take up the spot all the way in the back so no one can see me. Part of me wanted to go on this tour hoping that it would spark that *thing* in me that would make me want to go to college. But all it's done is given me this terrible headache.

I begin to lag behind the group until my steps falter and my toe catches on an uneven piece of pavement. I go tumbling down, scraping my knees and palms as I fall. My vision falters for a moment, slipping in and out as I try to sit back on my heels.

"Hold up!" I hear someone call out. There's the sound of shoes hitting concrete and then a shadow looms over me, bringing with it the smell of woodsy shampoo.

Miguel Fuentes squats in front of me as my vision returns. He's looking down with concern as he unclips the metal water bottle from his backpack. That stubborn lock of hair is still sitting on his forehead and draping over his left eyelid giving him a kind of rakish look.

"Here, drink some water," Miguel says as he hands me the bottle. I take it without question and greedily swallow down some water. "Take it slow or you'll make yourself sick," he warns me.

"Fucking desert," I groan as I take the recommended break between gulps. I'm not cut out for this climate. I'll take the surprise mold in your house from the consistently damp Pacific Northwest over this weather any day.

Emily breaks through the tour group, who are now back to staring at me from a distance. A tour and a show, they must feel so lucky.

"What happened? Are you all right?" Emily asks.

"I'm fine," I wave her off. "Keep doing your tour."

"Do you need emergency services?" she asks, her phone already out.

"It's just the heat," I assure her.

"I've got her," Miguel assures Emily. "You can continue the tour without us."

"Are you sure, Amy?" Emily asks.

"Please," I tell her, wanting the ogling eyes of the tour group off me.

Heat stroke wasn't the sign I wanted, but it was the sign I got: UCLA is not for me. *College* is not for me. My mom is going to be devastated, but nothing about this campus or the idea of going to school here appeals to me. And continuing Emily's well-rehearsed tour is not going to change that.

Emily gives us one curt nod before gathering the group back up and continuing on course.

"Thanks for the water," I tell Miguel as I pass it back to him.

"No worries," Miguel says, offering me a hand to help me back up. As soon as our skin touches, a static shock zips between us, knocking me back on my butt in surprise. "Jesus," Miguel remarks in surprise. "It's so dry today. Let's try again."

He helps me up this time without any surprises. I still feel a little woozy and I consider texting my mom, but she's probably halfway back to Tia's house. I want to let her have her girls' day.

"Do you have any cramps? Do you feel sick?"

"I'm okay," I assure him. "Go catch up to the tour. Thank you for your help."

"Ah, we have a martyr," Miguel says, clasping his hands together and nodding sagely.

"No!" I argue. "I just don't want you to miss out on the tour because I did something stupid."

"Oh, so it was *your* weather machine that brought us this lovely heat wave?"

That gets a laugh from me. "No! I'm the idiot who had Cuban coffee for breakfast and nothing else."

"Ouch," he says playfully. "Hurt by your own people."

I look up at him in surprise.

"How did you know I'm Cuban?" I ask suspiciously.

"Because *I'm* Cuban, and I've got great Cuban radar," he brags. "Ninety-nine percent accuracy. Which means I also know that jet fuel for breakfast does not a meal make. You need to eat something."

I look around. We're not far from where we started the tour, the Bruin bear still visible and the familiar smell of food-court fried food is wafting over from the building on my left.

28

I remember the drive in, cutting through Westwood Village to get to campus and seeing all the restaurants and coffee shops that lined the streets.

But Westwood Village is a fifteen-minute walk downhill, and I'm not sure I can manage that. I look over at the building that is emanating the smell of a mall food court.

"I'm going to have to eat Panda Express, aren't I?" I lament, too exhausted to care that I am displaying one of my worst traits: I'm a picky eater. It's not that there are certain foods I won't eat, like broccoli or ricotta cheese. It's just that there are certain preparations that I am completely against consuming. Most fast food falls on that list, but I do have a soft spot for McDonald's fries. Anything slathered in mayo and placed on a potluck table is an immediate no, and the only food courts I will go to are the ones my tia has taken me to in K-Town. And I have a feeling the UCLA food court isn't going to be nearly as good as the ones where you can get Korean fried chicken, gimbap, a katsu plate, delicious noodles, and Japanese cheesecake all in one place.

"I have an alternative solution," Miguel says, his lips quirking up in a sly smile. "You probably can't do the walk down to Westwood Village, but I'm parked in the garage around the corner, and I can drive us down to Diddy Riese."

"What's a Diddy Riese?" I ask.

"Ah, so you're not a local," he says. "It's an ice cream sandwich shop and an absolute Westwood staple. I'm sure ice cream will help you recover from the heat."

I look Miguel up and down, taking a moment to size him up. He's tall, easily over six feet, and looks like he probably plays some sport at school. He's got friendly eyes, and he seems like the kind of guy who's open and honest. I know I probably shouldn't take a ride from a stranger, but I am still feeling a little faint and he's been so kind since the moment I nearly passed out.

If anything, I have pepper spray in my purse.

"You know what?" I say, returning his friendly smile. "That sounds perfect."

I follow Miguel to his car, where he has another water bottle stowed away that he shares with me. We drive down to Diddy Riese and order ice cream sandwiches, running back to his car and the AC before they melt completely in our hands.

I'm swallowing my first ginormous bite before he's even back in the driver's seat.

"You really are hungry." He laughs when he sees that I'm already a quarter of the way through my sandwich.

"I really didn't think through this morning," I say, taking a pause so I don't add brain freeze to my list of ailments. "I've been really stressed about this campus tour because my mom is an alum and she really wants me to love this place and go to college here. She wants 'big things' for me," I say, adding in finger quotes with my free hand for emphasis. "And she's convinced herself that going to school here is how I'll do that."

"But you're not convinced?" he asks gently, immediately aware that this is not a topic I am comfortable discussing.

But this is a stranger, a guy I met during a campus tour and whom I'll probably never see again. My anxiety surrounding this trip has reached a head, and spilling everything to this complete stranger is easier than speaking to friends or family will ever be. Part of it *is* because he doesn't know me, my life, or the people in it. For him, this is just a story. But it's also because of his energy. He seems to radiate calm and makes me feel at ease.

"I'm not even sure I want to go to college," I say, admitting something out loud that I've been thinking quietly for months now. "I don't care about academia, I don't want to work a typical nine-to-five, and I don't want to spend the rest of my life in debt for something I could probably just learn on my own online anyways."

"I get what you mean," Miguel says, wiping off a smear of mint chip ice cream that has made its way to his cheek. He licks the ice cream off his finger, and I feel a blush rise up from my neck. I turn my focus back to my sandwich. "I don't love the idea of sitting in school for four years, waiting to do the thing I know I want to do."

"What do you want to do?"

"I want to be a cinematographer. In theory, you probably could work your way up to that level of work without college, but college certainly makes it a little easier to get there. I also think the arts degrees are a bit of a different experience compared to finance or communications. I would be taking classes that are hands-on, exposing me to real-world work before I graduate. Plus, some of the best cinematographers have gone to UCLA. It's a path well-trod."

"That's nice, having a path to follow," I say, considering the paths I know of that I could follow. My dad's, a path toward inheriting a family business that's struggling to keep the doors open. Or I could follow the path of my mom and Tia, getting a degree in some random field and spending the rest of my life not actually doing much with it in the end. Or the path my mom has envisioned for me, a life where I get a fancy degree and go to grad school and become some kind of respectable professional in a career that she can brag about.

None of those paths appeal to me.

"Making your own path is good, too," Miguel says, catching the wistful tone in my voice.

"I suppose I can," I say, considering my dream of going to culinary school. I know my mom would turn it down, insisting that I should go to college for something "practical." My dad would be offended that his personal education in how to cook is not enough for me. After all, if I want to cook for a living, I can just run the shop with him. But I don't want my world to be restricted by what's practical or the confines of the bakery's walls.

We finish off our ice cream sandwiches in silence and wipe off our sticky fingers with a few good licks and napkins.

"Was that satisfying?" he asks, taking my empty cup and stacking it with his. "Are you feeling any better?"

"I am," I say. "Although this is quite the unconventional lunch."

"Oh, so it's lunch you wanted? Why didn't you say? I can do lunch. I am quite the connoisseur of the LA food scene," he tells me with a winning smile.

"I couldn't even imagine living in a place with this many options. How do you pick where to go out for dinner? I would get decision fatigue every time."

"Most of the places in this city are window dressing, tourist traps and trend chasers. The locals know where the good stuff is," he says confidently. Then, a little less sure of himself, "I can show you, if you want."

"Show me what?"

"A more conventional lunch option. We're not far from some of the best Persian food you'll ever have. I know a shawarma place that will blow your mind."

"Don't you have things to do other than drive me around to restaurants all day?"

"Well, I did have the tour, but since we've skipped out on that my afternoon is free."

I check the time. Technically, the tour still has an hour left to go. And I told my mom I would take time to eat and explore after. But I didn't anticipate that I would climb into a stranger's car and go wherever he recommended.

But he hasn't led me astray so far.

"Sure, let's go."

We share a chicken shawarma in Little Tehran, where he tells me he would order us the knafeh if we hadn't just had ice cream sandwiches. The meat in the sandwich is tender and delicious, covered in crunchy vegetables and wrapped in thin lavash bread. We order the mint lemonade, which isn't the most appetizing color but tastes amazing.

I ask him about his work, and he shows me the cameras he's carrying with him today. One is a digital camera that has the retro look of a film camera, and the other is an instant camera. He snaps a shot of us, heads tipped toward each other with big goofy smiles on. When the picture prints, I'm mortified to notice a piece of parsley stuck between my teeth.

He takes another picture after I remove the offending piece of green, and he claims this print for himself. He offers to let me check out his digital camera, but I laugh off the offer because I'm not sure I could figure out how to turn it on let alone take a picture with it. He tells me how he fell in love with photography and what his favorite films are. I listen with rapt attention, absolutely charmed to see someone talk about something they clearly love.

"I want to go to pastry school," I say suddenly, giving life to something that has only existed as a vague idea in my head for years. "In Paris."

"That so cool!" he says, sounding genuinely interested.

I keep going.

"I want to be a pastry chef at a Michelin-starred restaurant. I want to develop recipes and write cookbooks. I want to travel the world and eat food from every corner of the Earth."

"That's quite the path," he says, impressed by my secret dream.

Miguel asks me a million questions after my admission, from my favorite dessert to the food city I'd like to travel to most. He makes it seem like a foregone conclusion that I'll get what I want, and his confidence in me sets something alight.

Neither of us want our lunch to end, and when Miguel mentions the food in Sawtelle offhand, I insist he has to take me there next.

Despite being fairly full from both an ice cream and chicken shawarma sandwich, we share a bowl of lechon and rice at a Filipino restaurant. The pork is topped with pickled cabbage, a fried egg, and a delicious tomato vinaigrette. If I could, I would follow this up with a bowl of ramen from across the street. And then cream puffs and a katsu sandwich. There's just so much good food, and I want to try it all.

"This is what happens when a small-town girl comes to the big city," I groan when we leave the restaurant. "I'm overwhelmed. I've eaten too much. I want to eat more. Everything looks so good!"

"How much longer are you in the city?" he asks.

"We leave tomorrow morning, this was just a quick trip for the campus tour." I try not to notice the disappointment weighing heavy on me, or how Miguel's face mirrors how I feel. I try to change the subject. "I feel kind of bad that I didn't even do it. The tour, I mean. What if my mom asks me about some weird campus tradition? 'Sorry, Mom, I had a terrible tour guide?' "

"Well, we can drive back to campus now and walk off some of this food and I can give you a tour?" Miguel offers.

"You're an excellent food guide, but I don't know about your UCLA tour guide credentials."

"Hey, my parents both went to UCLA, so I know a fair bit of lore. And between that and Google Maps I'm sure I'll be able to cobble something together. But first, boba?"

I can't turn down the offer of boba, so we stop in a shop and each order a drink. I get a passionfruit mango slushy with strawberry popping boba and Miguel gets milk tea with cheese foam and brown sugar boba. He lets me take a sip from his drink, and I offer him some of mine. Then we're back on the road toward Westwood.

My phone buzzes with a flurry of concerned texts from my mom.

Mijita, it's getting late. Wrap it up, I'm heading over now.

"Oh no," I say as Miguel turns into a parking spot. "My mom's on her way back to campus."

"Time for a speed tour, then!" Miguel jumps out of the car and runs over to the passenger door, pulling it open and offering me his hand. "Let's move!"

Laughing, I take his hand and we run out of the parking lot. I can hardly keep up between my full stomach and all the laughter that's bubbling out of me.

"Slow down!" I cry out.

"But you have to see the whole campus!" Miguel insists, tugging on my hand to make me run faster. "We have to at least get to the inverted fountain!"

I keep pace with him down the path and around the corner, where he finally brings our crazed run to a halt. We've made it to a large courtyard with a circular fountain. Instead of shooting up into the air, the water runs across a rocky surface before falling into a hole at the center, giving it its name. Around the courtyard are students walking around or studying on the benches and stairs.

"Okay, inverted fountain," Miguel says, out of breath. I'm doubled over, trying to settle my breathing and my stomach. "This is, uh, important. There's something about touching it. And then also not touching it."

"Wow," I say, "what insightful information."

"You can just tell your mom you didn't pay attention to the tour because you were really distracted by this handsome guy," Miguel says, shooting me a cheeky smile.

"You wish!" I cry out with a laugh, slapping him playfully on the shoulder.

"That's going to be my excuse when my mom asks me tonight how the tour went," he says, but this time the joking tone from before is gone. When I look over at him, he's watching me seriously, a timid smile tugging at the corner of his lips.

"Okay," I say, suddenly a little shy. "It's not the worst excuse."

"Come on, let's keep going."

"No more running, please," I beg.

"No more running," he promises, before setting off up a staircase. I watch him walk away, taking a moment to appreciate the sight of him. Tall, athletic, confident. In high school, his type is a dime a dozen. But there's something different about Miguel Fuentes, something that calls to me. An instant connection.

But we live a world apart. And it will stay that way, with him going to UCLA after graduating and me . . . well, I don't know what I'll be doing, but I'm certain it won't be that. If I only have the minutes left between now and the moment my tia's Volvo pulls up, I'm going take advantage of every second.

I run to catch up with him, and without thinking twice, I grab his hand with mine. Miguel looks down at me in surprise for a moment, like he's expecting some stranger to be there instead of me. But once he registers it's me holding tight onto his hand, his face breaks out in a smile. I return it.

Our tour continues at a meandering pace, and Miguel points at buildings and then reads their names off Google Maps. When we make it back to the spot where we left the tour, he takes a moment to stop and point.

"That's where some Cuban girl nearly passed out from heat stroke because she didn't eat breakfast," he says.

"It was the heat and the caffeine!"

"What a wimp, this temperature is nothing!"

"Okay, say that to the group of students we passed each holding up one of those personal spritzer fans you get at theme parks."

"Wimps, all of them."

Before I can come up with a retort, my pocket buzzes and my stomach sinks. This perfect afternoon with a handsome stranger is coming to an end. I pull out my phone and check the text.

"My mom's parking at the Trader Joe's and wants me to meet her there," I tell him.

"Okay," he says softly, "we can head that way."

We continue chatting, but the tone has shifted. Neither of us is looking forward to this ending. Our pace slows, trying to drag out our last moments together. His grip tightens for a moment before his thumb starts idly stroking the back of my hand. I lean in closer to him and drop my head on his shoulder.

The moment we reach the end of campus, our clasped hands drop and we turn to face each other.

"Thank you for the tour," I say.

"I'm always happy for an excuse to eat a bunch of food," he says with a smile. "Thanks for nearly passing out and giving us the excuse to do it."

Miguel reaches into his back pocket for his phone, and I know immediately what's going to happen next. We'll exchange numbers and follow each other on Instagram. I'll go home and we'll text back and forth for a couple of weeks, but it will feel only like a fraction of the chemistry we had in person. I'll see pictures of him hanging out with his friends, pictures where he's sitting too close to someone and it will drive me crazy. And the memory of this perfect day in LA will be overshadowed by the pale imitation we've made through text and social media. Our paths are not likely to cross again, our futures going off in very separate directions. It's a miracle our paths have crossed at all today.

So I put a hand down on his to stop him.

"No," I tell him, my voice serious and a little sad. "Let's just keep this here. In this moment."

"What?" he says in surprise, dropping the hand that's holding his phone. "What do you mean?"

"I'm not going to go to UCLA. I probably won't be back in LA for years. You're going to go off to Hollywood and become an award-winning cinematographer, and I'm going to be in Paris or New York or Milan working at some famous restaurant. If I were sold on going to UCLA things would be different. But I'm not sure we're ever going to see each other again. And I'd rather have the memory of this perfect day with you than a sporadic text thread where we just send each other memes about bread or something."

"A perfect day, huh?" he says as a smile slips on his face. Miguel returns his phone to his pocket and leans back to consider. "Okay, Ana Maria. We leave things here, then. A perfect day come to a perfect close, no open endings."

"Exactly," I say, relieved that he understands where I'm coming from. My pocket buzzes again, likely another text from my mom. I need to go. But my feet are planted, unwilling to take a step away yet. "I'll look out for your name in movie credits," I promise him.

"I'll keep an eye out for your cookbook," he returns.

Miguel and I could drag this goodbye out forever, staying rooted here until we have no options but to just stay together. But I have a life to return to in Port Murphy, with homework to finish and exams to study for.

"Goodbye, Miguel Fuentes," I say before stepping in for a hug.

His arms wind around my shoulders as I pull myself in tight. With my face pressed against his chest I'm overwhelmed by the heady smell of him, a mix of cedar and something unique. Miguel brings his face down next to mine.

"Goodbye, Ana Maria Ybarra," he whispers next to my ear, and the sound of his rumbly baritone sends a shiver down my spine that I'm sure he can feel.

We hold on for a beat too long, well past a friend hug. My pocket buzzes again, reminding me to return to reality. I pull back from him, and I can feel his hands drag, holding on to our touch for as long as he can.

"Good luck with UCLA," I tell him as I take one, two, three steps away from him.

"Good luck forging your own path," he says, tucking his hands into his pockets.

I take one deep breath and turn away, and it feels like I'm fighting against a magnet's pull as I try to put distance between us. Unable to resist it entirely, I look over my shoulder at him. He's still standing there, hands in his pockets with an almost wistful expression. I turn back around, determined this time to go to my mom.

But the gravity that pulls me to Miguel is too strong. An impulse I can't name hits me, and I'm weak against it.

I turn around again, but this time I run toward Miguel. His eyes widen in surprise as he watches me sprint toward him, but he stays still, waiting for me to reach him.

I come to a halt in front of him, gasping for breath, and his brows furrow as he watches me. But he stays quiet, curious to let whatever I have in mind play out.

Feeling braver than I've ever felt, I reach up with one hand to cup his jaw. It's sharp, with just the barest hint of stubble. At my touch I can feel his jaw clench, and I feel a jolt of power in knowing that my touch alone can elicit a response in him. I push it further, taking another step forward until our bodies are pressed flush against each other.

His breath skirts across my skin as we watch each other silently. Miguel's eyes rove over my face, reading my expression before finally landing on my lips. A hunger sparks in his eyes, igniting a flame in my belly.

Pushing up onto my tiptoes, I brush my nose against his, enjoying the warmth of our proximity. But Miguel remains motionless, waiting for me to make the move.

I smile before pressing my lips against him, a soft touch, just the faintest graze. And Miguel comes alive under my hands at that touch. A moan escapes his lips and brushes over my skin as his arms snake around my waist and pull me in. Warm hands brush over the bare skin at my back as his mouth opens to mine, and I can finally taste him. Sugary sweet and warm, his tongue dips into my open mouth and now *I'm* the one making sounds. I grip his face with both hands, enjoying the feel of his skin under my fingertips.

This is too sweet to ever forget. I've made things a thousand times worse for myself by kissing Miguel, but I don't regret a second of it. I may never kiss someone like this again in my life.

We pull back from each other, gasping for breath as I rest my forehead against his.

"I just wanted to make sure you wouldn't forget me," I whisper.

"There's no way I could forget you, Ana Maria."

CHAPTER FOUR

As soon as I make it out to the open street I let out a scream of frustration, in the hopes that my voice will drown out the echoes of Miguel shouting my name, chasing me. I pedal home hard, throwing all my confusion and frustration into getting me home as quickly as possible. Rose has tried calling me at least six times, and as soon as I'm off my bike I shut my phone down. I can't deal with her right now. First, I have to get a handle on the mess of emotions I've been cycling through.

I can't believe I betrayed my family like this. Rose was right when she said I'd broken the cardinal Ybarra rule by fraternizing with a Morales. I'm not the rebellious daughter (that's Sofía). I've always followed the rules my parents set, respected them—well, for the most part, anyway. Lately, it's been feeling harder and harder to live up to their expectations.

But hating the Moraleses has always been easy.

Even if I thought the feud was a little over the top given how much time has passed since the onset, I follow the rules. I don't speak to the Morales twins at school, even when Adrian Morales says something snide to me as I pass him in the halls. Sofía and I pull down every flyer for their bakery that we see on community boards or street posts. I give the wrong directions to every tourist who crosses my path looking for their bakery. For all the rules I've bent, I didn't dare touch the No Morales one.

Until six months ago when, without even knowing it, I had broken it completely.

I had kissed a Morales!

No, I can't think of that.

I drop my bike against the lavender bushes under the bedroom window. Sofía and I keep it unlocked on nights like this when we sneak out, not wanting to risk being heard coming through the front door. When I climb inside, Sofía is already in her bed, fully clothed and snoring. I don't know when she'd left the party, but at least she hadn't been there to see the whole scene. Hopefully she's still none the wiser about Miguel.

I pull off my top, throwing it down to a corner of my closet where it won't be found for at least half a year. It's been tainted by the memory of this terrible night. I change into my pajamas and climb into bed.

In just a few hours, my alarm will go off and Sofía and I will go help dad with the cake for the Barry wedding. I will go work in the bakery the rest of the day, continue to test my recipes at night, and research ideas for more by day. I won't have time to torment myself over Miguel. My schedule does not permit it.

But that doesn't stop me from burrowing my face into my

pillow and letting out a muffled scream, just as I've done many times since meeting Miguel.

"Levántate!"

I wake up with a start at the sound of my mom's chipper morning wake-up call. In our small house her shouts carry into our bedrooms despite the closed door. When I open my eyes I find that the pressing weight on my chest that I thought was anxiety is actually just my cat. And also maybe a little bit of anxiety.

Azúcar, the cat in question, watches me owlishly with icy blue eyes, and I wonder if she's begun to contemplate eating my face for breakfast.

"I don't want to," Sofía mumbles into her pillow, throwing her comforter over her head to block out the sounds of the morning. I shift slightly and this is enough to upset Azúcar. She jumps off my chest and slips through the tiny cat flap on our bedroom door.

I pick up my phone from my nightstand and realize I never turned it back on last night. I press the power button and dozens of texts from Rose load in, as well as a couple from James. I half expected pleading texts from Miguel but am suddenly grateful (and, annoyingly, a little disappointed) we never exchanged numbers. I ignore all the messages and look at the time.

"You better get up now if you want to take a shower," I tell my sister. "Mom let us sleep in, and your hair looks terrible."

"I'll just wear a hat," she mumbles.

"That's not part of the uniform," I point out.

"Dad won't care."

I roll my eyes and get out of bed. She's right, Dad probably won't care. Sofía, as the baby of the family, gets away with everything. I, on the other hand, pull my towel off the rack hanging behind our door and head to the bathroom. I need to wash off all vestiges of last night, because I swear even though I changed my clothes, a not-so-unfamiliar scent still clings to me. If anyone gets too close I worry they'll be able to smell the betrayal on me.

"Good morning, mija!" Mom says as I walk down the hallway toward the bathroom. "Apúrate, your dad just left to go pick up the van from Harry's."

Our delivery van had gotten a flat tire yesterday, and Dad had rushed it to his friend's shop for a fix. It seems like something is always wrong with the van, from the broken radio to the family of mice that had lived in the engine (they're probably the reason the radio went out in the first place). It's a miracle it still ran at all.

"Have you made coffee yet?" I ask from the bathroom door.

"Why? Are you tired?" Mom asks, appearing suddenly from around the corner. It's so fast I don't have time to duck away, but I still inch closer to the bathroom, hoping she can't smell the Morales on me.

"These early morning catering gigs are no joke," I say with a weak smile, shrinking under her gaze as she examines me.

"You can come back home afterward and take a nap," she says.

"Aha," I say, wagging my finger at her. "But I can't. I'm working at the shop this morning. No rest for the wicked." Little does she know how wicked I've actually been.

46

"I'll have café con leche ready to go in travel mugs for you and your sister," Mom assures me in lieu of giving me the afternoon off to contemplate my current circumstances. "And don't forget you have that stack of college brochures that came in the mail."

Ah yes, the college brochures I was planning on throwing in the recycling bin.

"Yup!" I say with false cheer as I hurry into the bathroom.

I take a quick shower, letting the water get so hot that I can't think of anything other than the feel of the water scorching my skin.

Ana Maria?

Memories of last night threaten to torment me, and I fend them off by brainstorming recipes.

Coconut arroz con leche with mangos. Dulce de leche croissants. Cuban Victoria sponge.

I scrub my legs, willing myself to forget everything from last night. But Miguel has had six months to embed himself into my mind, and he is not so easy to exorcise, even if he is a Morales.

The bathroom door opens loudly, and it's enough to startle me from my thoughts.

"Knock first!" I shout at Sofía.

"Whatever," Sofía says as she sits down on the toilet and begins to pee.

"Don't you dare flush—" I begin to shout at her, but I can already hear the clink of the toilet handle before the sound of rushing water. "*Sofía!*" I shriek as my hot water quickly becomes shockingly cold. I scramble to turn it off, the last of the soap suds slipping to my feet.

"Ugh, it's too early, I forgot," Sofía says by way of apology.

"You've lived here your whole life! How could you forget?"

"Girls, stop shouting!" our mother shouts from the kitchen.

I step out of the shower, and Sofía is pressed up against the bathroom mirror, attempting to apply her eyeliner in a mostly fogged mirror. After wrapping a towel around myself, I slide in next to her and bump her out of the way so I can brush my teeth.

"You're in a bad mood this morning," Sofía mutters as she stares in the mirror open-mouthed applying mascara. Her hair is already pulled up into a ponytail with a baseball hat she got from our uncle that says "¡Fuácata!" It's bright purple and doesn't match the white of our cater-waiter uniforms, but since we're just delivering a cake I know our dad won't complain about it. Sofía is an expert at rebelling within limits and it drives me crazy, but only because I can't manage to do it.

"Niñas! Hurry up, your dad is outside!"

Sofía, dressed and ready to go, leisurely strolls out of the bathroom as I rush out into our bedroom and change into my uniform. My hair, cut short to my chin for the summer, is easy enough to get towel dry quickly, but my bangs still need to be blow dried to look decent. I rush back into the bathroom and pull out the blow dryer and my round brush.

"We're going to be late," Sofía calls out from the hallway where she is sipping her café con leche as she leans against the archway.

I ignore her and quickly blow out my bangs, leaving the rest of my hair a wavy wet mess. I meet Sofía in the hallway, where she passes me my travel mug full of coffee. With the way this morning is going, I'm going to have to make myself a second cup when we get into the bakery for my shift.

When we go outside, I can see Dad through the windshield, tapping anxiously on his steering wheel as he waits for us.

"Morning, mijas!" he calls out through the open passenger window. "Speed it up!"

I glance down at my watch to see if we're running behind. We're not. But my family loves to make mountains out of molehills. Not that I don't understand my dad's anxiety around this wedding. This was one of our biggest cakes yet for a local news reporter with a big social media following. He's hoping this wedding will bring in lots of business for us, so he's been agonizing over this cake for weeks.

"Morning, Dad," Sofía and I chorus as we pile into the van. Dad has his phone in the cupholder blasting Celia Cruz, and I quickly pick it up and turn down the volume.

"Oye," he complains. "Don't mess with my music."

"You can hardly hear it over the sound of the engine, Dad," Sofía points out. "Why don't we just get a new van already? This one is days away from catching fire, I swear."

I roll my eyes. Sofía manages to live in an alternate reality where the struggles of our daily lives are not immediately apparent to her. My parents are very good at hiding our financial problems, but I've seen the books. We can't afford a new van. We could hardly afford the new oven we got for the bakery last year.

"Enough about the van," Dad cuts in. "Sofía, when we get to the shop I need you to run down to Michelle's and get the flowers. She should be in early this morning, so just knock on the

49

back door. Your sister and I will start loading the cake into the van when we get there."

"You got it," Sofía deadpans from the back.

Summer is the busiest season for the bakery by far. Port Murphy is on the Olympic Peninsula, right between Seattle and the Olympic Mountains. When tourists and locals alike swarm the national forests for hiking trails and kayaking trips they tend to stop into town for something to eat. The Pacific Northwest is also a desirable spot for a summer wedding, and we're usually booked out the entire summer for cakes.

The cake for the wedding today is a classic design, wrapped in fondant to look like draped fabric and studded with edible pearls. It is five layers, and once we get to the venue, Sofía and I will use our artistic eyes to expertly place cascading fresh flowers along the cake.

Dad backs into a parking spot in the back of Café y Más, and I jump out of the van and go into the bakery. Eddie, my second cousin, is hard at work in the kitchen getting ready for the morning rush. We're the only coffee shop around here open at seven on the weekends, and people in this part of the country *love* coffee. The morning rush is by far the worst shift to work, and I'm glad I'm on cake duty this morning.

"¡Buenos días!" I call out to Eddie.

"I have a colada ready for you guys on the counter," he calls back as he pulls out a tray full of fresh Cuban bread out from the oven.

"You're an angel!" I rush over to the counter and pour myself a shot of Cuban coffee from the colada. No offense to Mom's coffee, but *this* is what fuels me. Between the sugar and caffeine, I'll be ready to power through this early morning.

Together with Eddie's help, we load up the cake boxes into the back while the AC blasts. It's not quite hot in the morning yet in Port Murphy, but even just a little warmth could be enough to get the cream cheese frosting melting, making the cake layers slide around.

When we're almost done Sofía appears with a cardboard box full of flower arrangements. Before we're off, Eddie puts together a little box of treats so we can get something in us other than coffee. Sofía immediately tears into an empanada de carne and I pull out a pastelito de guayaba as we get back into the van and get on the road.

None of us are particularly chatty in the morning, so the ride is quiet. Sofía already has headphones on in the back seat, totally engrossed in whatever she's watching on her phone, and Dad takes the opportunity to turn up the music on his janky cup-holder phone speaker. I pull out my phone and begin to aimlessly scroll through social media.

My feed is full of images of my classmates having all kinds of summer fun. Tubing down rivers, hiking on Mount Rainer, international vacations with family, and summer college courses at various illustrious campuses.

I can't help but feel a pang of jealousy. My summer fun is going to be limited to the bakery, day and night. I don't have the money or time to spend on fun getaways. And even if I did, I have no way of getting there without a car. The most exciting thing I'm bound to do over the next three months is climb to the top of Rose's roof and stargaze while she tells me one wild story after another.

The last thing I had posted pops up next. It is a picture of a tray of pastelitos I had baked. It has gotten five likes. In my mind the picture looked cool, rows of laminated dough and bubbling filling. But the actual photo had been . . . well, it hadn't been good. I couldn't get the image in my mind to translate to what I was getting on my phone screen. The disconnect drives me crazy, and I rarely post because of it.

I scroll past it in frustration and the next thing that pops up is an ad.

It's a video that looks professionally made, full of beautiful shots of glistening pastries with luscious-looking fillings and perfect editing. It is, of course, an ad for Morales Bakery.

CHAPTER FIVE

I should just block Morales Bakery on all social media for my own well-being, but I need to be on top of what our competitor is doing. Even if I can't convince our dad to let us start an Instagram account for the bakery. Though, considering the track record for my own social media, it's probably better to not have one for the shop.

This ad is the video that propelled Morales Bakery into the stratosphere. People all over the country know about them now and travel to little ole Port Murphy to get a taste of their famous creation: the Dessert Burrito.

It has been featured in dozens of media outlets and influencer videos. Morales Bakery even has a website where you can buy T-shirts that proclaim: "Morales Bakery, Home of the Famous Dessert Burrito!" YouTubers drive into town to record themselves eating the monstrosity, and influencers take pictures holding the burrito next to the mural on the side of their bakery.

The mural is, of course, of an anthropomorphic dessert burrito.

The popularity of that monstrosity is beyond me. Nothing about it looks appetizing and, judging by the videos of people struggling to eat it, it is a bear to consume. My dad had turned absolutely apoplectic when he first saw the thing. "Burritos aren't even Cuban! How could they call themselves a Cuban bakery at this point?"

For months he would just mumble to himself about the burrito whenever the line outside the Morales Bakery wrapped around the corner while our sales dwindled.

Not being able to go into Morales Bakery myself, I had asked Rose to go on a covert mission on my behalf. Of course, she refuses to patronize Morales Bakery on principle, so she asked her lab mate in chemistry to go and bring back a dessert burrito to her house before they worked on a project together. While Rose and Bobby worked on their homework, I took the burrito to the kitchen table and performed an autopsy.

The following make up the monstrosity known as the Famous Morales Bakery Dessert Burrito:

For the tortilla, they use a thick, rather eggy crepe to hold the whole thing together.

The rice is a sickeningly sweet arroz con leche that is seasoned with cinnamon and star anise and made with too much condensed milk.

The beans are adzuki beans, which is really where the whole thing starts to go off the rails.

The ground beef is crumbled-up chocolate cake with red food coloring and added chocolate chips for texture.

The pico de gallo is made up of diced strawberries, mint, white chocolate shavings, and diced kiwi.

The lettuce is shaved coconut dyed green.

All in all, it is the most horrifying food creation I have ever witnessed.

But this video manages to make it look almost . . . appetizing? How much money did they spend to produce this? I mean, it's clearly paid off, judging by the lines outside the bakery.

I continue to watch the ad loop in horrified fascination. I have pitched so many new recipe ideas to my dad over the years, recipes way better than this stupid burrito, but he won't hear it.

"This is a traditional Cuban bakery."

"We don't need that fusion bullshit."

"Ay, mija, this is the same menu we've had for thirty years, it's not changing."

Which is why I had started my late-night escapades, working in the bakery to develop my own recipes that will never see the light of day if I stay in Port Murphy.

I finally scroll past the ad in frustration.

Soon after we pull into the venue—a rustic barn that has turned into a popular wedding spot since it has gorgeous views of both the water and mountains. Dad doesn't even bother telling me and Sofía what to do because we're already moving like a well-oiled machine. We unload the cake into the venue's kitchen, and Dad assembles it, making small repairs while Sofía and I prep the flowers. The bride pops in mid–getting ready to see the finished cake with her wedding party and immediately bursts into tears, causing her maid of honor to panic about makeup.

"Oh my God, Mr. Ybarra," the bride cries as her friends

helpfully fan at her face to help dry up the threatening tears before they fall. The entire bridal party is standing in the ballroom where the cake is currently sitting front and center for everyone to admire in their matching pink-satin robes. "You captured my vision perfectly, I love it!"

"I'm so happy to hear that," Dad says, absolutely beaming. Dad has a right to be proud, the cake is beautiful. Between my sister's artistic direction with the flowers and the elegantly draped fondant, the cake is stunning. It is made up of a white sponge with alternating layers of raspberry compote and fresh lemon curd. It's tart and fresh and by far one of the most popular flavors at the bakery. As the bridal party continues to titter over the cake, Dad pulls Sofía and me away.

"I'm going to pull the van out to the front. Why don't you girls grab our equipment from the kitchen and I'll meet you outside?"

Sofía and I give our dad a mock salute and part ways in the lobby.

"I can't believe people choose to get married in *barns*," Sofía says, at full volume, on our way to the kitchen.

"Sofía!" I hiss, slapping her on the shoulder.

"What? It's weird! This used to be full of cow shit and now people say their vows here, it's gross."

"Keep it to yourself," I snap at her.

Packing up is quick work. Sofía passes off the leftover flowers to the wedding planner, and I box up all our tools. I'm in front of the kitchen window, washing some spatulas, when a blur of white and something familiar streaks past. I freeze, wondering if the events from last night have me hallucinating Moraleses where there are none.

Panicked, I throw open the window and peer around the side of the building, where a smiling anthropomorphic dessert burrito winks at me before turning the corner.

"Oh no, oh no, oh no," I chant, dropping what I was cleaning down into the sink and running out of the kitchen. I nearly trample Sofía on my way to the lobby and latch onto her wrist to bring her along.

"Jesus, Amy, did you see a rat or— "

But I don't need to say anything, because at that moment, Valeria Morales walks into the lobby carrying paper bags emblazoned with the Morales Bakery logo. She doesn't look much like her twin brother. Adrian is well over six feet, with chiseled cheeks and a crooked nose from playing football. Valeria is a little shorter than her twin with a square jaw and big, light brown eyes. They both have light brown hair, but ever since we started high school Valeria has been dyeing it a dark auburn color that sets off the small smattering of freckles that erupt across her cheeks every summer. What they do share is their light olive skin tone, thin lips, and the blood of my enemy.

Her eyes bulge at the sight of me and my sister, but before any of us can do anything about our encounter, the sound of enraged Cuban men interrupts us.

"What the hell are you doing here?" I hear Dad's distant voice yell.

Mr. Morales yells something back that I can't quite make out, and Valeria just rolls her eyes at the sound and shrugs past us with the bags.

"Oh, fuck," Sofía whispers, understanding the gravity of what is happening.

This is an important job for Dad, and not just because of the bride's social media presence. Catering and cakes have been the primary reason we've been able to keep the lights on. Getting into a brawl with another grown man in the parking lot of an event wouldn't be a great look.

Without another word, Sofía and I take off.

When we burst out of the front doors, I take in the whole ugly scene. Our van is parked a few feet from the door, engine still running and driver's side door sitting wide open.

A few cars down is the Morales Bakery delivery van, shiny and new, with the back doors thrown open to reveal more brown bags filled with a delivery order. Adrian is sitting on the back bumper with a smug smile on his face as he watches the standoff between our dads.

"You didn't think to step in here?" I hiss at Adrian.

"And miss the show?" he replies, clearly enjoying himself.

He's always been my least favorite Morales.

"¡Mentiroso de mierda!" Dad shouts, sticking his finger into Pedro Morales's chest as the other man puffs up in defense.

"Nestor, por favor," Pedro says through gritted teeth. "Esto no es el lugar para esto—"

"El lugar? You want to talk about the right place? We agreed that weddings were mine. What the fuck are you doing here?"

"Making a fucking delivery!" Pedro shouts, finally losing his cool. "How was I supposed to know it was for a wedding party?"

"Why else would you be delivering something to a WED-DING VENUE?"

"HOW WAS I SUPPOSED TO KNOW IT WAS A WED-
DING? THEY COULD DO BAT MITZVAHS!"

"A BAT MITZVAH IN A FUCKING BARN? IN WHAT
WORLD WOULD SOMEONE THROW A FUCKING BAT
MITZVAH IN A BARN?"

"See, Dad thinks the barn is stupid, too," Sofía whispers
unhelpfully.

"I need to stop this," I say, anxiously looking over my shoulder as the wedding planner appears at the open door, looking very
concerned.

I run up to Dad and try to pull at his elbow, but he tugs away
from me and continues to get in Pedro's face.

"Si fueras una persona *decente*—" Dad hisses, and Pedro
cuts him off with a harsh laugh.

"Ah, y eso es lo que tú eres, ¿no? ¿Una persona decente? ¿Y
las personas decentes se comportan de esa manera? ¿Mientras
que los novios están a pasos?"

This makes Dad sputter with outrage, and I pull harder at
his arm.

"Papi, stop it," I say firmly. "Don't do this here."

"Listen to your daughter, Nestor."

"Don't say shit about my daughter," Dad growls.

Pedro says something else, but whatever it is ends up
drowned out by a loud bang. I duck, wondering if Adrian has
somehow gotten his hands on a grenade to make things worse.
The sound is enough to cut off Dad and Pedro, at least. We're all
silent as we turn toward the source . . .

Which just so happens to be our decrepit van.

"What—" But before I can finish my question, I'm startled by another popping noise and watch in horror as smoke starts to spill from under the hood. Even from this distance I can see the small flame that has erupted from the engine.

"I know this is your brujería," Dad says, turning back to give Pedro another glare.

"Papi, the van is *on fire*," I remind him. "You need to turn it off! Van! Gasoline! Fire! Explosion!"

This seems to be enough to get him to leave Pedro alone. As my dad runs toward the van, I hear Adrian laughing his ass off.

"Adrian, cállate and deliver the rest of the food," Pedro snaps at his son.

Dad manages to turn off the engine just as the already frazzled wedding planner runs outside with a fire extinguisher in tow. By now groomsmen and bridesmaids have come out to investigate the screaming and are now shouting "Fire!"

"New lore achieved," Sofía says from my shoulder. She stayed back while I tried to quell Dad's anger but has sidled up now that he's twenty feet away with his head in his hands as he watches our delivery van continue to burn. "The rivalry between their families was so heated that it once set a van on fire," Sofía says in a mock-newscaster voice.

"Too soon," I tell her limply as the wedding planner douses the front of the van with the fire extinguisher while the groomsmen try to evacuate everyone who is rubbernecking at the scene.

"I'll call Mom."

CHAPTER SIX

The van is dead. Very, very dead.

By the time the firefighters and Mom show up, the Moraleses are gone and the wedding party is eating tiny dessert burritos in the lobby where they can watch the rest of the Ybarra family drama unfold.

The bride, who was spilling tears of joy over my father's work thirty minutes ago looks like she's already mentally composing a negative Yelp review based on the way she's staring us down. I overheard the wedding planner say they need to push the start time of the wedding back because of all the fire trucks and police cars around. At least they're here because of the van and not because Dad and Pedro got in an actual fight. Honestly, it's probably a good thing the van burst into flames when it did, because I'm convinced that was the only thing that could have broken up the brawl.

Of course when Mom showed up, it wasn't long before there was more yelling.

"I told you to have Harry check under the hood when you took it in yesterday," Mom whispered not so quietly to Dad.

"We could barely afford the cost of the tire," Dad explained.

"Oh, but we can afford to have the girls get blown up?"

It went on like that for a bit until a police officer came to ask Dad some questions. While Mom and Dad speak to him, Eddie texts me to check in on when I'm coming to relieve him from his shift. His daughter has a dental appointment in an hour that he needs to get her to. I nudge Mom and show her my phone screen, and she sighs in frustration.

"Nestor, I need to drive the girls home. You finish up here and let me know when you need to be picked up," Mom says. We all cast a sidelong glance at the van, now slightly blackened and hooked up to a tow truck.

Mom ushers me and Sofía to her car, mumbling something along the lines of, "I don't know what he was thinking."

I consider telling Mom about the argument Dad had with Pedro before the van spontaneously combusted, knowing she'd get less mad hearing it from me than him, but by the stern look on her face as she drives us back toward Port Murphy, I know now is not the time. She spends most of the drive on the phone talking to the insurance company, attempting to get through to a human so she can figure out whether we can get another van in time for the cake delivery next weekend.

When Mom pulls into the parking behind Café y Más I bolt out the door, ready to get away from the ongoing conversation about deductibles and premiums. Sofía is passed out in the back seat like this morning never even happened, as if none of this affects her. I would give anything to know exactly what goes on in that head of hers.

When I get into the shop, Eddie is standing behind the front counter looking antsy. He lives in the apartment upstairs, which he moved into with his daughter after my abuelo passed away four years ago. Living above the shop means that he's got an easy commute, but being a single dad means his schedule isn't that flexible. It's clear that the van incident is making him run late for Josie's appointment.

"I'm here!" I call out, immediately going to wash my hands at the sink.

"Oh, thank God," Eddie says, throwing off his apron. "If I didn't have to run out the door right now I'd make you explain why your reply to my text was a series of flame emojis and a sad face."

"The story will be worth the wait," I promise.

Eddie gives me a quick wave as he hurries out. With him gone, and now that Port Murphy has gotten its fill of early morning coffee, the bakery is empty. It doesn't get much busier throughout the morning. A few people come in to grab some fresh bread, and one orders two dozen empanadas for a book club lunch, but that's about it. Depressingly, that's the most business we do these days.

The rest of the time is spent listening to Buena Vista Social Club while I watch the line across the street begin to form at the Morales Bakery. Is Miguel working there today? Probably, considering the twins were the ones helping with the delivery this morning. It's wild to think the guy I've been pining over for months is just a few yards away but more untouchable than ever. I swear I see a flash of dark hair and flannel through the Moraleses' window and quickly turn away, my stomach twisting in knots.

I plop back down at my stool behind the counter and pull up a blog post I had saved about how to take better pictures for food content. So far it seems like the first step is not using your camera phone, so I'm not off to a great start. The bell above the door rings while I'm reading, the first customer in over an hour.

"Buenas tardes," I call out without looking up, trying to finish reading the last sentence from the post.

"What's got you looking so down, Ybarra?"

I look up in surprise to see Rose barreling into the shop, which shouldn't really be a surprise at all. Rose has my schedule memorized and makes a point of coming down to the shop when she's bored. Which is frequently, since she is an only child with a single mom who works two jobs. My dad should just hire her at this point to make use of her constant presence.

"Could it be last night's betrayal?" she hisses dramatically as she approaches the counter. "I can't believe you kissed a—"

"Rose!" I cry as I vault myself across the counter and slap my hand across her mouth, silencing her before she could finish that thought. My frantic leap knocks over the iPad we use as our point of service and sends a small basket of Cuban coffee enamel pins spilling over the counter. I look over my shoulder into the kitchen as if my family materialized there just in time to hear Rose's proclamation.

"Naughty girl," Rose teases, pulling my hand from her mouth. "All these months fantasizing about a boy you barely know and turns out he's the enemy." She waggles her eyebrows like this is the best thing to happen to her since the time the guy at the shave-ice hut had a crush on her and gave us free cups all summer.

"That is a *banned topic* in this shop," I warn her, my hands moving to her throat in a threatening move. She throws me off, and I slip back off the counter.

"Fine, fine. When's your shift over?" she asks as she begins to collect the spilled pins.

"Four, same as usual," I say, continuing to eye her suspiciously. There's a security camera in the shop, but no one would have any reason to look at it unless something was reported. But still, the thought that Rose almost said what I did out loud had turned my blood to ice in my veins.

"The Debate Club kids are hanging out at Lacey's Diner tonight if you want to join," she says, thankfully dropping the topic of Miguel as she sits down on the counter.

"I can't," I tell her, not sounding regretful at all. Hanging out with the Debate Club is like hanging out with ten Roses at once. I love Rose, but one is enough for me. "After last night's setback I have to get more ingredients and revise my timeline."

"This competition is eating up our last summer together," Rose complains. She glances over her shoulder at me to throw me a pout, but the serious look on my face sobers her up. "You're going to kill it, Amy. You're getting yourself all stressed for nothing."

I scoff. I don't share her confidence. I'm sure I can create a kick-ass recipe. But the competition is more than that. *La Mesa* is known for their social media presence and stunning food photography. Winning is only possible if my recipe *looks* good enough to eat. And judging by my current Instagram account, that isn't the case.

"Do you want me to help?" she offers, completely genuine. "I can bring my ring light!"

"Thanks, but no thanks," I shoot back without even considering the offer, remembering the summer she decided she wanted to join the dance team and had forced me to practice routines with her that she later, embarrassingly, posted on TikTok. Rose and I would get absolutely nothing productive done if we were both in the shop together after hours with a ring light and camera. I *know* her. Suddenly there'd be half a dozen more TikTok dances on her page. She pouts at my rejection, but I can see the mischief in her eyes. She knows why I turned her down.

The bell over the door rings, and I call out "¡Buenas tardes!" before even turning to see who it is. When I do look up, I'm not surprised to see that it isn't a customer, but James from the Italian restaurant down the block bearing a takeout box that smells of wood-fired dough and basil.

"I come seeking a trade," he intones seriously.

"Is that a margherita pizza?" I ask, eyeing the box suspiciously. In the restaurant industry, food trades are a form of currency among local shops. Everyone that works at a restaurant along the main drag in downtown Port Murphy knows the system. If someone wants to get a coffee from us, they come in and offer the person working there something of equal perceived value. For the doughnut shop employees, a latte from our shop is worth one premium doughnut or two basic doughnuts. The Thai place on the corner usually trades pad thai for a Cuban sandwich, and Locicero's employees usually trade pizzas for pastries and coffee.

Café y Más and Morales Bakery do not make any trades with each other.

"You know it is." James confirms the pizza by opening the top to reveal the blistered crust and melted cheese. "Do you have any of those guava pastries left?"

"Just cheese and guava," I tell him. "But we do have a couple of chicken empanadas left. Sofía wanted me to bring one home after my shift, but she was a brat this morning so I'd rather trade them for the pizza."

"Fair deal," James agrees as he passes me the box.

"You want a coffee, too?" I ask, already turning toward the espresso machine.

"Definitely. I still have a headache after last night, and someone called in sick so I have to pick up a shift tonight, too."

"Oh, rough," Rose says as she opens the box and takes a slice of pizza for herself.

"The trials and tribulations of working for the family business," I say solemnly.

"I was surprised to see you at the party last night," James says, directing his comment toward me.

"What do you mean you're surprised?" Rose cuts in. She leans in conspiratorially toward James. "Our girl is a *party animal*."

"Ha ha," I say sarcastically from the hot case as I pull out the empanadas.

"You should come out more this summer," James says. "Dallas is throwing a Fourth of July pool party next weekend."

"Oh, I heard she's going to have her own fireworks show," Rose says giddily.

"I wouldn't be surprised, her family is loaded," James says.

I think back to my schedule in my head. The first submission is due in just over three weeks on July 18. It's not a lot of time to choose and develop a recipe, plus the time to shoot and edit the video. The competition was announced in May, so it's not like I've had no time to figure this all out, but I've been driving myself crazy trying to find the perfect recipe.

Guava whoopie pies, dulce de leche almond chess pie, oranais made with mango instead of apricot, tres leches eclairs. Nothing felt *right*.

If only I could actually make something that felt right and turned out good. Or turned out *at all*, considering my last batch of croissants is sitting at the bottom of the dumpster, unbaked and untasted.

"Maybe," I concede, knowing that this answer will mean I don't have to listen to either Rose or James try to convince me with reasons to go, but it also means I won't be caught in a lie when I inevitably don't show up. After my last appearance at a party, I think I'm ready to swear off of them for good. Too much danger for me there.

Rose's lips thin like she can see through my ruse, but she decides not to push me on it.

"Here you go," I say to James, passing him the box filled with my goods for trade and a colada of Cuban coffee for him to take back to Locicero's. "Could I put in a request for a pizza bianca the next time you come in for a trade? And maybe some of that broccolini?"

"I'll see what I can do," James says, shooting me one of his charming smiles as he heads out of the shop.

When he's past the window, Rose does a mock faint across the counter.

"Get off!" I tell her, swatting at her prostrate form. "If my dad sees you on the counter like this on the camera *I'm* the one getting in trouble."

"That James has such a cute smile, and he's always shooting them at you," she says dramatically. "Who knew you'd be such a hot commodity this summer? You should have seen the puppy-dog eyes Miguel had last night when you ran away. It was delicious."

"You just like to see people suffer." I give her another shove and she relents, finally sliding off the counter. "And I told you not to mention *him* here," I say in a threatening whisper.

"I know, I know." She waves me off. "But don't you want to know what happened after you left?"

"No," I lie immediately. "It's not important." But I can't stop my eyes from straying across the street again.

CHAPTER SEVEN

Rose stays for the rest of my shift. A couple of customers end up rolling in an hour before close to grab a late lunch and coffee, but the rest of the time is quiet. Rose, well trained at this point despite not being an employee, helps me with my closing duties. She empties out all the trash cans while I clean all the surfaces and sweep up.

"What's for dinner at the Ybarras' tonight?" Rose asks as she puts new bags in the trash cans.

"I think I smelled carne con papa this morning," I say as I count the cash for the till. "I can text my mom and ask."

Rose is a vegetarian, which means she can only eat one out of every ten meals served at our house. My mom tried convincing her that she could eat the arroz con pollo, she just has to dig out the chunks of meat. Rose was not sold on this tactic.

"Nah," Rose waves me off. "We still have some lasagna in the fridge."

Knowing her mother's schedule, it was likely a frozen lasagna. There simply isn't enough time in the McGinnis household for home-cooked meals. I know for a fact that most of Rose's meals are undressed bags of lettuce, tubs of hummus with carrots, and sliced cheese.

"I'll ask my mom to make her picadillo with fake meat this week so you can come over," I tell her in compromise. "It's the least my family can do considering all the unpaid labor you do around here."

"Deal!"

We lock up the door and set up the alarm before parting ways in the parking lot. Rose, like me, doesn't have a car and commutes by bike. Port Murphy is small enough to get around, and if we ever want to go farther out to the movies or the mall there is always someone to catch a ride with.

Less than a week after the solstice, summer is finally starting to sneak into the PNW. We've had five straight days without rain, and it looks like we aren't likely to get any more until the fall. The heat is beginning to climb, making what is usually a comfortable bike ride home a hot mess. With no clouds in the sky, the late afternoon sun beats down on me and sweat begins to collect behind my knees and at my temples.

We are still a few weeks away from the worst of the heat, but even now our century-old house is not up to the task of keeping cool in these exceedingly hot summers we've been having. We don't have central air in the house, and I remember that never being a problem as a kid. But now there are a few weeks every summer that leave the house so hot Sofía and I lay on the cool hardwood floor in our underwear with fans blasting us to keep us cool.

When I get home, I see the windows have been thrown wide open to allow a cross breeze to pass through the house to help cool it down. I can smell my mom's carne con papa from the front yard as I drop the kickstand on my bike and leave it on the driveway. My stomach rumbles from that aroma alone, an enticing mix of tomato, oregano, garlic, and beef. Stew is likely the last thing most people would want to eat on such a hot day, but I could never turn my back on a plate of hot stew and rice, no matter the season.

But trailing after the smell of dinner comes the sound of my parents' voices, raised and almost angry sounding. I freeze on the path to the front door, hidden under the trellis that is heavy with wisteria vines.

The sound of my parents arguing is not foreign to me. There have been seasons of discord between them, and although they have always tried their best to hide them from Sofía and me, we have picked up on them over the years. Though these seasons have come and gone, they have always been about one thing: money.

Before I was born, when my dad was young, the bakery did exceptionally well under my abuelo's reign. But when my abuelo's arthritis made it difficult to do anything in the shop, he had passed it down to my dad, his eldest son, who shared his passion for the business. Things went okay in the beginning, but shortly after I was born the recession came and Café y Más was hit hard.

Despite my mom's best attempts to keep the business together, my dad's . . . overbearing nature managed to make things worse. Whenever he made a purchase for the shop in secret and our mom found out, it would be a frosty few months in our house. To make up for the loss at the business, Mom would tighten the belt at home. Less fresh fruits and vegetables on the table, shopping at the dollar store, and learning how to DIY.

One year when our only toilet broke, our dad was ready to call for a plumber, but Mom stopped him and opened YouTube. There are things held together with duct tape around the house, but you'd never know because my mom is a master of illusion.

"Nestor, that is not a reasonable plan!" My mom's voice, frustrated and angry, spills from the house.

"Mi amor, it's the way we've always done it. It will work out, I promise," my father says, his voice softer, trying to calm the storm brewing between them. But I know my mother; this tone will only incense her further.

"Nestor, please," Mom says as her frustration mounts. "This business cannot stand on hope and wishes. The van is totaled, and insurance will only cover so much. We need to make cuts to the menu or find a different distributor. We need to make better—"

"No, we are not changing the distributor. My family has worked with them for decades and their quality can't be beat. This wedding season is all we need to get us through this. We already have enough cakes booked—"

"You're unbelievable."

It's times like these when the window in our bedroom is good not only for sneaking out, but sneaking in. Though sometimes I wonder if it's better to stroll into the house in the middle of a fight. If I do that, I'll have to see their faces, angry and ashamed, as they cut off whatever argument they were having for my sake. My dad will take my arrival as an excuse to end whatever discussion they were having and begin to talk to me about the schedule at the café or whether we were running low on garbage bags or something. This will only serve to make my mother angrier, and I can't bear to make her feel any worse.

I run past the front windows quickly, hoping they don't catch sight of me before I slip around the side of the house and through the lavender bushes. The window opens cleanly and I slip in. The bedroom is empty, Sofía probably out with friends, and I'm glad she's not here to hear this.

With the bedroom door closed, it helps to muffle the argument still going on in the kitchen. One of them will eventually realize the time and move the argument to their bedroom, where it will eventually fizzle out before Mom needs to get dinner on the table.

I close the window behind me and quickly put on my noise-canceling headphones before sitting at my desk. I know my parents love each other, I see it when they look at each other and in the little things they do for each other. But I also know that they are fundamentally different in how they view the world. My dad is a dreamer and my mom is a realist, and there is nothing in this world, not even love, that can truly bridge that.

Putting on the first playlist that pops up on my phone, I grab the top cookbook from the pile on my desk and continue where I left off. This cookbook is about Japanese desserts, and I'm particularly interested in the mochi doughnut recipe. This recipe calls for tapioca starch, which is derived from yuca, the same root vegetable Cubans make doughnuts with. Mochi doughnuts are everywhere now, but most people don't even know what a Cuban buñuelo is.

While I read and take notes, I spot Sofía with her headphones on walking up to the front door, and the distant rumble of my parents' voices fades. Sofía drops her stuff in our room but immediately heads to the bathroom for the shower she didn't take this morning. In the kitchen I hear the clatter of dishes and cutlery as Mom sets the table, so I quickly change and go out to help her.

"Hey, Mom," I say, giving her a kiss on the cheek as I take the pile of plates from her hands.

"When did you get home?" she asks in surprise.

"Not too long ago," I tell her as I place the plates on the dining table. There's a beat of silence as she takes this in.

"Do you want to help put together a salad?"

"Sure," I say.

While we work together I update her on our day, skipping the incident with the van and going straight to Rose dropping by and my plans to read some cookbooks for tonight. I leave out the trade with James, worried that this kind of behavior would feed into the argument she had with Dad earlier.

At the dinner table our parents manage to put the argument behind them and chat amiably with us. Our dad mentions next week's wedding cake, another five-tier monstrosity with the classic Cuban wedding-cake base: rum cake. He's so excited to be making it and has big ideas about how it's going to look. I immediately wonder how we're going to get a cake that huge to the venue without a van.

75

Mom must wonder the same because she pushes back from the table, annoyed.

"I have a bit of a headache so I'm going to lie down," she announces, dropping her plates in the sink before disappearing into her bedroom.

"You ladies have any plans for your day off tomorrow?" Dad asks us after Mom leaves.

"I'll probably just go to Rose's," I tell him.

"No idea," Sofía says. "Sleep in, probably."

"In that case, debemos hacer un despojo mañana mismo," Dad insists. "We'll go to the shop first thing tomorrow morning and grab some Florida water since we're out."

"We?" Sofía asks in surprise.

"Yes, you and I, since your sister said she had plans."

"I do have a plan!" Sofía protests. "Sleeping in!"

"After everything that happened this morning, we need to do a limpieza and you're going to help me." It goes unsaid that he wants to do this because he's convinced Pedro has cursed him and not because our van was ancient and held together by hopes and dreams.

"If you want me to stay home and help—"

"Yes!" Sofía cuts in.

"No," Dad says sternly. "Your sister and I have it under control. Enjoy your day off."

Sofía glares at me mutely, and I shrug in return.

The conversation ends there for the night as Dad gets up to add his plate to the sink before going to the bathroom. When the shower kicks on, Sofía and I begin to clean up together.

"They were fighting, weren't they?" Sofía says quietly as she passes me a dish to dry.

"Yeah," I tell her. "Money stuff again."

Sofía's mouth scrunches up, and she turns back to the sink. There isn't much more to say about it.

"I'm going to the bonfire party tonight," she announces. "I assume you won't be there?"

"No, and you shouldn't either. Those parties always get busted."

"I'll be fine." She brushes me off.

We hear Dad come out of the bathroom, which cuts off our conversation. He comes in a minute later and grabs a beer from the fridge and sits down in the living room.

My dad is always looking for external excuses for his problems. The van fire is because of brujería, the slow business is because of the dessert burrito, the discord at home is because of the rising cost of living. It's never because he's a little thoughtless or because his business can't keep up with the times. If he could just see the truth of his actions then maybe he wouldn't be falling asleep on the couch tonight to the ghostly light pulsing from the TV.

CHAPTER EIGHT

When my alarm goes off at midnight I'm not surprised to find Sofía's side of the room empty. In typical younger sibling vs. older sibling fashion, she's out to party while I get to work. I'm second-guessing my croissant recipe again and want to try something else tonight.

As I get ready to leave for the bakery, I wonder if Miguel will be at the bonfire party Sofía went to. If he's hoping I'll be there. If he'll be looking for me. What would happen if I went and we locked eyes over the flames—

I shake those thoughts from my head. I've had enough fires for today.

I sneak out, and as I pass the front of the house to get to my bike, I see my dad through the window, asleep on the couch. My heart constricts at the sight.

I walk my bike to the street and hop on where I can't be seen from the house, just in case. The cool evening air is bracing and helps to wake me up as I pedal toward downtown.

I lock up my bike behind the shop, disarm the alarm system, and prep my workstation. Tonight's project is buñuelos, one of the few Cuban desserts we don't serve at the shop.

Buñuelo translates to doughnut in English, and plenty of Latin American countries have their own take on them, but a Cuban buñuelo is entirely different from the American idea of a doughnut. The dough is made from yuca and malanga (and sometimes boniato and calabaza), starchy root vegetables that are usually found in savory dishes. The dough is fried and served in a sticky-sweet anise-flavored caramel. It's a classic Cuban dessert, but you're not likely to find it on a menu outside of Miami in the United States.

Before I pivoted to the croissant idea, I had been messing around with my abuelo's buñuelo recipe. I wanted to see if I could make a buñuelo in the style of a classic doughnut-shop doughnut. What would it taste like with a guava icing, or mango? Tossed in cinnamon sugar like a churro or finished off with a crispy coconut topping?

I had written off the idea a couple of weeks ago, thinking that I needed to do something fancier to impress the people at *La Mesa*. But after my croissants failed, I decided I'm not a particularly fancy girl, so why should my recipe be? A fun, playful twist on a doughnut definitely feels more *me*. After all, the best food comes from the heart, right?

Tonight, instead of making any icings, I want to prepare it in the traditional style with anise syrup. I put on my favorite cooking playlist and get to work. Once I'm in a kitchen, it's so easy to forget about burning vans and forbidden romances and get into the flow. It can look like complete chaos from the outside, pots boiling on the stove, an oven timer beeping, chopping and dicing, but for me it's all a well-choreographed dance. Every step is perfectly timed to ensure that every piece of the puzzle slots in together to produce the perfect product.

Once the doughnuts are fried and the caramel is ready, I make one perfect plate of buñuelos. The figure-eight-shaped doughnut is placed on a pool of anise caramel before getting topped with another generous spoonful. The doughnut is still hot and greedily soaks up the syrup. This is the prime opportunity for an Instagram photo, so I grab a piece of star anise and add it to the plate for garnish.

Like with most plates of Cuban food, the palette is overwhelmingly brown. I grab a lime, since I did use a small squeeze in the syrup, and throw that next to the plate. I look around the kitchen, trying to find something else colorful to add. My eyes land on a blue kitchen towel, and I add that into the mix.

Pulling out my phone, I open the camera and try out a few angles. But the lighting is terrible in this kitchen, and the buñuelos just look sad.

Frustrated, I grab my plate and take it out to the front of the shop and place it on one of the tables. The round top is a green Formica, and each table is decorated with a tiny glass vase with a small smattering of fresh wildflowers. In the summer it's easy to fill the vases with flowers from around town, from snapdragons to lilac, and in the winter we switch them out to fake flowers. There's a sugar container like the kind you'd see at old diners, a saltshaker full of salt and rice with a matching pepper shaker, and a napkin container covered in a pattern of Cuban tile.

My doughnuts are getting cold and I really want to try one, but I want to try one more time for the perfect shot. As I'm moving around the things on the table, a loud knock at the front door breaks me from my concentration. I drop my phone in surprise, the corner hitting the ledge of the plate and knocking it over enough to spill syrup all over my phone and the table.

"Damn it," I mutter, in response to both the phone and the fact that I've just been caught in the shop after hours.

I turn to look at the front door to try to see who it is, but the front light is off and all I can see is a shadowed form hunched toward the glass. Apprehension fills me as I eye the unfamiliar shape and my heart pounds against my chest as I consider what to do next. Without taking my eye off the mystery knocker, I try to grab for my phone and end up with a hand covered in syrup instead.

The stranger at the door must realize that I can't see them and pulls out their phone, turns on the flash, and points it directly into their own face.

This time my heart rate stumbles for a different reason.

Miguel Fuentes is standing outside the front door, his brows drawn down and eyes squinting from the bright flash he has pointed at his face. I feel that traitorous flutter in my stomach at the sight of him, my body not yet accepting that this boy is off-limits.

A look of recognition must cross my face because he turns his phone back around and turns off the flash.

"I just want to talk," he says through the glass, and even though he's back in shadow, I can feel his eyes on me, direct and focused.

I have a feeling turning off all the lights and pretending I never saw him isn't going to be enough to keep him away. I'm sure his cousins must have explained the deal between our families after last night, but if he's here, openly on the doorstep of Ybarra territory, clearly he's too stubborn to listen to them.

So it's up to me to set him straight.

I grab the chair from the table in front of me and carry it behind the counter. There's a wall that separates the front of the café from the kitchen, with a small window between the two. On the wall are shelves of various knickknacks, from bright yellow Havana license plates to the pothos plant that is older than I am. Framed photos of family from back in Cuba to the early years in Port Murphy. And there's the thing I'm looking for: the security camera.

I climb up on the chair and turn the camera over to face the wallpaper. Then I take the chair with me to the kitchen and do the same thing to the camera back there.

Only then do I return to the front of the shop, place the chair back in its spot, take a deep calming breath, and open the front door.

I only knew Miguel for a day, so I don't owe him much, not really. But he deserves better than me running away from him without having a conversation first.

When I open the door, he looks surprised, like he really thought I was just going to let him stand out there all night. Then he pulls out a white napkin from his back pocket and waves it like a flag.

"I surrender," he says.

"Do you speak for the whole family when you say that?"

"Just me, I'm afraid. The others wouldn't agree to it. Too proud. But I'm a Fuentes, and we're too romantic for blood feuds, really."

The blush on my cheeks is unavoidable. "I suppose if you wave a white flag I can let you into enemy territory."

"I won't combust if I step across the threshold?"

I laugh and grab his shoulder, pulling him into the shop.

"We really do have to hide in the back, though. Just in case someone passes by."

"Smells good," he notes, as he follows me into the back.

"I made buñuelos, if you want to try some," I offer, pulling up a stool for him in front of my prep table.

"You know I've been dying to try one of your creations," he says with a smile.

"It's my first attempt," I warn him as I grab a clean plate and begin to serve him my best buñuelo, the figure-eight shape clear and unbroken. "But I think they came out okay."

"Wow," he says eagerly as I place the plate in front of him. "Beautiful plating," he remarks.

"I've been working on that," I admit, thinking of my failed attempt to take a photo earlier.

"Do you mind if I take a picture of it?" he asks, pulling out his phone.

"You can't share it," I warn him. "People can't know I let you in here." I feel instantly jittery at the thought of being caught with a Morales in the Ybarra kitchen.

"I can take a picture with your phone then," he says, working me with his puppy-dog eyes. I consider his proposal. When the quiet stretches a little too long he drops the phone and leans in a little closer. "I saw you taking some photos in the front before I knocked."

"And they were all terrible," I complain.

"Well, lucky for you, you have an aspiring filmmaker here with an eye for the perfect shot." He holds up his index fingers and thumbs, pretending to frame the photo with a mock seriousness that makes me laugh.

I think of my sad feed and consider his offer. I need to start producing better content if I want to win the competition. Even if it's just one really good-looking picture among dozens of duds, it's something. "You can take a picture if you let me post it on my social media."

"Deal," he says quickly with his dazzling smile. I try not to get too distracted by his dimples and help him set up the shot. He incorporates the serving station, the caramel and undressed buñuelos peeking in from the corner. I watch as he adjusts the settings on my phone's camera and moves some sliders I never even knew existed, suddenly making the bad lighting look decent on screen. It takes him no time at all to produce the perfect photo.

"What do you think?" he asks, leaning in to show me the screen. My mind is overwhelmed by his sudden proximity, the familiar smell of his deodorant wafting over me, that I barely look at the picture.

"It's great," I stammer, inching away from him. I try to do it slowly so he won't notice, but I can tell he does by the sharp turn of his head. Caught, I take another step back, far away from him and that deodorant smell that has no right to be as intoxicating as it is.

The silence stretches between us, and I can feel the mood shift.

"Are we going to talk about last night?" he asks, and the bubble of calm that had fallen abruptly shatters.

I know now that I made a mistake letting him in here, letting him sweet-talk me and fall into this familiar repartee. The more we do it, the harder it is going to be to cut him off. And that's what I need to do.

"I assume Adrian or Valeria clued you in on the rivalry," I say, grabbing the dirty dishes and adding them to the sink.

"They made me a PowerPoint. I think there's going to be an exam at the end of the week."

"Well, you're clearly going to fail, because you keep breaking the first rule of the Ybarra/Morales rivalry: don't speak to the other side and certainly don't eat their food. My grandfather swore that your grandfather poisoned his water once."

"His water? How?"

"Laxatives."

A loud laugh bursts from Miguel.

"It's not a laughing matter, Mr. Morales. My grandfather almost shat himself to an early grave that day."

Another laugh sputters from Miguel as he tries to school his features.

"In all seriousness, our families do take this whole thing seriously. I'm sure you heard about the fight this morning." His slight wince tells me he has. "I know you're just here for the summer, but if my father finds out that I kissed a scion of the Morales family he *will* show up at your house with a machete."

"I believe it. I almost slipped up and mentioned you at breakfast, and Valeria all but launched herself across the table to shut me up. I owe her a new shirt."

"You're not taking this seriously, though," I tell him. "I can see it in your eyes."

"Of course I'm not!" he shouts. There's a laugh behind his words, but also a frustrated edge in his voice now. "Ana Maria, I *like* you. I never thought I'd see you again, and then bam, you show up in the unlikeliest of places. I was so excited last night, it felt like . . . like *something*. Destiny. Fate."

"Yes," I agree, "something fated to be star-crossed. As in, avoid at all costs unless you want to die an untimely death."

Miguel gives me a look. "You're not going to die an untimely death if you go on a date with me."

"A date!" I all but screech. "I let you in here because I thought you deserved a conversation instead of me just running away. But that's it, Miguel. This conversation is meant to be a goodbye."

"Ana, this is absurd. I'm not really a Morales. I didn't even grow up here, I have no skin in this game."

"Oh, so the laxative man Andres Guillermo Morales isn't your grandfather?" I ask.

"My mom left this town when she turned eighteen, she never got along with her dad, and—"

"But *I'm* from here, Miguel. You may think it's silly, but your family hurt my family and we haven't forgotten about it.

My parents mean the world to me, and I am not going to hurt them just to make you happy."

"I'm not asking you to do that," he says, frustration mounting. He wipes his hand across his brow and takes a calming breath.

"We spent one day together, Miguel. It's no loss to pretend we never met." The words leave my mouth, and I instantly regret them. A look of hurt flashes across Miguel's face. I've hit my target. But instead of victory, I'm left with a hollow feeling. I want to pull those words back in—it's a lie and it shouldn't have stuck.

"*Amyyyyy!*" A singsong voice breaks through the tension between us as the front door that I left unlocked rattles open.

CHAPTER NINE

You better be cooking up something tasty!" Sofía says as she barrels through the front door, the bells hanging above it clanging in alarm.

I look up at Miguel, all six feet of him, and do visual calculations, trying to figure out where I can stash him before Sofía spots him.

"Oh, buñuelos?" Sofía says, thankfully distracted by the table in the front with the plate of cold doughnuts.

The distance between us and the back door is too great. The path goes by the window to the front of the shop and then it's a long corridor to the back. At any moment while he makes his escape that way, Sofía could barrel into the kitchen.

Then my eyes land on the door behind him.

"I'm so sorry," I mouth, pushing him back off his stool and toward the walk-in fridge. He looks confused until I throw the door open, a blast of chilly air settling over us both before I quickly switch on the light and push him in. Miguel has the decency to at least look a little scared, although I'm not sure if it's because he's worried we're going to get caught or because I'm throwing him in the refrigerator.

"Amy?" Sofía asks, her voice closer as she approaches the kitchen.

"Hide in here until I get her out," I whisper to Miguel. He starts to open his mouth, maybe to fight me on my choice of a hiding spot, but I'm closing the door and shutting him in before he can get us caught.

"You sound drunk," I shout toward Sofía over my shoulder. "Alcohol shrinks your brain," I warn her, hoping my annoying older sister act will distract her from the lingering scent of boy in the kitchen.

"I had, like, two drinks," Sofía argues as she skips into the kitchen. "I wanted to see if you were around and could feed me." She says this with a sweet pout on her face, a look that is at odds with her general appearance. Sofía always looks like she's going to shove a boot up someone's ass.

"I'm cleaning up now," I tell her, pointing toward my sink of dirty dishes. "But you can have the plate I left out at the front. Stick it in the microwave or something."

Sofía looks over her shoulder at the plate.

"I don't really like buñuelos," she complains, "too much anise. Did Dad leave any leftover empanadas in the fridge?"

My heart nearly drops out of my ass as I hear Sofía make her way toward the walk-in. In my panic, I think of only one solution. I turn with the nozzle from the sink still in my hand and pull the trigger, spraying my sister with ice-cold water.

89

"*Amy!!!*" She screeches, deterred from her march on the fridge and now facing me with all her rage.

"That should help sober you up," I tell her calmly. "And no, there are no leftovers in the fridge, just cartons of milk and bins of lettuce. Eat a buñuelo and go home, Sofía."

Sofía is staring at me with her mouth agape, her hair curling around her face from the sudden dampness.

"You are insane," she finally says, her fists clenched.

"But it worked, didn't it?" I ask her.

"Sofía?" The front door clinks again, and I recognize the voice of Sofía's best friend, Jac. I'm relieved to hear him because he tends to be the responsible half of their duo. He's the sweet Filipino kid who used to live next door, and Sofía is his scary guard dog. "Is Amy cooking up anything good?"

"No," Sofía growls, "instead she's spraying me with water like a *dog*."

"I offered her buñuelos," I say reasonably. "A cold splash was the next best option."

"If Sof's not going to eat it, can I have the buñuelo?" Jac asks as he appears in the window in the front, the cold plate of doughnuts in his hands.

"Have at it," I tell him, and before I even finish speaking he's already scarfed down one of the figure eights. "Jac, will you please do me a favor and escort my sister home?"

"Sure thing," he says through a mouthful of food as he passes me the empty plate. "You missed a sick bonfire party."

"I'm sure I did," I say as I toss his plate into the sink.

Sofía grabs a towel from the counter and wipes down her face before angrily throwing the towel back at me. Sofía will be out for revenge for my water trick, but knowing her she'll do it when I least expect it. She is methodical with her revenge. But it's better to be on my toes around her for a week than to have my secret Morales exposed.

"I'm going to clean up here and then head home. Please leave the window unlocked," I ask her.

"We'll see," she says haughtily before sweeping past me and back into the front. "Come on, Jac," she says before swiping a bag of potato chips and stepping out the front door.

"Good night, Amy!" Jac says pleasantly as he closes the door behind him.

Once they're past the front window I run to the front of the bakery and lock the door and turn off the lights. Then I'm back in the kitchen and throwing open the door to the walk-in fridge, where Miguel is crouched on the ground with his arms tight around him, shivering.

"Oh my God," I practically wail. "I didn't think you'd get so cold, I'm so sorry." I reach out and grab his arms. His bare skin is cold and covered in goose bumps. He stands up slowly and once we're out of the fridge I close the door behind him and begin to rub his arms aggressively, trying to warm him up. "Miguel?" I ask warily.

"Did you really hose down your sister to prevent her from finding me?" he asks, and it's the last thing I expect him to say. A laugh bursts from me and I rest my head against his chest, so relieved that we made it through Sofía's sudden arrival without being caught.

"I really did," I say, remembering the look of surprise on my sister's face.

"You're a wild card, Ybarra," Miguel says before he wraps his arms around me and pulls me in for a hug. I press the side of my face against his chest, where I can hear every inhale and exhale and the beat of his heart. My arms reach around behind him and I begin to rub his back, still trying to warm him up.

Miguel rests his chin on the top of my head and it all feels so *natural*. I've never been so physically comfortable around another person before. I avoid hugs and grudgingly kiss friends and family on the cheek. I'm eager to let go after holding hands, and I never sit too close to anyone.

But from the moment I met Miguel in LA I felt so comfortable around him. *I* was the one that reached out and held his hand. *I* was the one that pulled him in for a hug. *I* was the one that rose on my tiptoes, closed my eyes, and—

"I need to finish cleaning up," I say suddenly, my voice scratchy and hoarse as I pull myself from his embrace. I feel the cold rush in to fill the space between us, and this time I'm the one left shivering. "You should head home. Walking should help to warm you up."

Miguel watches me, his brows drawn down in either confusion or hurt. I turn away.

"What happened with our abuelos is decades old," he says, his voice stubborn. "Someone has to bury the hatchet."

A bitter laugh escapes me. "Oh, and that's going to be you? The Morales that isn't even from Port Murphy?"

"Why not?" he challenges. "Admit it, someone needs to end this stupid rivalry. Why not the outsider?"

"Miguel, you really don't get it." I sigh, leaning back against the counter and rubbing my forehead. "My dad and your uncle *hate* each other. Like, slashing-each-other's-tires kind of hate. And your cousins aren't much better, by the way. Adrian spread a really nasty rumor about my sister when we were in middle school. You're not going to waltz into town and erase all of that. You have to respect that our families have drawn boundaries and that you're not outside of all this bullshit just because you rolled in from LA."

Silence stretches between us for a moment.

"Okay, so we'll hang out in secret then," he says, like it's the obvious next step in this problem.

"What?" I say, a little flabbergasted by the way his mind works.

"Our families hate each other but *we* obviously get along. And if that isn't going to change things for them, then we can just continue doing our own thing. In secret."

"I'm sorry, are you living in an early-two-thousands romcom? Because that is the only universe in which secretly being friends would work. Our families are *Cuban*. It's in their DNA to be up in their children's business. I'm fairly certain my mom does background checks on anyone I befriend. That's why I have only one friend."

"Hence the secret part," he says. "Like right now, with me hiding in the deep freeze and you fending off your sister."

"That was not the deep freeze," I correct him. "You would not have survived the deep freeze, that was just the walk-in fridge."

"It felt a hell of a lot like a deep freeze," he says.

"Do you want to test out the *real* deep freeze? Because that's where my father is throwing you once he finds out about our secret relationship."

I'm dead serious as I say this, but I can see that Miguel is trying hard to keep from laughing. And I can't say I blame him. To an outsider, I'm sure this whole thing is hilarious. Maybe ten years from now when I'm the pastry chef at a fancy restaurant in New York City, I'll turn to my coworker and say, "Hey, you want to hear a wacky story about my family and our hometown?" And we'll laugh at how insane the whole thing is.

But as someone who is still living in the middle of the whole thing, it's hard to find the humor in it.

Miguel's face slowly sobers when he sees that I'm not joining him for the laugh. He sighs, sounding a little defeated.

"I really wish it were different," I tell him, softly this time, the irritation gone from my voice. "But you'll go back to LA at the end of the summer and return to your life. So there's no need to stir up trouble here, okay?"

"Yeah," he says.

We stare at each other in silence for a moment, and I take the time to really look at him, to see if the truth of our situation has finally penetrated. It must have because his shoulders are slumped and he looks defeated. For a moment I feel a pang of something, guilt maybe, but I brush it off.

"Head out the back," I say, gesturing toward the back door with my head.

He doesn't move for a moment, and I'm terrified that he'll say something. But he seems to be an expert at reading me, because he follows my instructions without saying a word. When the back door closes behind him, my knees give out and I press my head against the aluminum of the sink, hoping the cold will shock some sense into me.

I finish cleaning the kitchen in a blur, unable to focus on anything but the task in front of me. After I close up I hop on my bike and pedal hard, working up a sweat and focusing on the movement of my legs.

It doesn't hit me until I'm back in my bedroom, Sofía snoring safely in her bed while I change out of my shirt. It should smell like oil and vanilla like it always does after working in the kitchen. But as I pull off the shirt, there's a new scent there, one that's snuck in and lingered on the fabric.

I can't seem to rid myself of Miguel Fuentes.

CHAPTER TEN

I need to focus," I tell Rose the next day as I stare down at my calendar. After she told me all about the Debate Club hanging out at the diner, she was supposed to be helping me talk through my competition entry, but she will not give up the topic of Miguel.

"Okay, fine," she relents, flopping back on to her bed. "But he's not going to go away, you know. Ari told me that Miguel and his mom moved into the Morales house. It looks like he might be here to stay."

When I rolled up to Rose's house this morning, I was tempted to tell her about last night. It was on the tip of my tongue when I walked into her kitchen, but I stopped myself. Last night wouldn't even be worth mentioning because I'm not going to see Miguel again. But if there's one thing a small town loves, it's gossip, and newcomers are always the number one topic of discussion—hence Rose's intel from last night.

"I think the doughnuts are a worthwhile avenue," I tell her, trying to change the subject and direct her back to my more pressing issue. "I made them again last night, and they were really good. The dough is pillowy on the inside and nice and crisp on the outside. I think they could be a hit."

"So the croissants are out?" Rose says, finally back on track.

I sigh. "I feel like the last batch being ruined was a sign from the universe to scratch that idea."

"You have the recipe part of this competition in the bag, regardless of which you choose," Rose assures. "Whatever you come up with, you will knock it out of the park." There's a weighted pause before Rose rolls over and turns her intense green gaze my way. "Your problem is your social media."

I groan and flop back on to her carpet. The glow-in-the-dark stars we stuck to her ceiling as kids stare down at me. Besides the video requirement, social media isn't explicitly a part of the competition, but looking at the history of past winners, they all had really good-looking social feeds. And it makes sense from the perspective of the magazine—they'd want the finalists to have produced images and videos that would look good on *La Mesa*'s socials. Plus, there's that old saying that the eyes eat first. If I submit an amazing recipe but a shit video where my food looks blah, my chances of getting selected as a finalist certainly don't look good.

"I think you just need to be more consistent. Practice makes perfect, right? The more you do something the better you'll be. And once you have my ring light your stuff will look better," she assures me.

I take out my phone and pull up the photo Miguel took last night. No ring light, no fancy setup, and yet he got a stunning picture of the buñuelos. The crispy exterior of the doughnuts is shiny from the caramel, and the colors look so rich and vibrant instead of just brown and bland. It took him all of two minutes to produce this shot.

Damn him.

"You're right," I tell her. "I should post more."

I open Instagram and without making any additional edits, I make a new post using Miguel's picture.

In the kitchen experimenting with buñuelos! Have you tried them before? #buñuelos

I hit post without thinking twice and sit back up.

"Okay, it's time for a snack," I proclaim, jumping up from the floor. I pull Rose up from the bed, an easy feat because she's always eager to eat whatever I whip up in the kitchen.

Rose's house is practically my second home. Every inch of it, from the plaid curtains to the stained carpets, is embedded in my very soul.

Being raised by Cuban parents in a predominantly white town means that our family does things a little differently. As a kid it can be frustrating, especially when it came to parties and sleepovers growing up. Sofía and I were not allowed to attend coed parties until high school, and to this day sleepovers are banned.

I know there is some irony in that because we have become masterminds of sneaking out at night, but it is important to note that we always end up in our bedroom at the end of the night.

The sleepover rule was broken only once, and it was for Rose. Being the child of a single mother who did not have a boyfriend meant that her home was safe enough to stay at. I'm sure when my mom relented in elementary school she did not expect me to escape to Rose's house for entire weekends in the summer, but with the ability to FaceTime me at a moment's notice to make sure I was still alive, she let it slide.

I always loved Rose's house because it seemed to be full to the brim with stories. It's an old Victorian that's sagging in places today but was once lovingly built by her great-great-grandparents. The house has managed to stay in the family generation after generation despite the family's ups and downs.

That means that there are treasures around every corner in this house, from the molding in the kitchen that has cataloged the family members' heights (including mine) for decades to the stacks of photo albums in the living room.

I've always been so fascinated that Rose's history is so succinctly captured in this house. My history has been cast across this continent from coast to coast and across to the Caribbean.

When we get into the kitchen, I start pulling things out to make grilled cheese sandwiches. I decide to add some thinly sliced apple to the sandwiches since there are plenty lying about.

Rose puts on some music and continues to update me on the Debate Club shenanigans, which are never-ending because the group is filled with a bunch of hot-headed type-A nerds who think arguing is a sport.

Admittedly, I start to tune her out until she says, "Amy, your phone is blowing up right now."

"Is it my mom?" I ask, not wanting to move away from the stove to get a better look. Grilled cheese can go from perfect to burned in no time, and I'm not taking my eyes off these babies until they are on our plates.

"No, they're all from Instagram. Did you hire a bunch of bots to start following you and liking your posts or something?"

"What?" I ask, still a little too distracted by cooking to understand what's happening. "No, I did not buy bots," I tell her, flipping the sandwiches down on to the cutting board. I give them each a crosswise cut and plate them up.

"I can't handle the suspense, I'm checking your Instagram right now," Rose announces, sitting back down on her stool and unlocking my phone.

I drop our plates in front of her and then quickly sidle up behind her to see what's going on.

When she opens Instagram, the first thing I notice is the notification icon with a red dot and the message icon with a boggling number on it. Rose taps on my notification feed, and it is absolutely inundated with a flurry of likes. Most of them are for my new post, but as Rose scrolls I see there are a string of likes from the same account across several of my photos.

"What the hell is going on?" I ask, absolutely aghast at the sudden attention my mediocre account has suddenly gotten.

"Did you just go viral?" Rose says, *still* scrolling down the notification page. I snatch the phone from her hands and try to figure out what is happening.

Amid all the likes are dozens of comments and a few dozen new follows. I continue to scroll until I get to the source of this sudden popularity.

@ShutterShyGuy mentioned you in a story: Check out my friend's food Insta! She's a kickass chef and definitely needs to write a cookbook.

"No way," I mutter under my breath, and before I can stop her, Rose is peeking at my phone to see what's caught my attention.

"ShutterShyGuy?" she says, reading out the handle. "Who even is that?" Rose reaches an arm over me and clicks on the handle before I can stop her.

I have no doubt in my mind that this mysterious profile belongs to Miguel, and my hunch is only further confirmed when his profile loads up on my screen.

@ShutterShyGuy

1493 Posts | 257K Followers | 837 Following

Miguel Fuentes (he/him)

Just a guy with some rolls of film to waste. LA -> PNW

Canon AE-1. Fujifilm X100v. Mamiya 6. Canon 7.

iPhone 14 Pro.

I guess all bets are off in his mind, and he decided to find my social media. At least he found the account I've blocked my family from viewing. I hope he was smart enough to block his family from viewing his stories. I really should be angrier about the whole thing, but the sudden influx of likes and follows sure does feel nice.

I take over the phone and begin to scroll down his feed. He has three pinned posts at the top of his page. One is of an older woman turning away from the camera with an embarrassed smile on her face. She's half in shadow with a bright blue cloudless sky behind her. There's a slightly harried look about her, hair thrown in a messy bun and the collar of her blouse slightly askew, but despite that she looks effortlessly beautiful. The love behind this shot is clear, and I don't have to read the caption to figure out who this is. Something about her features is familiar to me, something about the nose and the eyes. She's definitely a Morales, likely Miguel's mom.

The second picture is a self-portrait of Miguel. He's sitting in a diner booth, the segmented gray light from the blinds behind him making him glow a little around the edges. He's leaning forward a little, one hand holding a familiar Styrofoam container full of Cuban coffee and pouring it into a small cup, like the kind you might pour a serving of cough syrup into. On the yellow Formica table is a white plate with two croquetas, a slice of lime, and a plastic single-serving sleeve of saltine crackers.

He looks gorgeous and a little mysterious in the picture, and I'm tempted to click on it to read through the scores of comments I'm sure the post has.

But the third square is what really captures my attention. It's a frame from a video, cropped to a square to fit the format of the feed, but I immediately recognize what video it's from.

"Oh my God," I groan. "*He* made the dessert burrito video. He's the reason Morales Bakery went viral." I think back to our goodbye in LA, where we vowed not to look each other up on social media. I wish I had broken that stupid rule on the drive back to my aunt's that night, I would have figured out who he was immediately and not spent the last six months pining over that day in my memories. "He really is the enemy," I mutter, utterly defeated.

Rose snatches the phone from my hand, and I don't have it in me to fight her.

"Oh jeez," Rose mutters, still on my Instagram account. "I think maybe you should just avoid opening Instagram for a little bit."

"What do you mean," I say around a bite of grilled cheese.

"What if I become your social media manager, huh?" she says, slathering on her chipper tone, the one she uses to distract people. I know her too well to let that work on me.

"What is going on?" I ask, dropping my sandwich and reaching for my phone, but she swipes it out of my reach before I can grab it.

"Miguel has a lot of followers and, uh, they're passionate about photography," she says, her brows furrowing because even she can tell she's not doing a good job of lying. She sighs and drops the phone on the counter. "There are just some comments about the quality of your posts. I mean, plenty of people are saying the food looks delicious or that they want to try a recipe but . . . some are being pretty mean."

"Oh God," I mutter before dropping my head down on the cold tile countertop. *I* know that my camera skills leave something to be desired, but I didn't think it was bad enough to warrant hate comments. "I'm never going to win that scholarship. *La Mesa* will take one look at my Instagram and be like, ew, not her," I whine into the countertop.

Rose, a person who loves to hug and cuddle and touch, practically vibrates with the need to physically comfort me. But she knows me well enough to know that a comforting arm rubbing my shoulder is the last thing I want. Instead she rubs her hands together and steps into problem-solving mode.

"Listen, you have time to fix up your feed. And what really matters is your recipe and story, which are going to be killer, I know it. You'll take my ring light today and you're going to keep working hard, and it'll eventually click, okay? Don't let this get you down. Not all the comments are bad. People love that recent post. There were plenty of really nice comments on that one. See?"

She opens my phone again and pulls up the buñuelos post.

@JragonJamie353: These look so tasty! 🖤
@alysin_wonderland: okay we have to try these
@meg_on_eggs. I love Cuban food!
@KT_Curry: omg 🍴 need this
@crabgurl89: damn those look so good

I wail despondently and drop my head back on the counter.

"I didn't even take that photo. Miguel did," I mutter against the tile.

"What?" Rose says, dropping the phone and leaning in close to me.

I turn my head to the side so I can look her in the eyes as I confess.

"Miguel took that photo."

"You tramp!" Rose screeches, slapping me on the shoulder with a sly smile on her face.

"I didn't mean for it to happen! He showed up at the shop last night while I was working on a recipe, and I thought it would be okay if I let him in so I could apologize for running away from him the other night. He's not from Port Murphy, he doesn't get the rivalry. I just wanted to, I don't know, tell him face-to-face that we can't be friends."

"And then he somehow ended up taking pictures of your food?"

"Yes," I say, trying to find an argument to defend myself

with, but I can't think of anything. "It's weird, okay? You can't just turn off a switch on a relationship."

"Relationship?" Rose repeats with a laugh. "You knew each other less than twenty-four hours!"

"Okay! I messed up!" I yell, snatching back my phone from the counter and shoving it in my pocket. We sit in silence for a moment, and Rose finally starts to eat her sandwich, which is cold and congealed by now.

She takes a bite and watches me, her gaze considering.

"It is a really good picture. And he got you a bunch of new followers," she says softly. "So I guess it wasn't all bad. But you've got to stop this, Amy. I know you. You're going to get hurt if you don't cut this off now. I'm just worried about you."

"I know," I mutter. I only need to imagine the look on my father's face if he ever found out I kissed a Morales to know she's right. Upsetting my parents that much when they're already dealing with so much isn't worth it.

Miguel is just some guy, after all. Family is what really matters.

CHAPTER ELEVEN

After Miguel's story expires, the hate comments on my posts begin to dwindle. I'm honestly surprised by how many followers I got out of the whole thing and I feel like I need to capitalize on it, so when I get home from my shift that night I go straight to my bedroom and scroll through my camera roll searching for anything remotely shareable.

Instead of finding anything I can work with, I scroll back to Miguel's picture of my buñuelos. No matter how hard I try to focus on the scholarship, all roads in my mind end up leading back to Miguel.

I type his name in the search bar on Instagram and open his profile. I tell myself it's so I can get him out of my system. Maybe I'll see something that gives me the ick, some fault that will have me run away screaming. Him being a Morales should be enough to keep me away, but my brain hasn't been able to absorb that properly yet. Maybe in a week it'll finally hit me and I'll get the same feeling looking at him that I do when I see Adrian or Valeria at school.

But his feed proves to be spare in regard to details about himself. The photo of his mom that he has pinned just says, *Mami, San Diego*. The captions give me next to nothing to learn about him. The pictures are mostly of beautiful landscapes around Southern California and of his friends. Horseback riding in the desert, laying out by a pool, skateboarding in a parking lot at night.

And not one single ick in the hundreds of photos I scroll through.

If anything, I think I only make things worse for myself. Miguel is insanely talented. From the grainy videos of his friends at a skate park to the intimate portraits of friends and family, it's clear he has an eye. Not to mention the stupid viral burrito video that continues to be the bane of my existence.

I finally swipe away from Miguel's profile and resume my pointless search for a new photo to post. If I can't get the money saved up for culinary school, I'm going to be forced down a path of my parents' choosing: working at the shop indefinitely or mindlessly attending another four years of school.

Azúcar is spread out on my bed above me, snoring at a volume you would assume would be impossible for an animal of her size as I scroll through my phone.

"Why are you making that face?" Sofía asks, her head hanging upside down from the edge of her bed.

"I'm trying to figure out what to post on my food Instagram," I say, as I edit the same picture for the fifth time.

"Just post whatever," she tells me, "people can tell when you're being a try-hard. They don't like it."

"A *try-hard*?" I repeat, throwing my phone down on my bed to glare at my sister.

"People can tell when you're not being authentic," she says sagely before rolling over and sitting up.

"I'm not a try-hard," I explain. "I'm a perfectionist. There's a difference."

"Mm-hmm," she says, turning her attention back to her phone.

I look back down at the photo I've been trying to edit and undo everything. It's a picture of a metal container with espuma, the sugar-and-coffee concoction that makes Cuban coffee what it is. You take a few drops of your freshly brewed espresso (typically made on a stovetop Moka pot) and add it to a cup with a few spoonfuls of sugar and then begin agitating it aggressively. After a while the sugar-coffee mixture thickens and comes together into this beautiful light caramel color. When you add the rest of the brewed coffee to the mixture you should get a delightful layer of sugary foam on top.

It takes a while to learn how to do it right. If you don't whip it enough the sugar just dissolves into the coffee and you don't get the iconic layer of foam.

Making espuma is an art form. My photo showing off my espuma is not art, but it's mostly fine.

I post the picture as is with a caption about the art of espuma. The next day, I lose ten followers.

I try to spend the next few days working and focusing on my

application and recipe. I *also* try to expel thoughts of Miguel from my mind, but he seems to be everywhere I look. When I'm in the shop and go into the walk-in fridge I remember how cold his skin was when I finally pulled him out. When I'm home trying to take photos of something I remember the way his hands held my phone as he took pictures.

In an attempt to get him off my mind, I call Rose. She is explaining to me the very intricate drama that is playing out in the Debate Club this summer since Gage Magnussen was elected as president for the second year in a row.

I'm only half listening as she goes on to explain how Lor Edwards tried to sabotage the vote and just admitted to it last week. Most of my attention is focused on my phone as I scroll through Miguel's Instagram. Again.

It seems my last conversation with him finally stuck because I haven't seen him. He hasn't stopped by the shop while I work, he hasn't tried to reach out to me online, and he hasn't messaged me on Instagram.

It should feel fine. Miguel wasn't in my life before last week. And in the week he *has* been in my life it's been in stressful bits and pieces.

And yet.

The one photo he took of my food was so good. It was contest-winning good. If our families weren't bitter enemies, if I were from a *normal* family, I could ask him to help me with this scholarship. It would make my summer so much easier, having someone like him on my side to help me.

I swipe back over to my feed. Everything I've tried posting since Miguel's photo has completely flopped. I tap on his picture of my buñuelos. If the stuff I submitted for the scholarship competition looked like this, I wouldn't be nearly as stressed out.

I go back to Miguel's feed and open his stories, taking the chance that he might see that I've been watching them. There's a picture of Adrian and the Morales family dog dancing, a selfie of Adrian and Miguel from what looks like the roof of Morales Bakery, and as of five minutes ago a picture of a slice of cherry pie from Lacey's Diner with a bunch of *Twin Peaks* stickers.

I *could* take up Rose on her offer to help. She could help me produce okay content, certainly better than anything I could do on my own. But Miguel? Miguel's help would seal the deal.

"Rose, can I call you back later?" I say, closing Instagram and sitting up.

"Ugh, you're sick of hearing about the Debate Club, aren't you?"

"No, I just want to hang with my mom and sister in the living room, they're watching something together," I lie.

"Okay fine," Rose says. "I haven't even told you the best part of the whole thing, but we can get into that later."

"Can't wait," I say before hanging up.

I drop my phone and check Sofía's side of the room. She's still in the living room watching a Spanish TV show with our mom. I can hear her cackling as our mom cries over whatever doomed romance is happening on screen.

Without thinking too much, I jump out of bed and grab my jacket.

In the living room, my sister is sitting on the floor, one leg draped over the end of the couch and the other folded in like a pretzel. Our mom is wrapped up in blankets on the chaise part of the couch with a half-empty glass of wine on the end table next to her.

"Rose needs help with something. It should be pretty quick, so I'm going to head over now," I tell them as I walk toward the front door. "I'll be back before ten."

"Do you want me to drop you off?" Mom asks from her cocoon. "The forecast said it might rain."

"I'll be fine," I assure her. I'm so nervous, I feel like they can both see my secret plan floating over my head on a sign that says, I'M ON MY WAY TO A MORALES.

"Okay, be careful," Mom says. "Love you."

"Love you, too."

And then I'm out the door.

CHAPTER TWELVE

Lacey's Diner is an easy ten-minute ride from my house, mostly downhill. It's not normally an arduous ride, but tonight's stress has me all worked up. Sweat runs down in fat drips from my elbow creases and collects in my eyebrows, where it drops down directly into my eyes, making them sting. It feels like the final warning from the universe to turn back, to change my mind and not go through with this plan.

I pride myself on being the "good" daughter, the one who picks up after herself and helps the family without being asked. But honestly, it's not a hard title to come by when my competition is Sofía, the spoiled baby of the family. I do the things my parents expect of me and avoid most things they don't want me doing.

But I'd be lying if I said I was *always* the good daughter. I've had alcohol (always followed by several glasses of water), I've snuck out of the house (usually just to go to the bakery), and I've lied to my parents (by telling them each in turn that I want what they want for my future, even though I want neither for myself). My parents likely know that I'm not always the good daughter—if the stories about my father's youth were any indication, he knows all our tricks. But they at least know I'm always going to make a smart decision in the end.

I cannot in good conscience say that tonight is a smart decision. But I don't entirely believe it's a wrong decision either.

I brake at the bottom of the hill to catch my breath. On the corner sits Lacey's Diner, a classic mid-century diner that has been here since before my family set foot in Port Murphy. The food has always been mediocre, but it's open twenty-four hours and serves bottomless coffee. Being a diner in the PNW, they definitely lean into the *Twin Peaks* aesthetic, but they at least come by it honestly. In the daytime the diner is surrounded by huge evergreens with the peaks of the Olympic Mountains peeking through the boughs. At night it sits like a warm, glowing escape at the bottom of the hill, catching hungry wanderers in its orbit.

I follow the hazy butter-yellow light spilling from the windows of Lacey's and rest my bike against the side of the building next to the dumpsters.

Pulling up the hood of my jacket, I begin to prowl the parking lot, searching for a car I've only seen once. Even though I only have a vague recollection to go from, I am fairly confident I can find Miguel's car based on the fact it's going to be the only car in the lot with a California plate.

I still haven't spotted his car when I pass by the front windows. Inside, Lacey's has the classic L-shaped layout, with a bar running along the length of the restaurant with a matching bank of booth seating against the front window. Inside there's a line cook with one of those stupid paper hats, and the two waitresses are wearing their retro 1950s diner uniform. The counters and tables are all yellow Formica with bright red seats accented with chrome. Cheap wood siding covers the bar fronts and most of the walls, and the decor is made up of garish neon lights and kitschy PNW-themed bric-a-brac.

There are a couple families out for a late dinner seated in the window booths closer to the front door, a group of guys I recognize from the swim team seated toward the back of the restaurant, a couple on a date sitting at the counter, and the Morales cousins with friends sitting in the booth directly across from the jukebox.

Adrian is sitting all the way back in the booth, his arms spread wide over the back like he owns the place. He has a smug smile on as he tells a story to the entire table, soaking in their admiration like the attention hog he is. To his right is Dallas, who is eating up everything he's saying like he's the most interesting guy on Earth. On his left is his main sidekick, Lane Sanders, ready to hype him up even further.

Valeria is sitting across from them but looking out the window. I'm fairly certain she won't be able to spot me in the dark of the parking lot, but just in case, I squat down and hide behind the car in front of me. There are two other people in the booth, but I can only see the backs of their heads from my vantage point.

However, there is no doubt in my mind that the head at the end is Miguel's. I have no right to know the back of his head as well as I do, but here we are.

I open Instagram and pull his profile back up. I still have a chance to hop back on my bike and go home. I don't have to go through with this.

But I know if I want to stand a chance at winning the scholarship contest this summer, I need Miguel's help. Just looking at his feed now is a clear reminder of his talent.

Without thinking about it any further, I take the plunge and hit the message button.

I type out and delete a dozen messages before I finally land on something.

CocinaGuava: Hey. I want to talk.

There. I hit send and hope for the best. I look up from my phone and scan the parking lot again. And there, at the end near the pole for the diner's sign, is a car I recognize with California plates. I cross to the other side of the parking lot where there's more shadow and creep toward Miguel's car. I squat down on the side that's hidden from the Moraleses' view and wait.

My phone buzzes in my hand and I whip it out, nearly dropping it on the concrete before catching it.

ShutterShyGuy: Is this a test? Am I supposed to ignore this?

I turn around and look through the car window. From this angle I can see Miguel's side of the table where he has turned away from the group and is looking down toward his lap.

CocinaGuava: Not a test. I think we should try out your idea.

ShutterShyGuy: Custom hats for cats?

A snort of laughter escapes me.

CocinaGuava: No, but I don't think you should give up on that. Can you get away for a second?

I turn around to watch him again to see what his reaction is

115

to my question. He looks up from his lap and glances at Adrian, who is still monopolizing the table's attention with his story.

ShutterShyGuy: Yeah. I'm at Lacey's right now but I can make an excuse to leave.

CocinaGuava: Great, let's meet up. In secret.

I don't have to say anything else before Miguel is getting up from the booth and waving at his cousins before dropping a twenty down on the table and heading out. He runs out to his car and hops into the driver's seat without noticing me, the gremlin crouching next to his passenger door.

He has his phone out once the door is closed, and he's calling me through Instagram. I figure now is as good a time as any to let him know that I'm right next to him. I knock on the glass of the passenger door.

Miguel nearly jumps out of his skin and fumbles with his phone, clearly trying to hide the fact that he was just trying to call an Ybarra in case it's one of his cousins at the window. He turns to me, wide-eyed and terrified, and I can't help but laugh.

He lowers the passenger-side window once he's recovered enough and shoots me a threatening glower.

"You could have told me you were stalking me," he says.

"I saw your story with the cherry pie and I live nearby," I say by way of excuse. He unlocks the car and pops the door open for me.

"Get in here before one of my cousins looks outside," he tells me.

"They can still just walk up to the car," I point out, getting in anyway.

"We can go on a drive while we talk," he says.

116

"Just like old times," I can't help but point out, remembering the last time we were in this car together in LA.

Miguel starts up the car and pulls out of his spot while I try to work up the courage to begin this conversation. He waits patiently for me, not jumping in before I'm ready to talk.

"I think we should try the hanging out in secret thing," I say nervously, worried that he might no longer be interested. He glances over at me in surprise, but there's something more to his face. Excitement? Hope? "The honest truth is that I need help and you're the only person I know that has the skills necessary to help me out."

"So you want to use me?" he clarifies, his eyes back on the road making it difficult for me to read his expression.

"I'm trying to win this competition this summer," I tell him instead of confronting the fact that I do, in fact, want to use him. "Remember how I told you about my dream of going to culinary school? I've been able to save up some money, but nowhere near enough to pay for tuition and living expenses in Paris. And with graduation coming up, I know my mom is going to be on me about college. If I win this competition, it'll set me up to do the program in France by the end of next summer."

"What's the competition?" he asks, and I explain to him the whole setup, including the very important social media angle.

"I know my recipes are good, but I can't manage to make them look appealing in photos and video. The only people who engage with my content are friends or random Cuban people looking for a recipe to help them recreate their abuela's arroz con pollo or something. And then I posted that picture you took of my buñuelos and it blew up. You made my food look so good."

"Because your food *is* good," he tells me. We've made it to downtown Port Murphy, and he's taking one of the side streets that leads down to the waterfront. He stops in the empty parking lot and turns off the car.

I try not to think of the other nighttime uses for this parking lot. It's not like Miguel would know this is a local hookup spot—he's only lived here like five minutes. And besides, this is a conversation about *friendship*.

"I know it's kind of shitty to change my mind about us hanging out to use you for your photography skills, but I'm desperate. I really want to win this competition. I need something concrete to prove to my parents that the dream I want is . . ." I struggle to come up with a word.

"Attainable?" he offers.

"Yeah." I nod. "Something like that."

"Can we still hang out after the competition?" he asks.

"Yes," I agree quickly. "And you're free to use me for any goals or dreams you're trying to accomplish."

A cheeky grin spread across Miguel's face. "Yeah?" And I'm suddenly very aware we're in this dark car, facing each other in our seats. Miguel has his arm around the back of my headrest, and I'm watching him warily now, noticing the change in his expression. He looks contemplative, his eyes too dark to read clearly. Then he reaches out and catches a stray lock of my hair, tucking it behind my ear.

His fingers linger there for a moment and an embarrassing full-body shudder passes over me.

Miguel will go back home to LA at the end of the summer, I tell myself. Miguel is a Morales, I remind myself.

"Miguel," I say softly, a note of warning in my voice. "The deal is for secret *friendship*." I try to sound firm, but even I can hear the tremor in my voice.

"Friends," he repeats, pulling his hand back and leaning away from me. "Right."

Being friends with a Morales is already crossing a line I never thought I'd cross. I can't take it any further. No matter how much I want to.

"Well, Ybarra," Miguel says. "Looks like we have a deal."

CHAPTER THIRTEEN

I can't believe you're roping me into this farce," Rose complains the next day in her kitchen. We're giving it a deep clean and reorganizing things to make it more aesthetically pleasing.

"Your house is like Switzerland, okay? Neutral. It's the only place we could feasibly do this," I say as I move the blender from the countertop to the bottom of the pantry.

Before dropping me off at Lacey's to get my bike last night, Miguel and I exchanged numbers so we didn't have to communicate through Instagram anymore. I put him in my phone as "LA Food Critic" and he put me in his as "Bake Lively."

"Text me what content you think you need to record and we can make a shot list," he told me. "Do you have a place where we can secretly do this project together? I assume the restaurant is out. As are both our houses."

"Right." I had considered this, and while I didn't love the solution I'd come up with, there was an answer. "We can probably use my best friend's kitchen. Her mom works two jobs and

is never home, so we have more than enough time to film there."
I'd have to borrow some kitchen equipment from either my house or the restaurant, but hopefully that won't be too much of a problem.

"That should work. Can I stop by to scope out the place to see what kind of equipment I should bring?"

"Sure, Rose and I will get the place ready tomorrow. I'll text you."

What followed was an awkward goodbye where I went in to give him a kiss on the cheek and he went in for a hug and then I all but flew out of the car to my bike.

"You know I support you in everything you do," Rose says now, a cleaning rag in hand. "But I do think this is a really bad idea."

"You've made your views very clear! But he's really good at what he does and I *need* to win this competition, Rose. My mom emailed me like seven links about colleges in Washington and their hospitality degrees."

"Hospitality?" Rose shudders at the suggestion. "You'd have to deal with tourists *every day*. What a nightmare."

"It's what my mom was going to school for when she met my dad. I think she had a dream of starting her own boutique hotel or something." A dream she gave up for my father's dream. I'm not entirely sure if she regrets it, but I imagine some part of her must. When the dwindling sales and debts start to pile up, an alternate universe where you made a different decision must seem appealing.

With my senior year coming up, the future—specifically *my* future—has often been a subject of discussion over dinner. My father inherited Café y Más from his father, and he hopes to one day pass down the bakery to me. And I *love* our family bakery. I do. But truth is, I dream of *more*.

My mother dreams of more for me, too. That's why she set up the tour for UCLA. She tried to get me to fall in love with the school and with LA. It's not like she doesn't love the family business, too, but I know it's not the future she wants for me. She wants me to have something more secure than running a bakery that is always on the edge of closing down. Law school, medical school, business school, something prestigious that would result in me getting fat, steady paychecks.

But that expectation grinds at me just as much as the expectation of taking over the bakery. Because I want both: to bake *and* do something more, something bigger. But I don't want those things in the same way my parents do.

I want to go to the Cordon Bleu culinary school in Paris. I want to be a head pastry chef at a Michelin-starred restaurant. I want to travel the world, learning techniques and flavors from every corner of the Earth.

And that is a future neither of my parents would approve of. It would break my father's heart for me to turn down his bakery for something fancy in New York. And my mother would just see the instability of it all, the chaos that is the food industry.

So I need to win this scholarship, which will prove to my family that I can: a) save the money required to attend pastry school, and b) be good enough at baking and creating my own recipes that this is a reasonable career path for me to follow.

"Woof," Rose says. "So she wants you to pick up where she left off?"

"Not unlike my dad," I mutter.

"The only thing my mom cares about is me not becoming a teen mom. If I avoid that, it's a win in her eyes," Rose says, no trace of bitterness in her voice. "How does this look?"

The McGinnis kitchen wouldn't be featured in *Architectural Digest* or anything, but it has its charm. Since the house has been in her family for generations, not much has changed through the decades, including the kitchen. Most of the details from the last remodel in the 1960s remain, from the light teal cabinets and dark teal trim to the butter-yellow tile countertop and backsplash. The floor is a green-and-white checkerboard with red-and-black trim, and the windows have café curtains with a vintage floral print.

We've managed to clear most of the clutter from the countertops, mostly piles of mail and stacks of magazines. The air fryer (Rose's favorite kitchen tool) and other small appliances have been moved to the dining room or whatever cupboard could fit them. We're left with a blank slate for filming.

"I kind of love the colors," I say after a moment's consideration. "It reminds me of my abuela's neighborhood in Miami. All the houses are pink and aqua and yellow and everything is so green and lush."

"I'm glad you think so," Rose says, frowning at the kitchen. "My mom's been dying to update it. We spend most dinners just discussing what we'd do different."

"Well, I don't love the tile countertop. All the grout is impossible to keep clean. But it does look cute."

A knock at the back door cuts off our conversation.

"He took your rules seriously," Rose notes, sounding impressed.

"I was very stern with him."

The rules were a little extreme, but if we want to keep this thing a secret, we have to be extra cautious. Everyone knows that I only have one friend: Rose McGinnis. And everyone knows Rose McGinnis lives in the old McGinnis house on the corner of Cedar Street and Eighth Avenue. The road her house sits on is a popular road for cutting around traffic and has lots of eyes on it during the day. So if her house is going to be our meeting ground, Miguel has to park in the back, behind the rhododendrons and hydrangea bushes, and he can only approach from the back door.

I have Rose do the honors of letting Miguel into her house, welcoming him in through the small mudroom and into the kitchen.

He looks devastatingly handsome today, unfortunately. I was hoping being clear about this being a friends-only thing would mean that he would show up looking like a troll, but I'm out of luck. His hair is carelessly rumpled, and he's wearing a plain black tee with jeans that fit him *too well*. I avert my eyes and focus on the gear that he has slung over his shoulder: a camera bag, a long, soft suitcase that looks like it could carry a trombone, and his backpack.

"Welcome to Switzerland," Rose says, holding the door to the kitchen open for him.

"Oh, retro," Miguel says appreciatively as he takes in the kitchen. "Ybarra," he says with a jerk of his chin in greeting.

"Fuentes," I return.

"Where can I set this stuff down?" he asks.

"You can put it down on the island," Rose tells him, showing off the freshly cleared space. "You really brought the whole studio, huh?"

"Ana Maria said she really has to win this thing, so I left nothing up to chance," he says as he drops his things down. "Plus, I thought it might be easier to bring everything over now and leave it here until we're done filming. That way I don't have to be lugging it back and forth. One of my cousins might catch on."

"Where did you tell them you were going today?" I ask.

"I said I wanted to go on a hike to a waterfall to get some pictures. The Morales twins are not known for being the most outdoorsy," he explains. "What's yours?"

"Oh, I don't need an excuse to be at Rose's."

"Amy is like a sister to me," Rose says proudly. "That means I have my eye on you, Mister," she says, trying to sound threatening but Rose can't help but be cute instead. She's all of five-foot-three and is wearing her blond hair in pigtails—you can't get much more adorable than that. But Miguel holds up his hands in mock surrender anyway.

"Do you need me to swear on something? I promise I'm just here to help Ana Maria. I live outside this family feud," he assures her.

"Leave him alone," I say with a laugh, slapping Rose with a tea towel. "We should get started."

Miguel bends down and opens the mystery suitcases, which turn out to be the travel cases for some studio lights he brought over.

"No way!" Rose says with delight when he unfolds the soft boxes. "These are so much better than my ring lights. Can I use these to record TikToks?"

"You know how to use them?"

"She's a theater nerd," I tell Miguel. "And she pretty much knows how to do everything. She found a lamp at Goodwill last summer and turned it into a sconce."

"A hardwired sconce," she adds. "I know my way around a light."

"A real renaissance woman, huh?" he says with a laugh. "Sure, you can use them. And since you're so knowledgeable, help me set these up."

Together we get the lights and tripods set up. He has two digital cameras set up plus my iPhone for additional footage. He explains that this allows for multiple angles without having to reset too much. We shoot some test shots to see how everything looks, and he makes some creative adjustments to Rose's kitchen. ("Maybe the *I Love Lucy* clock in the back should go in the dining room for now.")

Miguel pulls out a very fancy-looking shot list that he has both printed *and* laminated. He has some ideas on how recipes can be stacked on the same filming day, and I make some adjustments to account for rest time and other variables. All in all, we will record twelve recipes total, with plenty of B-roll that I could use for other posts.

Which means I need to hurry up and decide what my showstopping recipe is going to be. Now that I have the concern of filming things off my plate, I'll really be able to zero in and focus on my recipe development.

"What are you getting out of this?" Miguel asks Rose as he begins to pack his cameras back up.

"I get to keep all the leftovers," she says gleefully.

"Even though she's a vegetarian," I point out.

"I'm a vegetarian, but my mom isn't. She deserves good food, too! It's her kitchen, after all."

"It's the least I could do for Poppy, really," I say. "After all, she produced one of my favorite people in the world." I reach for Rose's face and affectionately pinch her cheeks.

"And what are you getting out of it, Mr. Fuentes-but-might-as-well-be-Morales?" Rose says suspiciously after brushing my hands away so she can turn a stern look on him.

"Me? The joy of being a rebel, I suppose. My cousins are so straight-laced, I have to live up to my bad boy reputation in comparison."

"Bad boy?" Rose says with a laugh, pulling away from me. "I can't see it."

"What? I'm the cousin that's just rolled in from the mean streets of the City of Angels in a haze of cigarette smoke and sunshine. I have a mysterious past and a dark secret."

"Am I the secret?" I ask, half curious, half joking.

Miguel mimes zipping his lips shut.

His phone buzzes then, cutting off our conversation. He checks it and frowns.

"Time to head out?" I guess.

"Yeah, family dinner."

"I should have all my ingredients delivered here tomorrow. I'll need a day to prep everything, but after that I'll be ready to start filming."

"Perfect. Text me the time and I'll be there." Miguel picks up his camera bags, the only equipment he's taking back, and heads back out of the house. Once we hear his engine kick on, Rose turns to me with a mischievous smile.

"He's not half bad for a Morales," she says.

"It's because he's actually a Fuentes," I point out.

"He was also very well behaved," she says, picking up one of the laminated shot lists to inspect it again.

"What does that mean?" I ask.

"Don't be coy." Rose grins, her eyes peeking out from above the sheet. "As much as I think this arrangement is a bad idea, I can see why you were pining after him for all those months. The chemistry between you two is through the roof."

"Do not," I say, wagging a finger at her in my best attempt to look threatening, "start with that."

"No wonder you decided to do this at my house," she continues anyway. "If I wasn't here as a buffer you would definitely jump his bones."

"Oh my *God*," I screech, finding the nearest throwable thing—in this case, a seat cushion—and aim it straight at Rose's head. "We are *friends*, Rose! I can be friends with a boy, okay?"

"Oh, yeah, like who?" she asks, tossing the pillow back at me. "James? That boy has a raging hard on for you, too, Ames."

"I wish you would go back to espousing the wrongs of speaking to a Morales instead of whatever harassment this is," I tell her.

"Aw," she says with mock sweetness before walking over and trapping me in a hug. "I'm just here to keep you honest, Ybarra."

CHAPTER FOURTEEN

I spend the next two days after work at Rose's house, organizing my ingredients and making sure I have all the tools I need. Thankfully Rose's grandmother was quite the baker and has a beautiful collection of glass Pyrex in bright, fun colors that I think will look great in the videos.

Rose has decided to take on the role of set and costume designer for this project, so she's been at Goodwill trying to source extra props. So far she's found a beautiful set of Depression Era pink glass plates, an adorable 1950s-style pinafore apron in a soft yellow with little cherries, an amber glass sauce pot, and a couple of plates from a 1970s set with painted flowers and a gilded edge.

She also insisted that she will be doing my hair and makeup for the shoots and has even pulled out her instant camera to take continuity shots of all my outfits according to recipes.

When I tell her I didn't need her to do this much, that letting me use the kitchen is enough help, she brushes me off.

"Are you kidding me? This is going on my résumé. Kids applying for theater school these days have like professional-quality YouTube channels and are using Final Cut Pro for *fun*. I need to pad my résumé, and this is the perfect opportunity." After that, I don't try to stop her and let her have free rein on the visuals.

The schedule we land on gives us two weeks to shoot everything we need and a little under a week to edit the videos. We're on Tuesdays and Thursdays, and I got my dad to switch my schedule at work without any fuss or questions asked. That gives me just enough time off to perfect my recipe for the competition. Miguel's cousins might start to get suspicious about his frequent hiking, but I've left that up to him. Hopefully just seeing each other in person two days a week is safe enough for us not to get caught by anyone.

With all the preplanning we did, our first filming day goes off without a hitch. Rose and Miguel end up making a great team, and they work together to keep everything running.

"Don't worry about how your hands look," Miguel says.

"I'm not worried about how my hands look," I say defensively, shaking them out and rubbing them on the apron.

"Oh, she definitely is," Rose says from her chair, a barstool on which she has taped a sign that says, "Production Designer." Miguel has a matching chair that says, "Director," and my chair just says, "The Talent."

"You keep resetting your hands," Miguel points out. "Don't worry about that. The focus is going to be on the food."

We all discover very quickly that I'm a nervous wreck when the cameras are on me. Miguel makes the executive decision to focus on shooting content that is food-forward, insisting that the less said, the better.

"Social media food content isn't about creating a video someone can follow along step by step," he explains when I begin to look doubtful. "It's about inspiring someone."

We decide to do some voiceovers to add a story to the recipe, but I don't need to be concerned about laying out step-by-step instructions for the viewer.

That helps with the anxiety a little.

We decide to start with the recipes that require the most time first, so if anything needs to be reshot we don't end up running out of time. On the menu today is Cuban lechon, frijoles negros, and guava and cream cheese whoopie pies.

Once the pork starts roasting in the oven, Rose makes a gagging sound.

"I hate the smell of meat cooking," she complains from her seat. "I'm going outside. Text me when you need me."

Rose leaves through the mudroom, and I'm suddenly very aware this is the first time I've been alone with Miguel since we struck our deal. Turns out Rose might not have been so far off when she said she was a buffer between us.

"You haven't told me what your winning recipe is yet," Miguel points out as he resets one of the cameras.

"I haven't entirely decided," I admit. "I keep going back and forth on it."

"Why don't you tell me what you're choosing between and I can help you narrow it down. What's the competition looking for?"

I take a break from chopping onions and wipe my teary eyes with my shoulder.

"Well, it needs to be a dish with a story. But pretty much everything I cook has a story because I learned to cook Cuban food from my family's restaurant. My abuela's favorite snack was queso blanco with a slice of guava paste and the first time I tried it I lost a baby tooth. And I was always so underfoot in the kitchen as a kid that my mom always ended up giving me distracting tasks like counting the exact amount of raisins to add to the picadillo. There is no way for me to separate food from my family."

"Okay, so if everything has a story about your family, which dish has a story about *you*?" Miguel asks, looking up from the camera.

Since I agreed to be secret friends with Miguel, I've avoided certain things. Like being close enough to smell him or touch him at all. I think maybe he's made these same rules for himself, because when he looks up and I meet his gaze, I realize it's the first time since we made our pact that I've looked him directly in the eyes like this. Totally focused and alone.

I break our gaze immediately and look back down at my diced onion.

"I don't know," I admit. "I have one recipe, but . . . I think it's pretty simple. It doesn't really have that wow factor."

"What is it?" he asks.

"Cuban doughnuts," I admit, a little embarrassed by the idea.

"Based off those buñuelos you made?" he says excitedly, and I look up at him in surprise. "That would be so cool!"

"You think so?" I ask quietly.

"Of course! Were you thinking of making them different flavors?"

"Yeah, I have a whole slew of flavors I want to try. Cuban ones like churro, mango, tres leches, guava. The churro one has sugar rubbed with lime zest and a little bit of anise as a nod to the original recipe. I also want to try some flavors inspired by not only Cuban foods, but flavors of the Northwest, like strawberries and coffee."

"My mouth is already watering," Miguel says with an encouraging smile. "The best of both worlds, a classic diner food with a Cuban twist."

"Exactly! I want to find a way to reinvent the Cuban pastry classics through the lens of modern techniques. Using alternative starches for doughnuts isn't unheard of, there are doughnut shops out there already using malanga and yuca for doughnuts, but most people don't know it. Buñuelos are delicious, but it's rare for people to ever have them because they are either inaccessible or made with anise, which turns a lot of people off. I want to take something I love, something very Cuban, and make it my own. It's kind of like . . . what I want to do after school. I don't want to leave Cuban cooking behind, but I want to explore and learn and test the boundaries of what Cuban food is. My dad thinks that anything that veers from the traditional way of doing something is an insult and inherently wrong, but . . . I think we should question tradition sometimes."

"I think you have it," Miguel says softly. "That's the recipe. That's your story."

I decide to risk it and meet his gaze, to gauge how serious he is. When I look up he's stopped fidgeting with the camera and is

133

smiling at me encouragingly. I smile back at him, still so surprised that someone I've only known for a matter of days understands me so well. I look back down at my hands, trying to veer away from that train of thought.

Luckily, Rose chooses that moment to make her grand return. "Okay, it's finally starting to smell good in here again."

I jump like Miguel and I have been caught but recover quickly. "Now I guess I just need to make sure it tastes good."

We continue our recording session, getting several shots on the process of making the perfect pot of Cuban black beans (made meatless for Rose) and a shot of a butter knife scraping across the crispy skin of the lechon.

"I think we have used you enough for today," I tell Miguel. "No need to record me cleaning up the kitchen."

"I'll take a slice of the lechon and a whoopie pie as payment," he says.

"Isn't that dangerous? How are you going to explain the leftovers to your family?" I ask.

"My mom and I are staying in my uncle's basement, and we have our own kitchen," Miguel says. "I doubt my mom would even notice, and no one else even goes in there. It's safe. Plus, I'll hide it behind a tub of mayonnaise or something."

"Foolproof," Rose comments.

"If you say so," I tell him, beginning to pack up some leftovers for him. "See you Thursday," I say. As I hand off the containers to him, his fingers brush across mine. I flinch at the contact, the feeling of our skin touching hot and electric.

"You good?" Miguel asks as I quickly pull my hands from

the container and brush them across my apron. I can't help but notice that there's a faint smirk dancing on his lips.

"Yeah," I say quickly. "I'm good. See you Thursday."

"You said that already." His smile is full blown at this point. He slings his camera bag over his shoulder and heads out the mudroom door before I can embarrass myself further.

Thursday follows in the same pattern. We set up, go over the set list, and Rose makes small adjustments here and there to match up the set and my outfits as we go through the recipes. Today I'm making croissants made with lard instead of butter (like Cuban bread), a Cuban twist on tiramisu, and what I've decided to call the Vicky sponge, a Cuban take on the classic Victoria sponge. It has the two sponge layers flavored with a little rum, guava jam, and a mascarpone whipped cream stabilized with a little bit of instant vanilla pudding. It was a contender for the final recipe, but it ultimately lost because I couldn't think of a better story than "I watched a lot of *The Great British Bake-Off* one summer."

Rose is thrilled that no meat is involved anymore (with the exception of the lard in the croissants, which she is unhappy about but is relieved it doesn't come with the smell of roasting meat) and spends more of her time shadowing Miguel and asking him what he's doing.

"I'm switching out the lens on this camera for my zoom lens. It's going to give me a really crisp image of the foreground and then that bokeh effect on everything else that's out of focus. It's nice for these detail shots." He runs through how to change the lens with Rose, and I can see the gears turning in her head as she learns more.

135

"You're a real pro," Rose says, definitely impressed.

Miguel shrugs. "Not really, I just have a rich dad who is emotionally distant and makes up for it by buying me camera equipment. The rest is just dumb luck."

"Hardly," I cut in as I continue to stir the dulce de leche that I'd been working on for the last half hour. "You have an eye for this stuff," I argue.

"That can be learned, given enough time and effort. More than half the battle is having access to the equipment and learning the technical stuff."

"Ah, so you don't believe in talent, huh?" Rose asks.

"Not really?" Miguel says, resetting the camera. "I think people can be called to something, for sure. But to believe that something, some skill, is just innate and not . . . worked for or even faked with enough money, I'm not sure I can get behind that."

"Is this what he was like the first time you met him?" Rose asks me. "Just like . . . this total bummer energy?"

A bark of laughter escapes me at that description of Miguel.

"Hey!" Miguel says, frowning at Rose.

"Listen, you started this by being self-deprecating, I'm just calling it like I see it," Rose says. "It's just that Amy's never really liked anyone before, and if this was what you were giving off—"

"Rose!" I hiss, mortified that she's brought that up. "Please develop a filter."

"Oh, no, I have to hear more about this," Miguel cuts in.

I turn and point my whisk, covered in thick dulce de leche, at him in my best attempt to look threatening.

"Do not encourage her. This is an off-limits topic."

Rose, to her credit, redirects the conversation and asks Miguel about life in Los Angeles and how many celebrities he's met. She's absolutely fascinated with his stories about life in California and how much he has to drive to do anything or get anywhere. I'm grateful we've safely navigated away from forbidden territory and are no longer talking about me.

Once we've gotten all the shots we need for the day, Rose helps Miguel pack up the equipment as I start to clean up the kitchen.

"So how does this rivalry work with parties?" Miguel asks Rose as they breakdown the lights together.

"How do you mean?"

"Tonight is Dallas's party, and she's kind of dating my cousin." Rose makes a fake gagging sound. "And you were at the same party I was at with my cousins when we met. So how does that work?"

"Well, there are definitely camps," Rose says. "The Ybarra one is admittedly small."

"It boasts one member, and you're looking at her," I cut in, motioning to Rose.

"And while, yes, Dallas is currently in the Morales camp, parties are kind of like no man's land. Our school is so small and we all know each other so it's hard to get too territorial. We just do our best to avoid each other. Adrian is usually too focused on himself to care, and Valeria is too focused on having a good time to want to waste any of it on noticing Amy."

"Honestly, Sofía and Rose are the most likely to cause trouble at any given opportunity."

"So yes, we will be at Dallas's tonight," Rose says. I open my mouth to protest the use of *we* because I haven't agreed to be anywhere, but Rose continues on. "What did you tell your cousins about your public encounter with Amy?"

I cringe at the memory of that night. Miguel rubs the back of his neck and bites his lip, which causes my heart rate to spike. *Focus.* I turn back to the counter and begin to scrub it with vigor.

"They really just handed me my excuse," Miguel says. "Valeria said, 'I see you've met one of the Ybarras.' And she explained the family rivalry to me. No one really thought anything of it."

"Well, don't look at us, don't speak to us, and if you walk into a room we're in, leave. The hosts usually prefer it if we don't cause a scene," Rose explains, as though she really is an Ybarra by blood. Miguel doesn't question it.

"Small towns are wild," Miguel says with a laugh.

After Miguel leaves, Rose and I finish scrubbing down the kitchen together. When I try to worm my way out of going to the party tonight by insisting I need to get ready at my house, Rose locks the mudroom door and glares at me.

"You need to take a break," Rose says, reading my mind instantly. "I promise going to the party tonight will be fun. Dallas always has the best food."

I feel like a pot of water about to boil over. I'm *tired*. Between work, prepping for filming, cooking for six straight hours, and spending my nights agonizing over the essay for my application, I just want to go home and take a bath. But I can see it in Rose's eyes that she really wants me to be there tonight, to go out and have fun. She can see how stressed I am and wants to give me the opportunity to let off some steam. And I have to admit, it would be nice to spend some time together, just the two of us, outside the kitchen.

So I give in and follow her upstairs.

Rose gets set up at her vanity to start on her patriotic makeup look that features a giant blue star at the corner of her eyes and outlining it with rhinestones. She tried pitching me a red-and-white-striped lid with a glittery under eye speckled with gold stars.

I turned her down.

"You know," she says, mouth agape as she applies mascara, "Miguel really is nothing like his cousins. He's like, much more chill and interesting. Plus, he's a grade-A—"

"I don't want to hear it!" I cut her off from the floor where I'm curling my hair. "He's off-limits. For *many* reasons."

"Fine, fine." Rose sighs. "Such a shame."

"If you bring him up one more time, I'm not coming tonight," I warn her.

Rose pouts dramatically at me and gets up from her vanity to inspect her outfit. She's gone all out to match her makeup look, pairing a red jean miniskirt with white fishnets and frilly white socks and one of those graphic tees with art that looks like it's from an old educational children's book but has a bunch of kids summoning demons on it. We wear nowhere near the same size, so since borrowing anything was out of the question, I kept on my outfit from filming, a yellow pinafore apron dress with a short-sleeved white button-up shirt underneath. My mom regularly complains that I dress like an old woman, especially compared to Sofía, who dresses the part of an angry teenager.

But I like dressing comfortably and simply. I want to look

like I could be off for a picnic in a meadow, carrying a basket full of freshly baked treats and sandwiches with the crusts cut off.

To avoid ruining her look for the night, Rose asked Gage, president of the Debate Club for the second year in a row despite being a junior, to give us a ride to the party. No chance of me running away on my bike tonight.

I text Sofía to see if she is coming tonight, and she just replies "duh" with no further explanation of her plans.

Two honks outside announce Gage's arrival as Rose is putting finishing touches on her makeup look. She groans, throwing the lipstick in her purse, and we clamber down the stairs and outside.

Gage drives an ancient Subaru Outback that is already full of half the debate team, leaving Rose and I to climb into the trunk. Inside, Gage has his preparty playlist blasting while Abi and Avery argue at full volume in the back seat about the best way to prepare a hot dog. Noah kindly hops out from the passenger seat to close the trunk door for us once we're settled, and Colby turns around from the middle seat to greet us.

"Did you hear about the fireworks?" he asks us without preamble.

"Dallas's fireworks?" Rose says, sitting up and facing the front. I get too motion sick to do that, so I'm just laying prone staring up at the upholstered ceiling. It's ripped in one corner and starting to sag.

"Oh my God," Avery cuts in, momentarily ending her argument with Abi. "Dallas apparently scored, like, professional-quality fireworks from her uncle, and there's going to be this full-on fireworks show tonight."

"Orchestrated by a bunch of drunk teenagers?" I comment from the floor, already imagining the forest fire that Dallas's party will start.

"She's going to be doing it from the dock, it'll be fine," Colby assures me. I'm still not convinced, but everyone else is excited. "Her uncle also scored a keg."

Dallas's uncle is her mom's half brother and only five years older than we are. He's definitely skeezy because he shows up at some of Dallas's parties to hang out with—and occasionally hit on—high schoolers. Rose embarrassed him by rejecting him and verbally eviscerating him in front of an audience, and now he avoids her like the plague, which I appreciate.

"I brought sparklers," Abi adds. "I want to take those pictures where you write stuff with them."

"Oh, you know who's really good with a camera?" Rose starts, and for some reason I can sense exactly where she's going with this. My hand snakes out and pinches her thigh so tight she lets out a surprised yelp.

"Don't scream while I'm driving!" Gage warns from the front.

"Why did you do that?" Rose says, slapping my hand away. I make a face at her and then her eyes widen as she realizes she was about to let Miguel's name slip out. "Oh!" She breathes before collecting herself and looking back up at her friends. "I am! I'm really good with cameras now. It's my new hobby. ISO. Shutter speed. Apertures."

"Since when?" Avery asks.

"Since this summer. It's my new hyper fixation."

Thankfully the conversation moves away from cameras

quickly before Gage makes it to Dallas's street. Now that we've slowed down, I sit up and look around. The street is already full of cars that have parked on the side of the road, a good walking distance away from Dallas's place. We park with the rest of the common rabble, and Noah jumps out to open the trunk for us, reaching out a hand to help Rose take the very short step down to the street. I shimmy out behind her and follow the group toward the house.

Dallas's place sits on the sound, far away from the other multimillion-dollar homes in a secluded plot of land hidden by dense evergreens. Once you make it down the winding driveway—full of the other rich students' nice cars that can't possibly park in the ditches on the side of the road—the full monstrosity comes into view. The house was built in the late '90s with obvious tech money. It's a sprawling, relatively boring-looking house complete with a lighthouse on one end. What's really impressive is the backyard, where there is a massive heated swimming pool and a private beach. I can already hear the music blasting from speakers outside and see bright, flashing lights.

It's definitely too cold at night to really enjoy going in the water, but I hear some splashing coming from the brave few who have decided to enjoy the pool.

When we walk through the front entrance the grand staircase has been blocked off with a tinsel curtain and a sign that says, DO NOT GO UPSTAIRS. WE HAVE CAMERAS AND WE WILL CATCH YOU. Music is blasting from all sides, and balloons, disco balls, and more tinsel lead the way toward the kitchen.

Slowly the group we came in with disperses, Abi catching sight of someone she knows from French class and Avery running to the bathroom. Gage and Colby cut off to the backyard without grabbing a drink, and Noah stays with us, chatting with Rose about whales or something.

I feel like a live wire walking through the party, just waiting for the moment I bump into a Morales. Specifically, Miguel.

When we step into the kitchen, the host turns around and greets us with a big smile.

"Welcome!" Dallas cries out, throwing her arms out in an effusive greeting. She's holding a sippy cup in one hand filled with a bright blue drink and a genuine welcoming smile on her face. She runs up to us and throws her arms around Rose and me. "I'm so glad you guys made it. I know I'm hanging out with Adrian and I'm supposed to be, like, ignoring you or whatever, but I will never forget the time you let me cheat off your algebra exam," she tells me in a mock whisper. "You're my girl for life."

Dallas is clearly a few drinks in, because while I did let her cheat off me in algebra, I have never been one of her "girls." We're friendly in class and wouldn't dump pig's blood on each other or whatever, but my invite to this party is out of courtesy more than it is friendship.

"Us girls have to look after each other," I say, glad at least that she's decided not to ice me out.

"And I mean, I don't know how much longer I'm going to entertain Adrian anyway, because his cousin is in town and he is *so* much hotter," Dallas continues.

"Oh, is he?" Rose says, and I can practically hear the smile on her face.

"Shh, don't tell!" Dallas says pulling away from us to make a serious face and press her finger to her lips. "Anyway, help yourself to whatever's in here and there's some food outside. Oh, Riley!" she calls out, catching sight of someone behind us and walking away.

Rose opens her mouth, and I silence her quickly with my hand.

"Noah," I say, since he's still glued to Rose, "why don't you go get a drink with Rose?"

"What about you?" Rose asks with a pout. "You're not working tomorrow. Kick back with us."

"I'm working on my application tomorrow," I tell her. "I should try to find Sofía, anyway. Make sure she's not getting up to anything too crazy."

Rose continues pouting, but Noah is more than happy to pull her away.

Knowing Sofía, she's probably going to stay close to where the fireworks will be happening. I head out to the back patio, slipping between groups of people laughing and talking. I spot the Morales crew by the pool, where Adrian is showing off the freakish ability to enjoy the water on a cool night so he can have his abs on full display. Valeria is sitting on top of the artificial waterfall made up of real rocks and plants. Miguel has his feet in the pool, and he's chatting back and forth with his cousins. Unlike his cousin, Miguel is still wearing his clothes, but he has the arms of his flannel rolled up to reveal the sinewy muscle.

Focus.

On the outdoor kitchen countertop is an assortment of snacks, from pigs in a blanket to dips and even smoked ribs. I do a mental tally of what it must have cost to set up this whole party, from the decoration and food to the drinks. It would have cost Dallas close to a thousand dollars to put this together, and for her, that's a drop in the bucket. She could throw this exact party again next week and she still wouldn't hurt for money.

I'm not an envious person by nature, but it hurts being so close to wealth when I have to scrape tooth and nail to achieve a tiny fraction of this.

I swipe a handful of pigs in a blanket off the tray and grab a napkin before heading out to the back lawn. Some people already have blankets and lanterns out, ready for the much-anticipated fireworks show. It's hard to see in the dark, but it's easy enough to spot Sofía's friends. They have a blanket set up, and Jac is doing a handstand. He's walking around, switching between doing it two-handed and one-handed, and opening his legs in a split.

"Do a backflip!" one of Sofía's friends challenges, and Jac continues to do tricks across the lawn to impress them all. Sofía, meanwhile, is laying on her stomach facing the opposite direction and staring at her phone.

I plop down next to her and give her a friendly shove.

"Whatcha got there?" I ask, peeking over her hands at her phone screen.

Sofía tucks her phone into her chest and looks over at me with a frown.

"It's Mom," she says. "She wants me home in an hour, but that's when the fireworks start." She pulls her phone and types something out. "I'm making a case for the fireworks."

"This is what happens when you have a guy best friend, you can't use sleepovers at his house as a coverup. Wise up, little sister," I tell her. My parents think I'm sleeping over at Rose's house

145

tonight, which I am, so it's not entirely a lie. We just won't be at her house until later.

"The only reason that even works is because you almost never go out," Sofía complains. "Except for this week, actually." Her gaze snaps to mine, and her eyes narrow. "I've barely seen you. What have you been up to?"

Sofía and I are close. We're only a year and three months apart in age and have pretty much always gone to school together as a result. But we're not divulge-all-our-secrets close, not like I am with Rose. But I also can't bring myself to lie to her.

"I've been working on recording some food content at Rose's house. I'm applying for a scholarship that requires a video and original recipe to enter." I explain all the rules of the contest to her. "I've kind of been losing my mind over the whole thing," I say.

"Wait, so you *do* want to go to college?" she asks.

"Kind of. I'm going to use the money for the Cordon Bleu." I turn to my side to throw a glare at her. "Do *not* tell Mom and Dad. I'm waiting to tell them until I have enough money saved up."

"Hey, I'm supporting you in this, okay? You need to be the trailblazer and not go to college, so when I don't do it they can't get mad."

"Sofía, you are going to college," I tell her, in my serious older-sister tone. It may not be the place for me, but I could see Sofía thriving somewhere where she can explore multiple interests at once.

"Ugh, it's summer. I don't want to talk about this," she complains, rolling away from me.

"Okay, okay," I relent, dragging her back. "Don't go. I haven't seen you in days, let's just hang out."

Sofía groans like she hates the idea, but she rolls back anyway and launches into the latest gossip in her friend group. When everyone gets up to play a game of glow-in-the-dark bocce ball, Sofía stays on the blanket with me and we continue to talk.

Laying in the grass, we talk about everything except the subject of our parents and the struggling shop—and I also avoid the topic of a certain someone and the competition he's been helping me with. When people start making their way to the lawn, Sofía perks up, excited about the prospect of fireworks.

"Mom give you the okay to stay later?" I ask as she sits up.

"Yes, Jac will take me home as soon as the last firework goes off. This party kind of blows anyway," she complains.

"How can you say that? You've just been sitting here doing nothing," I point out. "With me," I add with a scowl.

Sofía shrugs and turns her focus to the guys lugging out boxes of fireworks to the end of the dock. Someone, I can't tell who, is screaming and running around with sparklers to announce the show, and that's my cue to get away. I do not want to be part of the chaos when Dallas's award-winning landscaping goes up in flames.

"Be good," I tell Sofía, planting a kiss at the top of her head before heading back to the house. I'm going against the current of the crowd as everyone rushes to the lawn to get the perfect spot to watch the show from.

If I had ridden my bike here, I would probably head home at this point, but since I have to wait for Gage, I need to kill time. I pick up a can of seltzer water from a bucket in the kitchen and amble in the direction I think the lighthouse is. The warning in the front staircase is probably more about keeping out of the family's personal spaces and might not necessarily apply to the weird lighthouse.

I tiptoe through the house, walking through the great room that has a deer head mounted above a fireplace and river rock on the walls. The great room leads to an area with a conversation pit, where I interrupt a couple and awkwardly run down the hallway. The house keeps going, unfurling room after room. I enter what appears to be a third sitting room with two over-stuffed couches facing each other and a row of windows that feature what I'm sure is a stunning view of Puget Sound in the daytime.

The next door leads me into what has to be the bottom of the lighthouse. It's a round space with lots of dark wood-paneled bookcases and a spiral staircase right in the middle. I close the door quietly behind me and take in the room. The bookcases span from floor to ceiling and have fancy brass picture lights at the top, illuminating every shelf.

Fascinated, I run my hand along the spines and walk around the perimeter. There seems to be no rhyme or reason to this library. Regency romances are shelved next to books about tax laws and Peter Rabbit. Some books appear to be valuable first editions or something and others are just well-loved paperbacks. I suppose that's better than having a library that's put together by an interior decorator with fake spines to make the home-owner look classy and well-read.

My curiosity piqued, I glance up the spiral staircase. It seems to go all the way to the top. The first booms from the fireworks show start, and the bright bursts of light filter down from the top level of the lighthouse. That seems like the perfect vantage point to enjoy the show from, considering I would be safe from both fire and potential trampling.

These stairs don't seem to have the same off-limits rule as the ones in the entrance, so I climb up. The next level is a continuation of the first. Some of the shelves are a little emptier up here, but the books look just as well loved. When I get to the next level, I stop at the top of the stairs and lean against the railing to take in the view. Panoramic windows line the walls and offer up a perfect view of the sound.

"Wow," I whisper, amazed that Dallas just . . . has this in her house. The fireworks show is in full swing now, filling the room with bursts of green and red and blue.

Then, out of nowhere, something touches the inside of my elbow, shocking me so thoroughly I fall down the stairs.

CHAPTER FIFTEEN

Oh shit!" Miguel reacts quickly as I begin to fall backward down the spiral staircase. He rushes over to catch me and in my surprise, I upturn my can of cold seltzer water all over myself.

Miguel manages to effortlessly sweep his arm around my back before crushing me in toward his body. I crash into his chest with a flustered "unf" and wrap my free arm around his waist to balance myself.

For days I've been avoiding touching him, handing things off quickly to avoid grazing fingers. I have taken routes around the kitchen to avoid passing too close to him so I can avoid inhaling the smell of him. I've managed to keep at least a kitchen island's worth of distance between us for a week.

Until now. I am pressed so firmly against him, all I can do is inhale the fresh scent of his clothes mingled with the musky smell that is uniquely *Miguel*. How is it even possible I can recognize his *scent*? Why does it feel like every memory I have of him is carved into my mind as though we've been close for years? Even without any skin-to-skin contact his touch is almost too much to bear. Every point of contact between us is sparking with possibility. My hand could reach under his shirt to feel the skin on his back. His arm around my back could slide down and— *Focus.*

I can feel the heat rushing to my cheeks, and I'm grateful that we're in a dark room together.

"I am so sorry," he says, leaning back a little to check on me. He pulls the sleeve of his flannel down and uses the corner to wipe away the water that splashed up onto my face and neck. Even through the thick flannel his hand is hot on my skin. "I didn't mean to scare you. I thought you'd seen me."

His voice breaks me out of the trance his touch put me in. I detach myself from him and finish climbing the stairs so I can avoid a second tumble and lean against the bank of windows to gather myself with some distance between us.

"I'm fine, just catching my breath," I tell him, in what I hope is a blithe tone, airing out the wet neck of my top in an attempt to dry it off. "You nearly took me out. Are you sure you're not a Morales assassin out to off the opposition?"

"A push down the stairs is too messy," he says seriously. "You know my family's style. Laxatives in the water."

"So you admit it!" I accuse him.

"I can neither confirm nor deny that my abuelo poisoned yours," he says solemnly.

"What are you doing up here being all creepy and alone in the dark anyway? I'm sure your cousin is out on that dock about to lose a finger to a firework," I joke.

"Oh, I'm sure he is. Valeria is keeping him in line, hope-fully." He walks up to the window beside me and gazes out at the lawn below us. "To be honest, the only people I really know here are my cousins, so it gets a little weird after a while. I can start chatting with someone, but then someone else brings up something about school or a person I don't know and I just fall out of the conversation." He sounds so lonely, and I fight the urge to reach out and touch him again. He sighs and runs a hand through his hair. "I just needed to get away for a little bit. And I really wanted to see the top of this lighthouse. I mean, who just has a lighthouse in their house?"

There's a lightness back in his voice now, and I try to match it. "It's a thing out here, honestly. Gianna, a girl from our school, has a full-on tanning salon in her basement," I tell him. "And Peyton, who's not even rich by these standards," I wave around at the lighthouse, "has a home theater."

"Wow," Miguel says. "And I thought this place was the boonies. I had no idea there was this kind of money out here."

"Tech money," I say with a dismissive wave. I turn around and face the lawn, mirroring Miguel's pose. A very impressive firework goes off, and the crowd outside cheers.

"Don't you need permits to set off fireworks like this?" Miguel asks.

"Fireworks are illegal here, actually," I tell him. "But Dallas probably thinks she's safe because she's far out enough to escape notice. Hopefully."

Miguel shifts his attention away from the window and turns to face me.

"So what brought you up here?" he asks.

I shrug. "This whole thing isn't really my scene," I admit.

"Much rather be sneaking into your family bakery and throwing unsuspecting men into the deep freeze?" he asks.

I give his shoulder a playful shove in response, and the touch electrifies me. *Kitchen island's worth of space between us*, I remind myself. I turn back toward the sky as more fireworks boom above us.

"I have a hard time relaxing. Doesn't exactly make me great at parties," I tell him. "It's like, every moment I'm not doing something productive, I feel this rush of guilt and frustration. If I'm not cooking, I'm reading cookbooks or watching videos or talking to my dad about food or working on my very complicated Excel spreadsheet that tracks my income and all my goals for Paris."

What I don't tell him is that day in LA with him was the first time I had actually let myself relax without any guilt attached. Part of it was because I was away from home and all the responsibilities and stress that came with it, but I can't deny a huge part was Miguel. And for some reason, my body remembers that about him. Something about Miguel makes me feel safe enough to take a break.

Which is dangerous, especially now with the deadline for this competition looming.

"And in the words of my sister, this party blows," I say, trying to lighten the mood again. But when I look over at Miguel, he's watching me with a pensive look on his face. It's hard to read his expression between the alternating blasts of vibrant red and blue bursting outside the window. "What?" I ask.

"Can I tell you the real reason I'm here? In Port Murphy, I

mean?" he asks me softly. Miguel turns around and presses his back against the wall until he's sitting on the floor. Curious, I join him, and when I straighten my legs, the toe of my sneaker bumps against his leg.

"Sure," I say, as though my sitting next to him wasn't invitation enough to continue.

"It's not just because my uncle offered me a job. My mom finally made the decision to leave my dad." He's quiet for a moment, knocking his head back against the wall and staring up at the ceiling, where it looks like a young Dallas had glow-in-the-dark stars installed. "He's been cheating on her for years. I've known it, she's known it, he's known that we've known it, and we just . . . lived like that.

"I never understood why she stayed with him. They met in college when she was an undergrad and he was already in medical school. They had been dating for two years when she got pregnant with me, and they just followed the script, you know? My dad's Cuban, too, and a Catholic only when it's convenient. My mom dropped out of college, they got married, and she supported him through school while raising me. I think she figured out real quick the mistake she made. My dad is a terrible father and a worse husband, but good Catholic Cuban girls don't get divorced. So she didn't."

I think of my mom, who married out of love and not circumstance. But even I could see the cracks in my parents' marriage, the ones they tried to fill with love and work. I can't imagine my father ever cheating on my mother, though, no matter how difficult things became at home.

"I think part of her was running off this idea that she needed to keep the marriage together for me. That I needed the stable two-parent household. But the last few years . . . You know he bought an apartment for his mistress the same month he told me that I'd have to pay for UCLA myself?"

"What an asshole," I breathe.

"Right? I think that was the last straw for Mom. Like, plenty of people have to pay for college themselves, it's not that. But the fact that he was spending all that money on the other woman while telling me I was on my own? The idea that living in that house with him was any better than me living with my single mother didn't make sense to her anymore." He pauses to sigh, running his hand across his jaw, his movements stiff and agitated. "I just wish she had done it sooner. Now I'm in this town where I don't know anything or anyone, and I . . . I miss home."

"I had no idea," I whisper. "I'm so sorry you're going through all that."

As much as I've been avoiding it since our secret friendship pact, touch had always been something that came easily between Miguel and me. I hardly have to think about it before I'm reaching for his hand and threading my fingers through his. Miguel grips back like I'm a lifeline and briefly brings our clasped hands up to his forehead before dropping them down in the space between us.

"My mom hated it here as a kid. She got out as soon as she could and then got trapped into a marriage with my dad. She never got the freedom she wanted when she was my age. And now she has to live in her brother's basement and start her life over in the one place she never wanted to be. How fucked up is that?"

I don't know what to say to him. I don't know how to quell this simmering rage I feel bubbling up in him. A rage toward the universe and the cards that we're dealt.

"But she is getting to start over," I say. "That is really brave of her."

"It is," he agreed. "My dad was pissed when she served him the papers. I feel . . . disgusted that I'm even related to him. That half of me is him."

"Hey," I say sternly, pulling on his arm and turning to face him. "You're not like him."

"You don't even know him—"

"I don't need to," I insist, grabbing his arm with my free hand and turning him to face me. "I know enough about you to know that you're not like that. You have empathy and you're kind. You saved me from heat stroke, fed me delicious food, and you listened to me talk about my hopes and dreams in a way that made me feel *heard* and supported." I give him a shaky smile. "And when I asked you to enter a very one-sided secret friendship in my favor, you gladly agreed. I don't think your dad would have done any of those things."

"I'm glad you think so," he says softly. His thumb starts gently stroking circles into the back of my right hand. My brain fixates on this point of contact, utterly hypnotized by the sensation of our skin touching in gentle glides. Is it as intoxicating to him as it is to me?

I glance up and try to read his face in the alternating bursts of colored light. His focus is held entirely by our clasped hands, his gaze hungry and almost . . . *pained.* An echo of that pain hums through me, a mix of frustration and longing. Miguel must feel my eyes on him because he glances up at me. I don't have enough time to wipe my face clean of emotion, and he sees everything laid bare in that moment.

His eyes flash as the truth of my feelings are made clear to him.

There have always been things trying to keep us apart. At the beginning it was distance, now it's our families, and soon it will be our diverging futures.

But right now, none of those things are in this room with us. Right now it's Miguel's breath skirting across the skin of my cheek, his thumb pressed to the back of my hand. It's my hand reaching toward the collar of his shirt. None of those things are trying to keep us apart.

I grip his collar, and a surprised gasp escapes Miguel's mouth as I give him a gentle pull toward me, sealing the distance between us.

His hand reaches up to cup my jaw gently, and I lean into the warmth of his touch.

"Ana Maria," he says huskily, my name slipping off his tongue like a desperate plea. "What are we doing?"

"I don't know," I say, my grip tightening.

"Ana," he groans, dropping his forehead against mine. "I can't do this just a little bit. I can't just kiss you now and go back to being whatever it is we're playing at and calling friendship."

I remember telling him something similar on that sidewalk so long ago before turning around and kissing him anyway. He's right. The frustration and misery I worked up over a kiss and a missed connection had been painful. But now that I know him? Now that I've seen him in my world, hanging out with Rose and in the hazy glow of Lacey's Diner, it's going to be so much more difficult to cut him from my life.

I pull back from him and let go of his shirt. He watches me warily, his hand still warm in mine.

"You're right," I whisper. "We have just a few weeks left before summer is over and you're back in Los Angeles. We shouldn't."

"Actually," he says, his tone more hopeful than before. "Mom was hoping we'd be back in LA by the end of summer, but Dad is fighting her on money stuff with the divorce. We can't afford to leave, so Port Murphy High it is. And since my last name is Fuentes, I don't think the guidance counselors will know to keep us separated," he says with a smile.

The thought of Miguel at school, in class with me, working on a project together, passing each other in the halls, seeing each other from across the dance floor at prom . . . That was the stuff of my fantasies up until a week ago. Now, they're a nightmare.

Being friends with Miguel for a summer was one thing. He would be here and then he'd gone by September. Our chances of getting caught were low enough that I was willing to risk it. But now that Miguel is going to be a regular fixture around Port Murphy. . . .

"Ana Maria?" he says gently, sensing my mood shift.

I let go of his hands and slide back on the wood floor. The fireworks show has stopped by now, and my phone is buzzing with text messages. Real life is flooding into this bubble with Miguel, and I can feel it threatening to burst.

"Why didn't you tell me you might not be here just for the summer?" I ask.

"I don't know," Miguel says, his voice cautious. "It just didn't come up. Mom was going back and forth for a while—"

"We can't do this, Miguel," I interrupt, trying to sound firm. "It was okay when you were a person that existed outside of Port Murphy, but you *live* here now. There's no way we can keep this a secret for that long."

I start to stand up, but Miguel reaches out a hand to stop me. "Wait, what?" he says. "Slow down, slow down. This shouldn't change anything."

"Of course it does!" I say, raising my voice. "This is a small town, Miguel. We could get by in the summer, when everyone is out of town and distracted by water sports or whatever, but in the winter when it's gray and wet twenty-four/seven and there is nothing better to do, people will be looking for something to talk about. You're a Morales for real now, and Port Murphy rules apply." I shake off his arm and stand up. "It was stupid to think a secret friendship would work anyway. I'm sorry."

"So that's it?"

"It's for the best, believe me," I say as my chest cracks open a little. I see how much this is hurting him, and it almost makes me want to take everything back. "Goodbye, Miguel."

I don't give him another chance to stop me. I fly down the spiral staircase and out of the lighthouse, running straight outside and down the driveway. Traitorous tears spill as I run to Gage's car to wait for him and Rose.

CHAPTER SIXTEEN

The next two days pass in a blur. I wake up, eat, work, and then spend hours rewriting my essay. This needs to be the thing that really grabs the attention of *La Mesa*. Because now that I've cut off Miguel, I'm not going to have the eye-catching video or social content I had been banking on. An entire week of work, gone.

I spend hours on TikTok watching cooking and food videos, taking notes of things I like and don't like, reading through comments and trying to figure out how I'm going to shoot the clips for my recipe next week. Hopefully Rose has learned enough to pick up where we left off and I can get something good without Miguel and his camera equipment.

Miguel.

When thoughts of him crop up, it throws a wrench in my progress every time. I could be in the middle of reading my essay out loud, making sure it flows well, and I'll suddenly think of the way my skin felt when we held hands at Dallas's party. Or I'll be running through a list of ingredients to order for next week and I'll think of the look on Miguel's face when he tried my buñuelos. It feels like my mind comes to a screeching halt, and it takes too much time to get back on track.

Rose tries texting me, but I can't bring myself to text her back. She knew something was up after the party when she found me waiting by the car. My tears were dry by then, but best friends always know. Just like she knew not to ask what happened with everyone else around. She just gave me a tight, silent hug. Then I woke up bright and early the next day and escaped before Rose woke up so I could avoid rehashing the events of the night before.

When she sends me a dozen texts in a row and tries calling me twice I know she's a second away from climbing on her bike and coming to check up on me, so I shoot her a quick text to let her know I'm working on my application and need total focus.

My mom knocks on my door Saturday night and tries to get me to watch a movie with her and Dad in the living room, but I tell her I'm too tired even though I hadn't left my room the entire day after working my shift at the shop. She frowns but decides not to push me on it.

By the time Tuesday finally rolls around, I'm running on fumes. I've been clocking in less than six hours of sleep a night and chugging Cuban coffee like it's water. Today would have been the next filming session with Miguel. His equipment is still at Rose's and I'm sure he wants it back, but he hasn't texted me since the party. Which means it's up to me.

Hey. You can come by and pick up your equipment from Rose's today if you want.

I take a scalding hot shower to try to wake up and help myself to cold scrambled eggs Mom left in the frying pan before jumping on my bike and heading over to Rose's.

When I roll up to Rose's driveway, she's already waiting on the front porch for me, her hands on her hips and a frown on her face.

"You're late," she calls out to me. "Call time for the talent is an hour before we start shooting. Now I won't have nearly enough time to do your hair."

I drop my bike down on her overgrown lawn and climb up the cream-colored wood steps as Rose berates me.

"It'll be fine," I assure her. "I don't have that much hair anyway." *And it's just us today.* But I don't have the energy to go over everything that happened at Dallas's.

"No, but you do look like the walking dead," she points out. "Have you been getting any sleep? Are you okay? What happened at Dallas's?" Her expression goes from concerned to stern in a split second. "And don't tell me nothing because I know you, and you wouldn't go radio silent like that if something hadn't happened."

"Can we please do this later?" Tears are already prickling the back of my eyes just thinking about telling her, and the last thing I need is a puffy red face when we film.

Rose narrows her eyes, trying to get a read on me. She must realize I'm still not ready to talk, even though I definitely owe her an explanation by now, and thankfully she shifts gears. "Well, if you're not going to dish, I will," she says. "I kissed Noah."

"You did not!" I gasp, this piece of info being enough to immediately snap me out of my days-long self-pitying funk.

Rose pushes me upstairs as she dishes. She goes into great detail about the merits of Noah as she does my makeup and hair and picks out my costume for the day. Rose is a romantic at heart and in love with the idea of love, so she's fairly picky when it comes to partners. But Noah really fits the bill for her, and I'm happy about this new development. She pulls out another retro 1950s apron that she scored at the thrift store this weekend and pins my hair up into a cute updo.

While styling goes on, I avoid looking at my phone. But even without checking for a notification, I don't feel or hear it vibrate. Miguel has not texted me back.

"Okay, I think this look is good for today. We can switch out the top for a sweater and change out the apron depending on how many recipes we get through. Are you starting on doughnuts today?"

"Yeah, my pièce de résistance: Cuban doughnuts," I say, trying to inject some cheer into my voice. This is the recipe I'm submitting for the competition, the thing I'm hoping will snag me a win. I've made it over a dozen times in the last week, tweaking things little by little until I landed on what might be my best creation yet. But I can't seem to whip up any excitement for it today. "I'll get started on the dough and fillings today, and we'll fry them Thursday."

"I have to wait two whole days to try these doughnuts?" Rose whines.

"Good things come to those who wait," I promise her as we leave her room and head down the stairs.

"I demand a best friend refund, this is not fair!" Rose cries out, throwing her arms wide as though appealing to the gods.

Mid-pose she freezes as she catches sight of something and drops her arms. "Oh, you let yourself in!"

"What?" I say as I turn the corner into the kitchen, thinking she's still talking to me. I trip over my own feet when I see Miguel in Rose's kitchen.

He's setting up a tripod with one of his cameras, and all the lights are already pulled out and set up. I'd be surprised we didn't hear him set up, but Rose had been blasting BTS in her room at top volume. There could have been a full-on home invasion downstairs and we wouldn't have heard it.

"You know, I was looking at some SLRs at the thrift store this weekend. I think I might buy one, but I was hoping I could get your input on which would be best for a beginner?" Rose asks as she drops her makeup bag on the kitchen counter, totally unaware of what she's just walked into. "I've never worked with a film camera before, but it seems like it would be a fun way to dive in. Oh, damn, I forgot the costume changes. I'm going to run upstairs, be right back."

Rose heads back up the stairs, past the spot where I am frozen in place, watching as Miguel continues to set up for the shoot.

Silence stretches between us as the sound of Rose's footsteps fades.

"You don't have to do this," I say finally, my voice a hoarse whisper.

"I'm a man of my word, Ana Maria," he says smoothly without looking at me. "I said I'd help you with this competition, and I'm going to follow through on that." He finally stops what he's doing to look up at me, and I'm taken aback by how little I

164

recognize the boy standing in front of me. There's something remote about his expression, something closed off and distant. Even when he was an absolute stranger to me that day in LA he hadn't looked like this.

I put that look on his face. He looks like this now because I hurt him.

That thought alone makes my stomach go sour.

"Don't worry, I'm not mistaking this for friendship or . . . anything else," he says, his tone acidic. "Once this is done I'll keep my distance, like a real Morales."

His words are like a gut punch, and I try not to physically recoil. Is this how he felt that night at Dallas's? What do I even say to him now?

"Got it!" Rose says as she rushes back into the kitchen, cutting through the tension. "Let's get started!"

Miguel turns his focus back to his equipment, and Rose begins to herd me to my spot at the counter. I feel jumbled and a little sick as Rose pins back a loose piece of hair. I'm not sure I can spend an entire day in the same room as Miguel, not like this. I'm not even sure I can bring my focus back to the task at hand. I wasn't prepared for this today and I'm not sure how to get past it.

I slap my cheeks lightly, trying to bring my attention back to the competition and cooking. My future is riding on this; I have to get my head back in the game.

I'm glad that we decided to go with a shooting style that focuses more on the food and less on me, because I'm a wreck the entire day. Miguel is professional yet distant with me, but friendly and chatty with Rose whenever she asks him process questions. When we wrap up filming for the day, Miguel packs things up like usual and says he'll see us Thursday.

When he walks out the door Rose shoots me a weird look but doesn't say anything. I help her clean the kitchen and ask her question after question about Noah, but once we wrap up and I'm getting ready to head out the door, Rose stops me with a hand on my arm.

"Do I need to slash his tires?" she asks. A surprised laugh escapes me and then I crumble. I fall into Rose's arms, probably one of the few times I've initiated a hug between us. But I'm just so grateful in this moment to have a friend like Rose, who can read my moods in an instant and who would do anything to protect me. She wraps her arms around me and squeezes tight.

"What can I do? How can I fix this?" she asks.

I sniff back my tears. "The only way you could fix this is with a time machine so we can go back and prevent the Ybarra-Morales feud from happening in the first place," I tell her honestly. I pull back, and Rose gives me a sympathetic frown.

"I still think it would help if you told me what happened," she says gently. And so I do. We don't come up with any solutions—don't even try to—but she listens. And in that moment, that's enough.

CHAPTER SEVENTEEN

The next day I wake up with puffy eyes but feeling better after telling Rose everything. I get up early for my shift at Café y Más and catch a ride with my dad. He's waiting for me in his truck, a beat-up old Chevy, with a thermos of Cuban coffee in his hand.

"Hop in, mija!" he calls out. "We have a corporate lunch to cater today!"

I'm glad to have the chaos of a catering lunch and a day in the shop to take my mind off the other things that have been cycling through ceaselessly for days on end.

Dad hands me the thermos after I buckle into the car, and I take a grateful sip. "Mmm, thank you."

"Of course, mijita," he says. He turns the radio on but keeps the volume much lower than usual. Once we've backed out of the driveway and are on the road, it's clear why. "I noticed you stopped coming into the shop at night to cook," my dad says.

I wince. "So you knew," I say guiltily.

"Of course I knew. I can tell when someone's been in my

kitchen. I'm glad to see you taking initiative. You know, all this will be yours one day," he says, a big, proud grin on his face.

He reaches across the cab and catches my shoulder in a firm grip.

"This shop is our American Dream," he says reverently. "It's a symbol of our family, of the strength and determination that lives in our blood. Proof that we can survive anything."

I smile back at him, and it's nearly a grimace.

What Dad is saying isn't anything new, but today it sparks a new kind of guilt. If I let the bakery go, what does it say about the family? What does it say about *me*?

"I assume Rose is keeping you busy with one of her projects and that's why you've stopped coming in? Or did you give up on trying to figure out my secret recipe for my rum cakes?" he asks with a goofy grin.

"Yeah, I've been spending a lot of time at Rose's working on a project," I say, not wanting to add that I've actually come up with a rum cake recipe that I think is better than his. I'll keep that secret, and some other ones, to myself. "I'll be back soon enough, you can't beat commercial baking equipment."

"Just make sure you're locking up before you go home," he continues. "And I know it's summer, but don't stay out too late, okay?"

"You got it," I tell him. "Who's the lunch for?" I ask, in an effort to turn the conversation away from me and my future.

"Some startup in Seattle is doing a retreat on the peninsula this weekend. Today is the first day, so hopefully they like what they get and order from us again this weekend."

"First? Of how many?" I ask.

"Five days," he says. I shudder at the thought.

"That's a long time to be on a retreat with your coworkers."

"It looks like they're going camping, too. Quite the getting-to-know-you exercise," Dad says.

"Sleeping in tents with your coworkers? That sounds like my nightmare."

"Hey," Dad cuts in. "I'm your coworker."

"Exactly!" I shout. "And you snore like a freight train. That's why we've only gone camping with you once."

"At least my snores keep bears away," he points out defensively.

When we get to the shop Eddie is in full swing, prepping for the early morning rush. There are baking trays full of Cuban bread, freshly baked pastelitos, and the sweet smell of Cuban coffee brewing.

I take over at front of house and turn over the open sign on the door. As I'm taking the chairs off the tables and setting everything up, our first customers start trickling in. Through the window across the street I can see a couple people heading into Morales Bakery for their sub-par coffee.

"¡Buenos días!" I call out to our customers as I slip back behind the cash register.

A day behind the counter at Café y Más is just what I need. The morning rush keeps me so busy that I don't have a spare second to think about the competition, my future, or Miguel. Once the worst of the morning passes, I go into the back and help my dad out with the catering order and pack things up for him.

Once everything is ready to go, Eddie and my dad head out and I'm left alone in the shop. I pull up a stool behind the cash register and scroll mindlessly on my phone. When the bell above the door rings, I stand up and drop my phone to greet the customer.

A couple, tourists from out of town by their looks, walk into the shop looking slightly confused. They take in the interior like they're looking for someone or something but come up short when they make eye contact with me.

"Hey," the girl says, pushing her sunglasses down the bridge of her nose. "Is this the place with that dessert thing?"

"The dessert burrito," the guy she's with, who's wearing the most hideous patterned shirt and short shorts, cuts in.

A full-body shudder passes through me, and I'm glad my dad isn't here for this interaction.

"No, we don't serve a dessert burrito here. But we have dozens of classic Cuban desserts available," I say, pointing out the case full of pastelitos, flans, and cookies.

"Oh, so you're not selling it anymore?" The woman asks, looking at the giant Cuban flag behind me.

If I wanted to be helpful, I would tell them that the place they're looking for is about five hundred feet behind them. But when it comes to the Morales Bakery, I'm never feeling helpful.

"Nope, we are not selling dessert burritos here," I say with my best customer service smile. "Do you want to order something else? Our house specialty are the guava pastries."

"What's a guava?" the guy asks.

I do not let my smile slip.

"It's a tropical fruit," I tell him.

"Kacey told me to go to the Cuban restaurant in this town to try that dessert burrito, she said she was just here last month," the girl says to her friend. She cannot fathom that a town this small in the PNW would have a second, more famous Cuban restaurant across the street. And I'm certainly not going to help her reach that conclusion.

"Come on," the guy says, clearly not interested in the tropical fruit desserts I have on offer, "let's just get beer at that brewery we saw."

"I'm going to call Kacey when we get there," the girl says, turning around and heading back out the door. "She did say she went to Port Murphy, right?"

Once the tourists are out the door I let out the frustrated scream I had been holding. I fold over and drop my forehead on the counter, depleted from that interaction.

One day, when I'm the pastry chef at a restaurant somewhere, I won't have to sit behind a cash register and try to convince people to try guava.

The bell above the door rings again, and I force my smile back into place as I stand up.

"Buenas tardes—" I cut myself off when I see who's walking into the shop. "Oh, thank God it's just you," I say, dropping the customer service pretense and shooting James a genuine smile.

"Bad day?" he asks as he saunters up to the counter. He's wearing a black polo shirt, which must mean he's working at Locicero's today.

"I just had some confused customers who walked in and asked for the monstrosity," I tell him.

"Ouch," James says, pulling off the tote bag he has slung over his shoulder.

"What do you have there?" I ask, trying to peek into the bag. I know he's here looking to trade.

"Your favorite," he says with a smile. "Tiramisu."

"Oh, you angel," I cry out, reaching out with grabbing hands, waiting for him to drop my prize in my hands. He passes it off to me with a smile, and I turn my attention to the bag's contents, where my prize for the day sits in a black plastic take-out container. This tiramisu is Locicero's bestselling dessert and with good reason. Because it's such a popular item, James rarely has the opportunity to bring any around for me, so it's always quite the treat when he manages to snag one.

I pull out the tiramisu and take a moment to admire its cocoa-dusted exterior. Perfect. When I look up, James is looking a little dazed.

"Dealer's choice," I tell him. "What do you want in return?" I look over at the hot food display case. "We have some empanadas de carne y pollo, or papa rellena. I know you don't really like croquetas . . ." I look over my shoulder at the kitchen. "I could make you a sandwich if you want. Cuban or pan con lechon?"

I'm still babbling about food when I turn back and look at James. He staring down at his feet with his brows drawn, like he's thinking really hard or something.

"James?" I prompt, surprised because he usually comes in knowing exactly what he wants. "Not hungry? Do you want a rain check instead?" He finally looks up from the floor and settles his attention on me. I'm a little thrown by the look he's giving me, like he might throw up.

"Go on a date with me."

What?

Oh. *Oh.*

A dozen responses shoot through my mind. The competition. I'm too busy. We're friends. There's someone else. There isn't someone else, actually. Not at all. Not even a little bit.

"No pressure," he continues when I don't respond immediately. "I didn't mean to, like, demand you go out with me. Just dinner tomorrow, at Locicero's. Super low key. You can have the tiramisu fresh, instead of a day old."

"Yes," I say suddenly, and it seems both James and I are surprised by my response. *Yes?*

Two weeks ago I know what my answer would have been: no. James and I have always been friends by virtue of both working at our families' restaurants on the same side of the street. During the school year he would give me rides downtown since we both had shifts after last period. He became a staunch Ybarra supporter when Adrian Morales pantsed him in middle school. He's funny and nice, and certainly not lacking in looks. I know plenty of girls at school that have crushes on him.

But *I* never did. Once high school hit I came to the realization that I would likely never date anyone from Port Murphy. The town is overwhelming white, and not just any white, but tall, blond, and athletic white. Back in the 1880s, Norwegians immigrated to the Seattle area in droves. To this day the ties to Norway are strong, with hundreds of people attending the Norwegian Constitution Day parade in Seattle.

What that ultimately means is that the people around here tend to look nothing like me and they usually aren't attracted to me, either. Rose, with her naturally blond hair and adorable freckles, has been inundated with admirers since middle school.

Valentines in her lockers and, once, a full-on brawl between two guys at school over her.

But I'm a Cuban girl with a sweet tooth. I'm a little taller than the average girl, a little curvier than the average girl, and a little darker than the average girl. Where my dad's side of the family is relatively European in ancestry, my mom's is more mixed, resulting in my coal-black hair and light brown skin. Sofía is the sister that came out looking a little more European, with a slender figure and a button nose.

Sofía doesn't notice the attention that comes her way because she's always been a little mean and scary to our peers. But I definitely notice the attention that doesn't come my way, the overheard conversations about the pretty Ybarra sister that aren't about me, and the feeling of being invisible when people used me as a way to get closer to Sofía or Rose. I used to feel more bitter about it all, but since putting my sights on culinary school in Paris, dating has been the last thing on my mind.

And even if none of that were a factor, two weeks ago I was still hung up on a guy I had met in LA last winter.

Okay, I'm *still* hung up on a guy I met in LA last winter.

But now I am determined to fully purge him from my system.

"Really?" James asks, openly surprised.

"Yeah," I say, trying not to let my voice waver. This date is exactly what I need.

It totally is.

"Okay," he says with a shy smile. "Perfect. I'll pick you up tomorrow night. Does seven work?"

"Absolutely."

CHAPTER EIGHTEEN

Thursday morning I wake up and get ready for the final filming session. While I'm rummaging through my own kitchen trying to find something to eat for breakfast, Mom walks in.

"Morning, princess," my mom says on a yawn. "You've been busy these past couple of weeks. I've hardly seen you."

"I'm working on a project with Rose, but we're wrapping up today," I tell her, pulling an orange out of the fridge. I start to head out of the kitchen, but Mom grabs onto my sleeve and stops me.

"No, no, no," she says as she pulls me into the kitchen. "You need to eat more than that."

"I can eat more at Rose's," I tell her, thinking of the menu lineup for today. Half a dozen flavors of Cuban doughnuts, mojito lemon bars, and guava lemonade.

"You're not leaving the house with just an orange in your stomach." Mom pushes me over to the breakfast nook and opens the fridge. "I'll make you a tortilla."

"Mom, you don't have to make me anything," I start, but she's already pulling the eggs and frozen hash browns out. I *do* really like her tortillas, so I don't argue anymore.

"Have you looked at those links I sent you?" she asks as she grabs an onion from the pantry.

"All those Washington schools?" I ask, wishing she had brought up literally any other topic. The tortilla was clearly a trap to get me to talk about my plans for the future.

"Well, since you didn't like the idea of going to UCLA, I thought you might like something more local." Mom grabs the good pan and sets it down on the gas range before filling it up with what some might say is too much olive oil.

"I actually think Rose is going to apply to UW for their drama school," I say. "In addition to Juilliard, Yale, and NYU. So it's more like a backup school for her."

"You shouldn't make a big decision like where to go to school based on what someone else does," my mom warns me. "Rose will always be your friend, but you can make new friends wherever you go."

That is patently false, given that I've only really made one close friend in my whole life. I doubt college will change that.

"Yeah, you're right," I say, hoping that by agreeing with her she'll drop the subject altogether.

I watch as she throws the onions and frozen potatoes into the pan before giving it all a few good twists from the salt mill.

"Well, what did you think?" she asks, unfortunately not deterred. "WSU has a great hospitality program, and UW has an excellent business school. It would be easy enough to take a weekend to tour both."

"I'm not sure I really want to do a hospitality degree," I tell her, which is about as close to the truth as I'm willing to get with her right now.

"Time is running out," she says unhelpfully. "You need to start thinking seriously about these things."

What if I just told her right now that I didn't want to go to college? That I didn't want a future in middle management spent climbing the corporate ladder? She makes me feel like she's trying to right the wrongs in her life by forcing me to make the decisions she would have made, but our lives are different and those choices she wants don't fit *me*. But how do I tell her that?

"I *am* taking it seriously," I assure her. I think she can hear something in my tone because she turns away from the stove to look at me. Her brows crinkle in an expression that is both loving and concerned.

"You know I just want the best for you, right? You're such a smart girl, there are so many opportunities for you out there. I just want to make sure you don't miss them, okay?"

"I get it, Mom," I tell her. She holds her gaze on me for another moment before turning back to the pan and flipping my omelet. I get up and grab a plate for her to serve it on and plant a kiss on her cheek. "Thanks for breakfast."

"Of course," she says with a smile. "Tell Rosita I give her my love, okay? She should come by for dinner this weekend. I'm making picadillo with that fake meat she likes."

Mom gives me a little squeeze on the shoulder before heading back to her computer in the living room. I eat the tortilla as quickly as possible—onions, potatoes, and eggs truly make for the perfect breakfast trio—and hop onto my bike and race to Rose's to avoid being late again.

I manage to get there on time, but Rose still rushes me to her room to get ready. As she's curling my hair, I watch her through the mirror, her brows furrowed in concentration as she works.

"What do you think about James?" I ask tentatively.

"That he has good taste," she says through the bobby pins she's holding between her teeth.

"What?" I ask, baffled. "He wears Toms. And you regularly tease him about that."

Rose puts down the curling wand and pops the bobby pins out of her mouth before turning an assessing look toward me. "I meant he has good taste because he's in puppy love with you like any halfway decent person *should* be. You're smart, funny, a great cook, gorgeous, and your best friend is really cool."

"Okay," I say, taking my eyes off her and tucking a piece of hair behind my ear. Rose slaps my hand away and fixes the piece of hair herself.

"You know who else has good taste?" she asks, her tone slightly needling.

"Noah?" I guess, and Rose rolls her eyes.

"Obviously, but we're talking about you right now. And you know the answer is Miguel. He likes you *and* he told me he once buried all of Adrian's toys in the backyard during vacation because he had said something mean to Valeria. I think we need to reconsider our stance on him."

"Rose!" I hiss.

"What? Does your dad have listening devices planted in my house? I can talk openly about how great this guy—"

"No you *cannot*," I hiss. "Because all the doors downstairs are unlocked and you *know* sound travels in this house. He could be downstairs setting up now."

Rose pouts, but the threat of being overheard by the person she's talking about is enough to keep her quiet. She returns to my hair, which is nearly finished anyway, and then does a final check on wardrobe before we go downstairs.

When we head down to the kitchen Miguel is there, having let himself in through the mudroom again. The cameras and lights are already set up, and Rose starts moving props around while I pull the doughnut dough from the fridge.

"Hey," I say to Miguel.

"Hey," he says in return but doesn't bother looking my way. It stings, but I tell myself again that this is for the best. This is what I wanted.

Luckily today's recipes require a lot of attention, so I don't have much to spare on Miguel. Most of the day is spent on frying the doughnuts and preparing them with a variety of toppings. I use white chocolate and heavy cream as the base for my fruit icing, adding freeze-dried strawberries and mangoes to decorate them. Then I have the dulce de leche, cinnamon sugar, and guava cheesecake toppings. I add a pinch of anise and lime zest to the cinnamon sugar as a nod to the original buñuelo. I decide to also make a batch of natilla, which I dip the doughnuts into before adding sugar to the top and torching it to get that toasted-sugar crunch from crema catalana. Miguel knows that the doughnuts are *the* recipe for the competition, so he's being extra attentive and purposeful with those shots.

"Before you put them in the fryer, let me switch out my lens so I can get a nice close-up of the dough cooking," he says while we're waiting for my timer to go off.

"Turn the tray ninety degrees," he tells me as I'm beginning to decorate the figure-eight shaped doughnuts.

"We should have a shot of you tasting them," he says once I finish decorating the last set. Rose fixes my hair and makeup and we take a shot of me eating the doughnut. He's using his iPhone for this shot and as I'm taking a second bite of my crema catalana flavor, the crispy sugar topping crackling as I bite into it, something on his phone breaks his focus.

His brows furrow for a second, and he turns away from me.

"Sorry, I need to take this call," he says, dropping the camera he has around his neck on the counter and stepping out through the mudroom.

"Those smell so good," Rose says, hovering over a tray of guava cheesecake doughnuts. I don't even swat her away when she reaches to steal one. My eyes are still on Miguel, who I can see through the glass door as he paces back and forth on the back porch.

"Earth to Amy," Rose says, appearing next to me and waving a hand—which is holding a doughnut that has a huge bite taken out of it—between me and Miguel. "What is up with you today? I know things are still weird between you and Miguel, but—"

"James asked me out on a date." It rushes out of me before I can stop it.

Rose sputters for a moment, clearly unsure of where her reaction to my attempt at distraction should land.

"That's why you brought him up earlier?" she asks. "What did—"

Rose is cut off by the sound of the mudroom door opening. Miguel pops in looking a little annoyed, and I notice that he looks more . . . bedraggled than usual. His hair is messy and he looks like he hasn't had a good night's sleep in days.

"I'm sorry, I have to cut out early. I think we're good on shots for everything, though."

"No, of course," I say, waving his concern off. "I'm sure we have everything we need."

"Good." He nods. "I have to head out now, but I can come by tomorrow to pick up my stuff if that's okay with you, Rose?"

"Yeah, I'll be around, no worries."

Miguel nods and without giving me another look he heads out. Rose and I wait in silence as we listen to his car start up, followed by the sound of crunching gravel as he backs out.

"I also need to head out," I tell her as I pull off the red gingham apron I've been wearing and hand it back to Rose.

"You mean you're just gonna drop this James bombshell on me and *leave*?"

"Do you mind boxing up these doughnuts for me? I'll pick them up later."

"You are not getting off that easy! I'm calling a BFF summit tomorrow," Rose says as I put my shoes on.

"Okay, okay, tomorrow. BFF summit. I'll be there," I say. I grab my bag and start toward the mudroom door.

"Ana Maria Ybarra, you have some 'splaining to do!" Rose yells after me in her best Ricky Ricardo impression, which is terrible.

"¡Hasta luego!" I call out as I tear down her street toward my house.

CHAPTER NINETEEN

I don't *need* three hours to get ready, but I decide to make the most of it. I take a shower and blow dry my hair. I scroll through TikTok to try to find hairstyling inspiration and find a tutorial on a way to curl my hair with a straightener. I end up hating the result and just pin back a bunch of random pieces until it looks intentional. The back looks awful, but if my date is staring at the back of my head we have a bigger problem.

I follow that up with a half hour of scrolling through makeup tutorials before deciding that I actually don't need to do a full beat for a date at the local pizza joint. A wing and some glitter on my eyelids will be enough. Sofía comes home in the middle of my scrolling and is now playing a game on her Switch that appears to be a power-washing simulator.

"I need your help picking an outfit," I tell her, not because I particularly admire her style but because I need help making a choice.

The normal butterflies I would expect to feel before a date

simply . . . aren't there. And because I don't feel nervous at all it starts to make me feel . . . nervous. Because part of me knows I made the wrong decision. I don't have any feelings for James beyond friendship. But maybe that could change? James is a nice guy. He does well in school, he's nice to his little sister, and he knows the struggle of working at your family's business. We have so much in common. And yet . . .

Maybe last year I could have convinced myself that I could grow to like him. I'd never really had any feelings toward someone before, so I didn't know what it should feel like. But now I know what that spark feels like with someone. And I'll know what I'm missing if I date James.

Look where that spark got you, I remind myself. *Not worth it.*

"That looks frumpy," Sofía says, giving me a quick glance before returning her attention to her game.

"It's not frumpy," I argue, looking down at my outfit. I'm wearing a white, long-sleeved ribbed turtleneck with a red floral midi dress on top. "It has a slit, it can't be frumpy if it has a slit," I point out.

"Yes it can," Sofía says, deadpan.

Frustrated, I step out of the dress and pull on my second outfit. It's a dark plaid pencil skirt with a green sweater. The sweater has a cute keyhole detail on the chest and is light enough to be comfortable for a summer night.

"What about this one?" I ask her, giving her a twirl. Sofía pauses her game and looks up at me.

"Is this for a date?" She asks.

"Yeah," I say, plucking at the sweater.

"You never go on dates," she says, her tone suspicious.

"Well I am now," I snap back at her. Sofía rolls her eyes in response.

"Unless he has a thing for frumpy librarians, this one is a no, too," Sofía says before resuming her game. "You need to show off your assets."

"My assets?" I repeat, looking into the full-length mirror on the back of our closet door. It's hard to be objective about your own body. It's especially hard to figure out what your assets are when all you can see are your flaws. Thighs that rub together and chafe, a flat chest that is still waiting for puberty to hit, a wide nose, and a really big forehead that I cover with bangs.

"Show off those gams," Sofía says over the dull sound of a power-washing machine. I take off the skirt and look at my bare legs in the mirror. They are longer than average, but my thighs have a fair amount of both fat (from pastries and pork) and muscle (from having to bike around everywhere), and I've always been self-conscious of them. "And your butt," Sofía adds.

My butt is a point of pride, to be fair. Sofía ended up willowy and tall and with a flat bottom, and my butt has always been the thing she's jealous of.

"I thought the pencil skirt did a good job of showing off my butt," I point out, considering the thing is pretty skintight.

"Just wear something short, for the love of God," Sofía says, clearly over helping me pick out an outfit. I decide to take her advice and pull out a corduroy overall dress that's embroidered with tiny flowers and goes to my mid-thigh. I decide to pair it with a scallop-hem white turtleneck and combat boots.

"Who are you going on a date with anyway?" Sofía asks as I look at myself in the mirror.

"James, from Locicero's," I tell her as I tug down the hem of the overalls. I swear I remember this being a little longer the last time I wore it.

"Bo-*ring*," Sofía says.

"Hey," I say, turning to face her. "James is cool. And cute."

"And?" Sofía prompts.

"And he's, uh," I rack my brain for something interesting I know about him. "His uncle has a boat."

"Oh wow, how romantic," Sofía says, deadpan.

I throw a pillow at her, which she blocks with her leg.

"I'll remember to mention his uncle's boat in my toast at your wedding," she continues.

"Go back to power-washing," I tell her, angrily stomping to my side of the room and closing the dividing curtain. Sofía laughs gleefully as she continues to fake-clean a fake house in her video game. If only she would put that same effort into cleaning her side of the room.

While I'm picking out my earrings, James sends me a text letting me know he's five minutes away. No chance of canceling now.

I'm putting on my azabache necklace, a custom piece made by my tia Camila that I wear almost every day, when I spot James's beat-up Honda Civic with a big "Locicero's Pizza" emblazoned on the side pulling up to my house. He steps out of the car and I panic, running out of my room to intercept him on the front porch. We are not doing the whole ring the doorbell, meet my parents song and dance tonight. I run past my mom, who's still working on her computer and barely has time to register me before I'm at the front door.

185

"I'm grabbing pizza with a friend!" I call out to her. "I'll text you when I'm on my way home."

"Be careful!" my mom calls back, her standard way of saying, "Goodbye, I love you."

James is halfway up the porch when I barrel out the front door and push him back to the street.

"I'm starving!" I yell at him, as though my frantic energy is due to hunger and not the thought of him meeting my parents and telling them he's taking me on a date.

"Oh, okay," James says, taking my high energy for a good thing. "I asked my uncle to reserve the good table."

"Can't wait!"

CHAPTER TWENTY

James wasn't lying, he did get the good table. Locicero's sits on the corner of the block, and there is one table tucked right against the curved glass. It gets beautiful natural light from the south-facing windows, and it feels like you're tucked into a tiny garden because of all the greenery growing on the trellis outside. There's bright white and purple passionflower and fragrant jasmine, pots full of gardenias and trailing pothos.

This is *the* table hot couples try to score before homecoming and prom so they can get that picture-perfect shot, with the white tablecloth and tea lights with real flames and not those fake battery-operated ones.

The two chairs at the table are tucked in close to each other so they can both angle out to face the beautiful scene outside the window. Beyond the greenery you can just see the sparkling blue water of the sound.

Objectively, it's the perfect spot for a date in Port Murphy.

But all I feel as the hostess walks us to the table is dread.

James looks so happy, and he's been chatting nonstop about his recent camping trip with his friends.

"So we start setting up camp, and Lewis pulls the tent supplies from the trunk and he freezes suddenly and I think a chipmunk or something is in the car but it turns out *he forgot to bring the tent poles.* Can you believe it? We just have a nylon tent, a camping stove, and Jack's attempt at lembas bread."

We get to the table, and James starts to sit down when he suddenly realizes he should pull out my chair for me, even though I'm already doing it myself. But when he goes to stand up, his foot gets caught up in the chair leg and he trips. I plop down on the chair to avoid colliding with him, and he rights himself quickly.

"Sorry about that," he says, red from embarrassment.

"No problem!" I say with false cheer. Can he feel how awkward this is? How not right this is? Do I just come out and say it? But what if things get better? He could just need time to chill out. I could just need time to get into it.

But the longer I think about potentially dating James, of kissing him and holding his hand, the more uncomfortable I get.

I pick up the small cardstock menu and try to focus on the food.

"The seasonal appetizer right now is fried squash blossoms. Do you like those?"

"You could fry anything up and I'd eat it," I tell him.

"Awesome."

We sit in silence as we look over the menu. I don't know why James is pretending to consider the menu when he should know it like the back of his hand.

"The brown butter corn casunziei is the summer special," he tells me over the menu. "It's definitely worth trying."

"I'll have that, then," I say, dropping the menu down and turning to look at James. He's all but gripping the menu in his hands and watching me almost warily. Can he tell that I'm not feeling this? A date shouldn't feel this weird, right?

"The Italian soda flavor for the summer is POG," he continues to speak as though he is my waiter for the night. "That one was actually my idea. My uncle was just going to do passionfruit, but I convinced him to do POG instead. And I know you love guava."

"Let's order that," I tell him, turning my attention to the window.

While we wait for the waiter to come, James goes back to the tent story. I follow along with nods and smiles but my mind is elsewhere. I could be finalizing the materials for the competition right now. I have the recipe written along with the essay, but I want to draft some captions for the videos. Miguel said he would upload all the raw footage for me this weekend. I only have a week left before everything is due, and I should be working on all of that instead of sitting at this extremely romantic table with someone I do *not* have romantic feelings for.

I desperately wish I had a time machine so I could undo saying yes to this date. I would then take it back even further and stop myself from biking down to Lacey's that night. Or maybe I should go back further, back to that day in LA so I could stop myself from meeting Miguel.

But I can't do that. So now I have to ruin another friendship tonight.

This table at Locicero's is popular, and some pedestrians who pass by peek in to see who scored it for the night. It's still bright outside with sunset two hours away. James and I are perfectly visible in all our awkward glory as he continues to tell me about their adventure without tent poles.

Then someone passes by whom I recognize. He has to stop at the end of the block because the do-not-walk light is on. While he waits for the light to turn, he glances over at the corner of Locicero's, where I'm sitting in plain view.

Miguel's eyes meet mine, and first I see the surprise on his face. He's wearing a Morales Bakery T-shirt and there's flour dusted on it. His emergency earlier must have been a call from a family member to come help at the bakery. And now he's here, his eyes sliding from me to look at James. Miguel's brows furrow as he takes in the scene, and I feel like I am going to throw up.

He shakes his head once and decides to cross without the light's permission.

I move without thinking. I jump up from my chair and startle James enough that he stops telling me about his camping trip.

"Amy?" he says, concerned.

"I'm so sorry, James," I say, picking up my purse from the back of the chair and slowly backing away. "I don't think I can do this. I just have a lot going on right now with this competition thing I'm entering and I need to concentrate on that." It's not fair, leaving him like this with such a thin excuse, but I have to get out of here.

James awkwardly stands up from his chair, maybe to try to convince me to stay, but I run out of the restaurant, nearly knocking over the waitress who is carrying our Italian sodas.

I tear down the street in the direction Miguel went. I can see his car parked farther down the road, and I pick up my pace so I can catch him before he leaves.

"Miguel!" I call out, desperate to get his attention.

I can tell that he knows I'm chasing him because his posture goes rigid and he speeds up.

"Miguel, please!" I call out, not caring who sees me running down the street calling after a Morales.

Something in my voice must have convinced him because he does stop. He doesn't turn to face me though, keeping his back to me as he runs a hand through his hair. I come to a halt beside him and double over as I try to catch my breath.

He stands still as a statue next to me, waiting for me to gather myself. I try to make eye contact with him, but he's looking at my shoes. His face is a perfect blank mask as he waits for me to speak.

"I'm sorry," I finally say. This gets him to look up, his brows furrowed as he considers me.

"What could you possibly be sorry for? You've done nothing wrong," he says genuinely with a weak shake of his head. He's trying to keep emotion out of his voice, but I can hear the hurt in his words.

"I shouldn't have said yes to that date with James," I tell him. "I shouldn't have done a lot of things. I seem to be making bad decision after bad decision this summer."

Miguel lets out a bitter laugh. "Me among them, right?"

Despite myself, my throat catches and tears start to well.

"No, no, that's not what I meant, that's not why I came after you—"

"Why *did* you run after me? Huh?" he asks, exasperated. "You made yourself very clear at Dallas's party. I'm respecting the line *you* drew."

"I didn't want you to get the wrong idea about what you saw back there, is all," I tell him. "He and I aren't together."

"That's it? That's what you chased me down to tell me?" he asks. When I don't respond, Miguel throws his hands up in frustration and pushes past me toward his car. I let him pass, struggling to think of something to say. What *am* I doing here? Why am I running after this guy who I have determined is off-limits?

"I'm sorry," I say again, my eyes locked on the Morales Bakery logo on the back of his shirt.

"Look, Ana Maria," Miguel says as he pulls open the door to his car. "I can't do this. I can't have you chasing after me to reassure me you aren't seeing some other guy when we can never—" He stops for a moment and takes a deep breath before continuing. "I don't think you understand how much you hurt me that night. I had just told you all these things about myself, things that I haven't told anyone outside my family, and you just . . . cut me off. Like none of it mattered. So, you can't do this. Because you're just going to throw me aside again. And I can't take that anymore, not from you. It hurts."

His voice breaks at the last bit, and he presses the back of his hand to his mouth. For a moment it looks like he might say more, but he just shakes his head and jumps into his car.

I watch him back out of the spot and drive away, stunned and frozen in place.

CHAPTER TWENTY-ONE

I'm so mad at myself. I want to scream, but I'm still in the middle of downtown and I don't want any witnesses to my breakdown. There is only one person I want to see right now. I begin to walk as I open my phone and text Rose.

I'm coming over now. Stranded downtown so I'm walking.

Not even one block into my walk and my boots start digging blisters into my ankles. I try to focus my attention on the pain instead of remembering the look on Miguel's face—somehow the blisters hurt less.

My phone dings in quick succession as Rose sends me a flurry of disjointed texts.

Stranded???

Downtown????

You need to pick up these doughnuts.

Aren't you supposed to be on a date with James?

Where are you right now?

Are you okay?

Instead of typing out a response, I call her.

"Explain, please," she says when she answers.

"I just walked out on my date with James," I tell her. "Actually, saying I walked out is generous. I basically ran away. And I am obviously not going to turn around to ask him for a ride, so I'm walking."

"Ugh, I wish my mom were home. I would take her car and pick you up. What happened?"

"I'll tell you when I get there," I assure her.

"But you're okay?"

I'm not, but I know she's asking something different. "Yeah, I'm okay."

"Okay. I guess I'll just have to wait here in absolute *suspense!*" she complains, and I manage a little laugh.

"You'll survive. See you soon."

I shoot a text to my mom and let her know I'm spending the night at Rose's before continuing my trek to the McGinnis house.

When I get to Rose's, I open the front door with my key and go straight to her room. She's sitting on her floor with a mirror and dozens of makeup products spread out on the floor in front of her. When she turns to look at me, one eye has a bright blue eye shadow look and the other has an aggressive wing liner in electric blue.

I don't say anything, I just collapse into her bed and start crying.

Rose, who normally never runs out of things to say or questions to ask, silently climbs up onto the bed with me. I curl into her and cry while she brushes my hair.

"I'm sorry this is the second time this week I'm crying all over you," I say, my voice muffled and thick with tears.

"Shut up, after all the times you've done this for me? It's the least I can do," Rose replies. "But I will be sending you my dry-cleaning bill."

I laugh but it quickly dissolves into sobs again.

I end up crying myself to sleep, and when I wake up the next morning, Rose is on the bed next to me snoring loudly. I slide out without disturbing her and head downstairs.

Ms. McGinnis is in the kitchen making herself a cup of coffee. She looks exactly like Rose, just thirty years older and way more tired looking. She's already in her scrubs and looks ready to head out to work.

"Oh, Amy, I had no idea you slept over," she says with a smile. "It's good to see you. Rose said you made these doughnuts?" she says, waving toward the half-eaten strawberry doughnut she has on her plate. "They're delicious!"

"Thanks, Ms. McGinnis. Do you want to bring a box in for your coworkers?" I ask her.

"Oh, that would be amazing, are you sure?" she asks.

"Of course, I made more than enough. Thanks for letting me use your house as my own personal test kitchen," I say, pulling out one of the bakery to-go boxes I have stashed with my baking equipment. I fill out the box with the doughnuts and some leftover mojito lemon bars.

"Oh, sweetie, any time. Someone should make use of this kitchen."

I grab one of the tote bags from the pantry and slide the box of baked goods inside.

"The girls at work will love these," Ms. McGinnis says as she takes the bag from me. "I need to head out now, but tell Rose that we're having dinner at my cousin's tonight, okay?"

I nod and smile as she takes one last chug of her coffee and grabs her doughnut before heading out. I make myself a cup of coffee and start tidying up Rose's kitchen. I gather all my materials, the extra ingredients, and the boxes of pastries. Rose already has all of Miguel's equipment put away in a pile by the mudroom door.

Is he even going to stop by today? Should I leave before he gets here?

Before that spiral of thoughts gets too far, I throw myself into deep cleaning. I wipe down the cabinet fronts and find an old toothbrush to scrub the grout on the countertop tile. Rose eventually gets up and comes downstairs mid-cleaning frenzy.

I'm pulling everything out of the refrigerator so I can clean inside when she comes up next to me. "Good morning," she says. I wait for the questions I know have been piling up inside her all night, but she simply pours herself a cup of coffee. She grabs the half-and-half from my pile on the counter, splashing it into her mug before taking a seat at the table.

She takes two full sips before finally asking, "Are you ready to tell me what last night was about?" *Sip.* "Does it perhaps have something to with what's been going on between you and Miguel?" *Sip.*

And just like that, everything floods out of me. From the awkward date to my chase down Main Street, I tell Rose the full story. Rose listens patiently, not cutting in while I explain the whole situation to her—not even when I have to pause to wipe my tears or blow my nose.

"No matter what I do, something about Miguel feels . . . inevitable. And I hate that so much," I confess, my voice wretched. "Logically I know I should stay away, but I just can't."

Rose gives me a sympathetic frown and takes a moment to collect her thoughts.

"I never thought I'd say this about a Morales—and for the record, most of them do suck—but Miguel really is a great guy," she says gently.

"I know," I say begrudgingly.

"He even stuck around and kept helping you with the competition after you friendship-dumped him," she continues.

"*I know*," I repeat, miserable.

"You guys really do have great chemistry together. And I like him, which is obviously the most important thing." She pauses and sighs. "But his family."

"But his family," I echo, resigned. It always comes back to his family. To *my* family. "I haven't even broken the news about wanting to go to culinary school to my parents yet. Can you imagine if I added Miguel to the mix?"

"You're almost eighteen," Rose points out. "You can make your own life decisions."

"Ha!" I cry out with laughter. "Rose, I'm *Cuban*. My parents will be up in my business for the rest of my life. My family does not respect boundaries. My grandfather tried to change my sister's name on her birth certificate."

"Really?" Rose asks, sidetracked by the new piece of Ybarra lore.

"Yes, he wanted her to be named Josefina after my abuela. And there is no escaping their control, because my parents ended up changing Sofía's middle name to Josefina."

"She always said she never got a middle name!"

"You know Sofía's favorite sport is lying."

"Okay, okay," Rose says, waving off this tangent of a conversation. "Listen, Amy. Life is short. We don't always get what we want. That's why you have to follow the things that make you happy, you know? Even if they hurt a little bit, finding happiness is always worth it. And I've never seen you as happy as you were that first week working on this project with Miguel. Or those first few days after coming back from LA. I've only ever seen you that excited and animated about two things: when you're in the kitchen working on your own recipes and whenever you're talking about culinary school in Paris."

She reaches out and grabs my arm, so I turn to face her. I drop my spray bottle of vinegar water (Poppy McGinnis does not have Fabuloso in her home) and face Rose.

"Those two things that make you happy, they both go against the things your parents want for you. What's one more?"

"Rose McGinnis Ybarra!" I exclaim in surprise. She holds up her hands and shoots me a cheeky smile. "My parents are going to take away your honorary Ybarra name if they ever find out you said that."

"I'm just saying. I think it might be worth considering." She glances at the pile of Miguel's equipment and then at the time on the stove. "Wasn't he going to come by and pick this stuff up this morning? It's almost noon."

"He might need some space after last night," I admit. "Do you mind holding on to it for a little longer?"

"Sure, but I *will* use it while it's here. Oh, speaking of, I need to hop on a call with Noah and Caroline. They were talking about shooting a short film this summer, and now that I'm basically a cinematographer I was thinking of joining the production. Are you good in here?"

I nod and turn back to the fridge. I clean for another half hour while Rose talks on the phone upstairs. When I've run out of things to wipe down, I text Rose and let her know I'm going to borrow her bike to take some of my baking tools back to my house. She shoots me back a thumbs-up emoji, and I grab some of the equipment. I walk out through the mudroom with my arms full, my back pushing open the door onto the porch.

When I turn around, I nearly drop my load of equipment directly on my feet because Miguel Fuentes is sitting on the stairs, his back leaning against the railing and his face turned up to look at me.

He looks a little disheveled in a white T-shirt and a rumpled light brown short-sleeved button-up. His hair is sticking up like he's been running his hands through it, and he has bags under his eyes.

"Oh, hi," I say in surprise.

"Hey," he returns with a wan smile.

I place my handful of kitchen odds and ends in front of the door and take a seat on the stairs across from him. How long has he been here? Did he hear my conversation with Rose? My heart starts racing, and it's like it's going to burst out of my chest as I try to think of something to say. Do I bring up last night? Fourth of July? Should I just leave him alone?

"I'm sorry about last night," he says softly.

"You don't have to apologize," I say quickly, waving my hands at him. "I've been awful to you."

"No, you've been honest with me. You were up front about how bad this whole thing with our families is. I should have taken you seriously from the start instead of pushing you. I just . . ." He trails off and he lets out a frustrated breath. "I've had a really shit time the last few months. I wasn't excited to move up here. So when I saw you it was like . . . the first time I had seen sunshine in months."

Something in me cracks open at his words, and the pit of anxiety at the bottom of my stomach begins to unravel. I think of the moment I heard my given name being called out at a party where people only knew me as Amy. How in the few hours we had spent together in LA, Miguel had changed the course of my life. I'm not sure I would have had the confidence on my own to go after pastry school if we hadn't had met. Miguel is important to me, regardless of how our families feel about each other and what that means for us. But I had never considered that I could be just as important to him.

"You know, I actually spent most of my life desperate to have the Morales last name," he says quietly, in the tone of a confession. "As you already know, my dad is an asshole. And his whole family kind of sucks, too. When my uncle and primos from my mom's side would visit, they were such a tight unit, you know? It was so different from what I saw on my dad's side of the family, and I so desperately wanted to be a part of it. But

Adrian was a little shit, and he would always make a point of saying I wasn't a Morales, I was a *Fuentes*.

"My abuelo would cut in and say, 'Well, if you want to be a real Morales, you have to eat oysters. All Moraleses love oysters.' When we'd go on family vacation to the Oregon coast we'd go to this restaurant, and while Valeria and Adrian were slurping down oysters, my abuelo would watch me. The thing standing between me and my dream of belonging was a shell full of snot. I could never bring myself to eat one."

Miguel sighs and scratches the back of his head, looking up at the clear blue sky.

"And then you come along and you insist I'm a Morales, the thing I always wanted to be, but to you it's a curse. Kind of twisted, huh? I finally got what I wanted and now I don't want it at all. I don't want to be a Morales if it keeps me from being with you."

I think of every time I had called him Morales in an attempt to keep him at arm's distance, thinking that the only person it would hurt would be me. But each time I called him by that name, it had twisted a knife in him I had never known about.

His confession lingers between us.

This is a make-or-break moment. I could truly end whatever this is between us, once and for all. We would be honoring the wishes of our families.

But I know that if I cut off Miguel, I wouldn't be honoring myself. Because Rose is right, Miguel makes me happy. And I deserve to choose happiness.

"I'm scared," I whisper, scooting across the stairs and reaching out to hold his hand. To my surprise, he doesn't pull back or draw away. Miguel gives me his hand and holds on tight to mine. I can't bring myself to face him, so I keep my head down and focus my gaze on our hands. "I haven't told my parents about culinary school. I haven't told my mom that I'm not going to college. I haven't told Dad that I have no interest in inheriting the family business. And I certainly haven't told them that I have this heart-stopping crush on a Morales boy." I exhale, a rush of relief passing over me as I finally get those words out. "I'm terrified of disappointing them, and, honestly, I'm a little afraid that they'll lock me up Rapunzel-style if I tell them about any of this. My parents have sacrificed so much for me and my sister. I don't want to throw it all in their face by going against their wishes. But I don't want to let that fear drive all my decision-making either, you know?"

I take a deep breath and look up at him. This time, we're not in the dark of his car or in a lighthouse at night. I can see him clearly in the bright afternoon sun, his expression laid bare for me. There's some trepidation there, an underlying fear that I might reject him again. But there's hope there, too, in the way the corners of his lips curl. He has faith in us yet.

"I think we should revise our deal," I tell him, watching his face closely.

"Yeah?" he says, his brows drawn, unable to read my tone.

"If you're still up for it," I say with a challenge and a smile.

"I think I might be." His lips twitch.

"We would still have to keep it a secret," I tell him. "But I think we can get rid of the friends part."

His face falls for a second, and his eyes watch me closely. Because as I say this to him, I lean in a little closer and let go of his hands. I reach up, slowly, deliberately, to cup his cheek. I see it the moment it clicks for him and his face breaks out in a smile.

This time he leans in closer, his arms snaking around my waist to pull me in. I drag my nose along the side of his, his warm breath ghosting across my lips.

"I think I can work with that," he whispers in a deep rumble.

I'm not sure which one of us closes the distance first. His mouth opens to mine and I fall into the kiss gladly. I slide into his lap, eager to close the space between us, to get so close I can feel his heartbeat against mine, to make up for lost time.

This is different from our first kiss, nothing like the desperate goodbye I stole from him last winter. This kiss is an invitation, the sweet promise of a fresh start.

CHAPTER TWENTY-TWO

Dating in secret is a lot harder than being friends in secret.

We convince Rose to let us use the house as our editing cave as we go over the footage we've shot over the last two weeks. We're good at staying on task for a few hours, but inevitably, I'll look over at Miguel as he's focused on the computer editing a video and something will come over me.

He's so beautiful, I'll think as I watch him work. *And so talented*, I'll think as I watch his hands move around the keyboard and track pad. The thoughts will become so overwhelming that I just have to rest my hand on his knee, to reassure myself that he is real and that he's here.

I'll feel his leg tense up at my touch and a sharp hiss will escape him. The laptop is easy enough to toss aside. We'll make out on the floor of Rose's bedroom until she comes in to check on us.

"Oh my *God*," Rose exclaims. "This is the third time today."

I sheepishly extract myself from Miguel, who I had been straddling while we kissed up against the foot of Rose's bed.

"It is not," I say defensively. "The second time was totally innocent, it just looked compromised." To be fair, I was probably minutes away from jumping Miguel when she walked in.

"I feel like I need to put some house rules into place," Rose says, crossing her arms across her chest with faux sternness.

"Hey, you were the one that convinced me to give this a go," I accuse.

"You were?" Miguel pipes up, now safely five feet away from me and working on the laptop again. "I owe you for that one."

"Yeah, well now I'm beginning to regret it. He has a car, you know. Why can't you be regular teenagers and find some creepy park at night to make out in?"

"Yes, but I raise you this question: ¿por qué no los dos?" I ask her with a smile.

Rose throws her hands up with a groan and stomps out of the room, but she can't hide the grin on her face.

"Rose is right," I tell Miguel, grabbing the pillows from Rose's bed and building a wall between us. "We need to get this work done. Enough fooling around."

"I feel the need to point out that you have been the instigator every single time," Miguel says.

"I don't know what you're talking about," I say haughtily, as I stack the pillows high enough for me not to be able to see him. "I've been working on my application over here very diligently."

Everything has been typed out and proofread at least four

times, so the last two steps are submitting the video and filling out the application form. The form has some basic questions about my background, what got me into cooking, and fun questions like: what is your favorite food-related memory?

These are all short-answer questions, but that last one has had me stumped for the last hour. Which is probably why it's been so easy for me to get distracted by Miguel out of the corner of my eye.

Almost all my memories are tied to food in some way. From the birthday when Sofía requested a pie to the face or the first time my dad let me cook with him. I remember the last few years with my abuelo, making café con leche Sunday mornings and reading the paper with him. Food has informed almost every single moment of my life, and it's so hard to pick a favorite.

But as my eyes keep wandering to Miguel, I think back to that day in LA. Leaving that UCLA tour was possibly the first step in my new life direction. When I left campus with Miguel, I knew I was picking the future I had chosen for myself.

I have a goofy smile on my face as I finally type out the answer to that question.

We work in silence for another hour, Miguel clicking away as he edits my video and me agonizing over scripts for my voiceovers. I'm stalking another food creator I love, looking for inspiration, when I feel a hand slide up my foot to grip my ankle. Down the hall the shower turns on and I can hear as Rose gets in and starts belting a show tune.

I drop my phone to look up at my wall of pillows, where one wiry arm has reached between them to grasp on to me. Before I can say anything, Miguel gives my leg one good tug and I go crashing through the pillows.

"Miguel!" I cry out on a laugh as my carefully constructed wall comes crumbling down on me. With one strong tug, Miguel has managed to drag me all the way to him. He sweeps a throw pillow off my face and settles down next to me, his head propped in his hand as he looks down at me.

"I'm ready to clock out for the day," he says as his free hand traces the edge of my blouse. Half of it is ridden up nearly to my bra from the force of his tug across the carpet, and the mere warmth of his hand near my skin is enough to drive me crazy.

"We're on deadline, Mr. Fuentes. Cutting out early isn't allowed," I tell him, faking a stern tone.

"I think I could make a case for it," Miguel says, his voice barely a rumble against the side of my neck. I can feel his lips hover there, at the base of my throat where my pulse is fluttering wildly. "I can be very persuasive."

"Don't I know it," I say on a gasp, my voice a fractured whisper.

Unable to play aloof any longer, I reach up and run my hands through his hair. With one hand at the back of his neck I try to pull him in, but he playfully resists me.

"You have to dismiss me first," he insists, his lips tickling my cheekbone.

"*Miguel*," I whine, pressing my body against him and moving my hips firmly against him. He shoves his face into my neck and groans. The sound of it sends chills through me and I smile into his hair. He lands a playful nip on my neck and I can't keep the game up any longer. "You win, you win," I insist, trying to lift his face back up to mine. "Work time is over."

When he looks up at me through his lashes he has a devilish smile on his face.

"I'll get you back for that," I warn him before finally catching him in a kiss.

Miguel returns my kiss eagerly, his hand pushing my blouse up farther and farther until I'm scrambling to get out of it. Frustrated with our progress, he sweeps the rest of the pillows out of our way and rolls over onto his back, taking me with him. Straddling his hips now, it's much easier to pull off my shirt. Miguel's hand grips my waist and he watches me with hungry eyes, making me feel suddenly shy.

"You're beautiful," he says, almost reverently, one hand brushing along my sides as he admires my curves.

"You're not so bad," I say as I lean down over him.

I know making out with my secret boyfriend while topless in my best friend's bedroom is not the kindest thing I could do to Rose. Our bedrooms are our sacred places and having someone else hook up in them is not ideal. However, Rose loves love, and I think she would understand this transgression. We're star-crossed lovers, after all.

The universe, however, seems to disagree. Just as Miguel and I are getting going again, all fevered kisses and wandering hands, there's the unmistakable sound of the front door opening and Ms. McGinnis coming home.

"Rose, whose car is that parked outside?" Poppy shouts into the house.

I bolt upright, hoping that the untimely arrival of Rose's mom was all in my head.

"Rose?" Poppy calls out again.

Poppy McGinnis is, by most standards, a cool mom. She lets me use her home kitchen as my own personal test kitchen. She didn't balk at my mom's crazy sleepover rules in middle school. She lets Rose dye her hair fun colors in the summer (always back to blond for school because of the dress code). But Poppy McGinnis is also a certified informant. If I do anything that seems even mildly like something my parents would disapprove of, she will report it to them. She respects my parents too much not to, especially after all the hours they have spent helping her out with Rose over the years, from dinners to daycare.

And Poppy McGinnis will most certainly report me making out shirtless with a mysterious boy to my mother.

I can hear the shower in Rose's bathroom still going down the hall, which has made it impossible for her to hear her mother's question. Then I hear the creak of the third stair, a very distinct *crrr-THUNK* that sometimes makes you feel like you're going to fall straight through the step and into the basement. Poppy is going to find us.

I look around Rose's room frantically, trying to think of what to do. My options are fairly limited. I could send Miguel out the window, but the roof is steep on this side of the house and would not work for a hasty retreat. That leaves me with only one option.

"Go in the closet, *now*," I whisper at him as I push him toward Rose's closet. Miguel scrambles, wide-eyed, toward the door. The closet does not offer much in terms of concealment. It could hardly be considered a closet by modern standards and is just as small and strangely shaped as most closets in houses that are over a hundred years old. The space inside is hardly two feet deep and only about four feet wide, and if this were any other person's closet, that would probably be enough to hide in if you tucked yourself behind some clothes.

But this is Rose's bedroom. The closet is half neatly hung-up clothes and half avalanche of failed outfits. A layer of dangerously pointy shoes lines the bottom along with stray cuts of fabric, old diaries, a box of mementos, and more clothes.

"Where do I hide?" Miguel asks plaintively, looking at the avalanche, his eyes wide with panic.

"Rose?"

Poppy is at the top of the stairs.

"In!" I hiss, pushing Miguel into the avalanche. He falls over cleanly and sinks in. He tries to move some things out of the way so he can hide better, but it's not enough. I grab a handful of clothes and tear them off the hangers, throwing them all down on him. "She's in the shower!" I call out to Poppy, hoping to gain us some time. I decide to take some of the pillows from my wall and add them to the Miguel pile. If you weren't looking for a person in the pile, you probably wouldn't notice him.

"Amy!" Poppy says cheerily as she pops open Rose's bedroom door. "I didn't know you were— Oh! You're changing!" She backs out of the room to give me privacy.

"Rose is letting me borrow a shirt," I tell her, reaching into the pile and grabbing something to throw on. It's a black sheer top with black opaque stars over the boobs. I throw it on in a panic.

"Is that your car outside?" Poppy asks.

"No, a friend is letting me borrow it today to return some kitchen equipment," I say, the lie coming out smoothly. I run over to the bedroom door and pop it open.

"Oh, that's nice," Poppy says pleasantly, completely oblivious to the scene in the bedroom. "Are you staying for dinner?"

"Not tonight," I tell her with a smile. "My parents are complaining that Rose has taken too much of my time and I need to report home for dinner."

"You tell your folks I say hello, okay?" Poppy gives me a kind squeeze on the shoulder. "You should make sure to come over on one of my days off, okay? We can make a girls' day of it."

"Of course! I'll bring the snacks."

Poppy gives my shoulder one more squeeze before disappearing into her bedroom. I close the door and all but run back to the pile. I unearth Miguel, who does a playful gasp when I uncover his face. I shush him with a stern look and help him stand.

"That's what I get for wanting to clock out," he says, brushing his clothes off as though he were removing dirt. "I think I prefer the deep freeze."

"Well you're going to like it a whole lot better than this: you have to leave out the window. We can't risk letting Poppy see you in the house."

"I'm always up for an adventure," Miguel whispers before leaning in to kiss me on my nose.

I go out the front door and meet him around the back of the

house to make sure the coast is clear. I text Rose and ask her to distract her mom while I get Miguel out of the house. She gladly takes on the role and puts on the performance of a lifetime regaling Poppy with a story about the short film she's officially signed on to do with Noah and Caroline.

I give Miguel a silent thumbs-up and he jumps down. Not wanting to waste time, I give him a chaste kiss on the lips and rush him to his car. I follow quickly on my bike and hightail it home.

CHAPTER TWENTY-THREE

With Rose's house out of the question (I can't risk her mom seeing Miguel's car again and beginning to question exactly which "friend's" it is) and only days away from the final deadline, Miguel and I try to find alternatives. The park at night quickly falls to the bottom of the list when we drive up and find his cousin's car parked in the lot. Any other spot in town is far too visible, and the inside of his car is fairly limited in terms of amenities.

That's how we end up in a twenty-four-hour diner two towns over on the day before D-Day.

We're stationed in a booth toward the back—I can make an easy escape if necessary from here—where we have commandeered a table for most of the day. The Wi-Fi is free and the coffee is good, so it's been the perfect spot to settle in as I agonize over hitting the submit button.

I want to get in the application now, a day before it's due, in case the website breaks or something goes wrong when I try to hit send. If something happens, I'll have a whole day to solve it. If it goes well, then I can move on. In theory.

Everything is finished. The video is perfect, showing off the process of making and frying the dough before decorating it with my colorful and artistic toppings. It looks professional but approachable, and I think Miguel was right to go with a voiceover that tells a story instead of a step-by-step kind of video.

I teared up a little the first time I tried recording the voiceover in the temporary sound studio we made from the trunk of Miguel's car. He collected what must have been all the blankets in the Morales house and used them as sound padding in the car, blocking out all the windows and covering every hard surface. We sat cross-legged across from each other in the trunk with the microphone between us as I read from my scripts over and over again.

The blankets also proved to make the car more comfortable for . . . other activities. Which we kept to a minimum, because we are on a deadline and if we parked anywhere too long with the windows covered up, even at night, we were bound to get unwanted attention.

"You've looked over everything at least five times now," Miguel says gently. "I think you're ready to hit send."

"I know," I groan, moving the mouse toward the send button. "But as soon as I hit send, it's out of my hands. I won't have control over it anymore." Instead, I will be refreshing the landing page on *La Mesa*'s site as I wait for the finalist announcement. I even set up a Google alert for my name already just in case. "Okay, I'm going to do it," I say, trying to infuse confidence into my voice. "I'm going to hit send."

The pointer hovers over the button, waiting.

"You've got this," Miguel says encouragingly, like pressing this button is some kind of monumental feat I need to overcome. And he's right, it is, as embarrassing as that feels to admit.

"Okay," I say again, nodding. But I still can't bring myself to hit send. Should I look over everything one last time? What if I spelled my name wrong somewhere, or worse, wrote Amy instead of Ana Maria? "Ugh," I groan, dropping my head to the table. "I can't do it. I need you to hit send."

"Are you sure?" Miguel asks.

"Absolutely. The deadline will pass me by at this rate if you don't. Here," I turn my laptop toward him.

"All right." Miguel pulls the laptop closer and settles his hand over the track pad. "In three . . . two . . . one . . . send!" I hear the click of the track pad and that's it. The application is out, and with it, all my hopes and dreams for the future. If I win this prize money, I will be able to set my plans in motion after I graduate. And if I don't? I'll have to convince my parents to let me take a gap year to save up money. That is not a conversation I look forward to having.

"Thanks," I tell him.

"Anytime." He closes the lid of the laptop and pushes it back to me. "So what do we do now?"

"What do you mean?"

"Our initial reason for being together is gone," he explains with a tone of mock seriousness. "Without this scholarship, I don't think you would have taken me up on my offer to be secret friends. I owe *La Mesa* big-time for that. Maybe I should subscribe to their magazine?"

"Well, first, you should. It's a great magazine. And second, I didn't decide to be your secret friend *just* to use you for your skills."

"Oh yeah?" he returns with a goofy grin.

"Even without the scholarship I'm sure something would have tipped the scales for me. You're really cute, you know. And you have those sad puppy eyes."

"Cute? Puppy eyes?" he asks incredulously as he reaches around my waist and tugs me closer to him. "I think you mean handsome and smoldering eyes."

"I knew it!" I exclaim as I poke him in the chest. "You are a secret romance reader, aren't you? You can't know about Forks, Washington, and the term 'smoldering eyes' without being a romance reader."

"I'm a *cultured* man, Ana Maria. That's all."

"Hmm," I say, my tone disbelieving.

"I think we should order pie to celebrate."

"You're just trying to change the subject," I accuse.

"Yes, but also, we need to celebrate this accomplishment. I saw they have a sour cherry pie and a mudslide pie on the menu. Are you game?"

I nod and he calls over the waitress. He surprises me by asking for the slices to go.

"Calling it quits already?" I ask, trying to mask the disappointment in my voice with a weak laugh. "The sun hasn't even set."

"I know it hasn't," he says with that goofy smile that screams mischief. "But this hardly seems like the right celebratory environment, even with pie. An accomplishment such as yours deserves something epic." He gestures widely at the drab diner, which has considerably less personality than Lacey's.

"I'd hardly call the trunk of your car epic," I point out as the waitress drops off two boxes. "Unless you're talking about the things we can get up to in there." I waggle my eyebrows at him in cartoonish suggestion.

Miguel frowns down at me, and I can tell that my comment has derailed his thoughts for a moment.

"I have a *plan*," Miguel says carefully. "Don't distract me."

Miguel pays for our pie and swipes the boxes from the table before sliding out of the booth and offering me a hand. I take it, not hiding the skepticism from my expression as I scoot out.

"You're sure you're not open to suggestions? I think the pie can wait," I ask, letting him lead me out of the diner.

"*Ana* . . . ," he growls, stopping in the middle of the parking lot to glare down at me. "You're being quite the menace tonight."

"Now that I've hit submit on that application, I'm free to cause a little mischief," I say, reaching up on my tiptoes to bring my face closer to his, trying to tempt him into a kiss.

But instead of giving in to my feminine wiles, he presses a finger to my lips.

"I will not stray from the plan," he says, his tone a little less firm this time. I've gotten to him, at least a little bit. "We can get up to some mischief after I see my plan through, I promise. But time is of the essence." He gives me a boop on the nose and turns back toward the car.

"This surprise better be mind-blowing!" I call out after him.

Miguel places our to-go pies carefully in the back seat and we climb in up front. As soon as the car is on, he switches the screen on the central console from the map to the music app in an attempt to hide where we're going.

He reaches across to my lap and grasps for my hand, pulling it in for a kiss.

"It's a good surprise, I promise," he says. He gives my hand one more squeeze before dropping it and pulling out of the lot. I wish I could say I'm able to keep track of where he's going by just watching where we turn, but since I don't drive and my parents rarely venture out of town with us, none of the sights are recognizable to me.

Miguel has our favorite driving playlist on as we wind down a cedar-lined empty road. Conversation starts up again, the subject of his plan left behind as we move on to other topics. As much fun as it is to kiss Miguel, talking with him is just as good (well, nearly). Time flies by as we jump from subject to subject, laughing and teasing as we go.

The conversation is enough to keep me distracted on our drive until I notice Miguel turn down a street with a No Trespassing sign posted.

"Uh," I say nervously as I watch a Private Property sign zip by. "Was your fun surprise committing a crime together? Because I'm not sure we have the same definition of fun."

"*Technically* we will be committing a very small crime," Miguel says admits. "But it's not the point of the surprise."

"Oh, just a fun criminal by-product, okay," I say, a nervous edge creeping into my voice.

"We'll be fine," Miguel promises, reaching across to grab hold of my hand again and give it a comforting squeeze. "I came here by myself first to check it out ahead of time."

The dense tree coverage begins to thin out, and the winding road turns quickly from paved to gravel. Our destination peeks out from between the trees, a splash of white and red against the blue sky.

"Is that—" I cut myself off and turn to stare at Miguel in surprise. "Have you just taken me to the world's tiniest abandoned lighthouse?"

Sitting at the top of a small hill is a squat lighthouse, its clapboard exterior covered in flaking paint and overgrown weeds. It stands three stories tall but manages to only be about two-thirds the size of Dallas's decorative lighthouse. There's a small single-story house attached to its base, a few of the windows busted open and red tiles missing from the roof.

Despite the lighthouse's dilapidated condition, there's something charming about the whole thing. The small structure is surrounded by a quaint white picket fence, and the field is covered in wildflowers.

"I wanted us to have a lighthouse redo," Miguel explains softly. "We can't go inside because, you know, it's on the verge of collapsing, but there's still a really nice view."

My heart leaps at the sweetness and thoughtfulness of the gesture. I lean over the center console and give Miguel a quick kiss.

"Definitely better than a diner," I say. "Thank you."

"Of course," Miguel says before giving me another peck. "Plus, I wanted to take some pictures out here during golden hour, so it's a bit of a win-win." I swat him playfully on the arm, and we both turn to get out of the car.

Miguel grabs the takeout containers and a hidden tote bag.

Holding hands, we walk up the overgrown path toward the lighthouse. At the top of the hill, Miguel pulls out a blanket from the tote and spreads it out on the ground. He sets down his camera bag gingerly before helping me sit down on the blanket.

"I'm ready to tear into this pie," I announce, opening the to-go containers for inspection. Miguel plops down next to me and begins to fiddle with the settings on his camera.

There is something magical about the sheer simplicity of diner pie, a delightfully nostalgic beauty about the no-frills presentation and humble fillings.

The cherry pie has a perfectly golden and crispy lattice top, with dark cherry filling glistening on the inside. It looks like a perfect picture of fruit pie, the filling staying firm instead of spilling out from the edges. A good pie.

Then there is the mudslide pie. It has four distinct layers, and as soon as I have my hand on a fork, I'm tearing in, curious to discover all its parts. A buttery Oreo crust, an airy espresso cream cheese mousse, a decadent chocolate mousse, and topped with homemade whipped cream. Bits of Oreo crumbs and a decorative swirl of hot fudge decorate the top. It is mouthwateringly good.

I don't even have to taste the other one, this is my slice.

Miguel doesn't fight me, happy to keep the cherry for himself.

We eat our pies slowly, savoring our time as the sun sets. I ask Miguel about growing up in LA and his dad's side of the family. I tell him about Port Murphy High and which teachers to avoid. We talk about cities we want to visit and dreams we want to accomplish.

Between bites he picks up his camera and takes a few shots,

insisting he needs one of me because I managed to get chocolate all over my face. When I'm full of pie, I lie down on the blanket and continue to watch Miguel with his camera.

My heart aches at the sight of him, the focused look on his face and the careful motion of his fingers as he adjusts the settings. In this moment I'm so grateful I took the leap of faith to try this with him because nothing in my life has ever felt as wonderful as this.

A thin thread of golden light hovers above the sound, illuminating the whole world in the warm glow of sunset, matching the warmth I feel throughout my entire being.

I want to capture this moment, to look back on this image of him and remember everything I feel right now. While he's distracted, I reach into my pocket for my phone so I can get a sneaky picture of him. But my phone's not there. Confused, I look around the blanket. When was the last time I used it? The diner? In the car?

Miguel senses my sudden distress and puts down his camera. "What's going on?" he asks.

"I can't find my phone," I say, grabbing my purse and upending its contents onto the blanket.

"Did you leave it in my car?" Miguel asks.

"Maybe?" I say as I look at the random spread of contents from my bag. Altoids, wet wipes, three different lip glosses, a tiny white cat charm Sofía made for me when she was in elementary school, and my wallet. But no phone. "What if my parents tried calling me? What if they've already called the police and reported me as a missing person?"

"It's been less than eight hours since the last time you saw one of your parents, I'm sure no one has called the police," he says reassuringly. "Yet."

"Miguel!" I screech.

"You would at least have seen text messages come through on your laptop," Miguel says calmly as he starts collecting our trash. "We'll find it, don't worry."

Anxiety mounting, I jog back to the car and search the cup holders, under the seat, and in all the nooks and crannies but nothing comes up. Miguel calls my phone and we both stand there in silence waiting to hear the vibrations but all we hear are literal crickets. I have to imagine someone would have answered it if I left it at the diner.

"Where do you think it is?" Miguel asks.

"Maybe back at the shop?" I had a closing shift at work today, and Miguel picked me up three blocks away in a dank alley. In my rush to meet him I might have left my phone under the counter. Or it fell out of my bag on my covert operation to sneak into Miguel's car. "Can we stop by downtown before you take me home? I'll run inside and check to see if I left it there."

"Sure thing," Miguel says before starting up the car and heading back to Port Murphy.

"I'm sorry to have cut our lighthouse date short," I say softly. "At least I didn't run away this time."

"Maybe third time's the charm," he says reassuringly. "I'll find a bigger lighthouse next time, one we can actually go inside." His joke helps lighten the mood for a moment, but I still panic the entire drive back.

When we get to town, Miguel pulls into the alley behind

Café y Más, and we make sure my dad's car isn't in the parking lot. I jump out of the passenger seat and wrangle my keys out of my bag. When I hear the driver's side door click open I turn back to Miguel in surprise.

"You can wait in the car," I tell him. "I'll only be a minute."

"Let me just keep you company," he says with a smile. "It's dark."

"I sneak out of my house in the middle of the night and come to this shop *regularly* by myself," I assure him.

"Do I need to remind you about the disproportionate amount of serial killers that come from this part of the country?"

I know it will take more time fighting Miguel on this than just letting him accompany me for the minute it will take me to search for my phone. Besides, it will be helpful to have a second pair of eyes to help me look.

"Fine," I relent, unlocking the door to the shop. But when I open it, instead of being greeted by a dark kitchen and the sound of the alarm, the lights are on and music is playing. The next moments seem to pass in slow motion. I step in and turn toward the alarm, my muscle memory taking me through the normal steps of coming into the shop at night. Everything else seems to register a moment too late, and there's no time to warn Miguel before he's stepping into the kitchen behind me.

CHAPTER TWENTY-FOUR

Dad must have heard me open the door, because he pops out from the office in the back, his arms carrying a cardboard box. He looks confused at first, surprised to hear someone coming in through the back door. But when he sees it's me, a grin breaks out on his face.

"Papi!" I cry out in surprise, hoping that Miguel can back out quickly before Dad notices him. "What are you doing here?"

It all happens so quickly after that. First, there's delight in his eyes as he takes me in. But then, Miguel must make a sound or move behind me because Dad's eyes jump to him. He jolts in surprise at the sight of him and then his eyes begin to burn with something else. I know immediately by his face that there is no way I will be able to convince dad that Miguel is just some friend and not a Morales. He is so clued into the Morales family that he can already recognize the new family member in town on sight.

He probably has a printed-out family tree with pictures that he curses every night before he goes to bed.

Dad closes in on us in three angry steps, and I nearly trip over myself as I back up toward Miguel, trying to create a physical barrier between my dad and the Morales boy.

"Papi, please, I can explain!" I cry out. I don't have to look behind me to know that Miguel is still standing there, frozen in shock.

"No lo puedo creer," Dad seethes. "Este niño es el nuevo Morales, ¿no?"

"Miguel, go, *now!*" I call out over my shoulder as I hold up placating hands to my dad.

"Señor Ybarra," Miguel says calmly from behind me, and I want to scream because he should be running to his car right now if he knew what was good for him. "Yo no tengo malas intenciones con tu hija, te lo prometo."

"Este hijo de puta—" Dad takes a threatening step toward Miguel.

"Papi!" I scream, throwing my hand up at him in a sad attempt to keep him away.

But Dad swats me away like an annoying fly before grasping Miguel by the collar and pulling him into the kitchen.

"Papi!" I cry louder this time. I've never been scared of my dad before, but right now I'm terrified. Miguel is still holding up his hands in supplication as my dad forcibly drags him through the shop muttering obscenities in Spanish. "Papi, let him go! Let me explain!" I cry out as I chase after them.

"Voy a llevar este meao de gato to his uncle's place right now and set things straight," Dad growls. "I cannot believe you would do something like this to me."

"His family doesn't know! He's not like the rest of them. Please, Papi!"

"You can't trust those people!" Dad shouts over his shoulder. "They're lying, thieving pieces of shit! The whole lot of them, esa gente toda está podrida, ninguno sirven. You *know* that!"

Dad throws open the front door of the shop and pushes Miguel out. I scramble to the front counter and quickly find my phone in a drawer. I text my mom and Sofía the quickest message I can type to get them out here: *SOS at shop, come NOW.* Then I'm chasing my dad and Miguel out the door.

Port Murphy at 9:00 p.m. is certainly no ghost town. There are two couples outside of Locicero's drinking wine on the outdoor patio. Some bar patrons from down the street are smoking cigarettes on the corner, and the local wine store is having their monthly drink and draw, where I can see several inebriated people's attempts at painting a bowl of fruit through the window.

But to my surprise, Morales Bakery has the lights on and there seems to be a crowd of people milling around. They normally close at five and are not known to host late-night events in town. It feels like all of Port Murphy is on Main Street tonight, watching my father manhandle the guy I like across the street as he continues to shout in Spanish.

"Señor Ybarra, por favor," Miguel tries again as my dad shoves him toward the door to Morales Bakery.

"Open the goddamned door," my dad growls.

Inside the shop, the Moraleses seem to be hosting a party. People are standing around with glasses of wine and small plates, chatting over the vibrant sounds of salsa pulsing through the speakers. All eyes are on us the moment Miguel pulls open the door, my father's mood like a dark rain cloud on the party.

"Papi, let's not do this in front of everyone," I hiss from behind him, giving the sleeve of his shirt a half-hearted tug. But Dad is beyond reason at this point and is already stomping into the shop.

"PEDRO!" he shouts in his deep, booming voice. The party-goers are stunned silent by his bear-like entrance, and they all stand in silence watching him as the speakers continue to bump Celia Cruz's soulful voice. "GET YOUR ASS OUT HERE RIGHT NOW!"

There are gasps and titters all around the room as people take this show in. Dad still has his grip on the back of Miguel's shirt, his knuckles white and shaking. I glance around the room in panic and lock eyes on Valeria, who is watching this whole scene unfold in frozen shock.

Pedro pushes his way through the assembled crowd wearing a Morales Bakery T-shirt and looking just as pissed as my dad. The anthropomorphic burrito on his shirt stares at me with a gleeful smile.

"Miguel, what is going on here?" Pedro asks instead of acknowledging my dad, and I can practically feel the fury in him double.

"I caught your nephew sneaking into *my* shop with *my* daughter," Dad accuses, finally pushing Miguel toward his uncle and letting go of his shirt. Miguel stumbles a few steps, and his uncle reaches out an arm to steady him. "Tienes que mantener a tu sobrino lejos de mi familia si tu sabes lo que es bueno."

"If your daughter's sneaking around with boys at night, you're the one that needs to be keeping a tighter leash at home," Pedro says with a smug look on his face.

"Can we please not do this here?" I beg, trying to break some of the tension with my calm voice, but my dad is pitching forward, ready to fight Pedro over his comment.

"Ana is right, can we take this to the back?" Miguel says, and my dad lets out a strangled sound.

I look around, trying to catch sight of Valeria again, hoping that maybe she can knock sense into either of our dads, but instead I lock eyes on Adrian, who flashes me a smug smile. I flinch when we make eye contact, startled by how close he is to me.

"You and your dad are trespassing on a private party, Ybarra," Adrian says calmly, as though our fathers aren't having a screaming match behind me. "We're unveiling our new menu item tonight, which you've rudely interrupted. You've disturbed all of our guests with this outburst."

I've been too distracted by my dad and his temper tantrum to really take in what's happening in Morales Bakery tonight. But Adrian's words have me suddenly on edge, the sounds of the argument behind me fading as I turn my attention to the party. I look over Adrian's shoulder and some guest's head moves just enough for me to see the poster displayed on one of the tables of food.

It's designed in the familiar splashy colors of Morales Bakery, advertising their new menu item: the Cuban Doughnut. On the table is an assortment of figure-eight doughnuts in a variety of flavors. Mango, coconut, guava, tres leches, cinnamon sugar, and citrus. I take another look around the room and finally see what it is everyone is holding and eating. Small plates full of a creation achingly familiar to me. I had worked on these dough-nuts for months, adjusting the recipe until the texture was just right. I had come up with those exact combinations of flavors.

And I had documented almost that entire process in front of Miguel Morales Fuentes's camera this summer. I hadn't posted the videos for my doughnuts yet, so there's only one way Pedro Morales got his hands on this recipe.

Hating the Morales family had been something I was born into and that I had accepted as family tradition. The story of betrayal was secondhand, but I did my best to hold on to that same anger that burned like a torch in my abuelo. But after two generations, I couldn't sustain a torch, not really.

I can sustain a hell of a lot more than a torch now.

My grandfather had his recipes stolen by the Morales family many moons ago, and here I am, watching as the cycle repeats itself. And all because I decided to break the number one rule of being an Ybarra: never trust a Morales. I turn away from the grinning Adrian and lock eyes on Miguel.

"I trusted you," I rasp, and Miguel's attention turns from his uncle to me. "I trusted you," I say again, sterner this time, "and you used me."

He's staring at me, slack-jawed and brows furrowed, his mouth working to say something but no sound coming out as my dad and his uncle to continue to argue.

"I guess you finally get to take on the Morales name like you always wanted, huh? It's not eating oysters, but it's giving a big fuck you to that stupid Ybarra girl!"

"No, Ana, no," Miguel sputters. "What are you talking about?"

"The fucking doughnuts!" I scream at him. "You stole my fucking doughnuts!"

He looks flabbergasted, and his mouth flops open and closed like a dying fish as he struggles to come up with a response.

"You're both trespassing on a private event!" Pedro cuts in, finally realizing that my dad isn't the only one screaming anymore. "Leave now, before I call the police."

I continue, careless of Pedro's threat, pointing at the poster and table full of doughnuts. "You stole my recipe and gave it to your family's shitty bakery."

"You stole my daughter's recipe?" Dad growls, his attention turned to this new confrontation, new fuel for the rivalry's fire. The fire hadn't been properly fed in decades, and tonight it's getting its fill.

"Ana Maria, I would *not* do that to you! I did not do that to you!" Miguel has remained calm, but I can see the desperation rising in him now.

"How else do you explain this, then?" I ask, stepping over to a table where a discarded doughnut sits next to a postcard advertising Morales Bakery's newest menu item. "This is my idea, these are my flavors!"

"You Ybarras always think so highly of yourselves," Pedro scoffs. "You're not the only ones in this town capable of *thinking.* This is *our* family recipe."

"The only thing your family is capable of is THEFT!" Dad interjects. "You know half of your bestselling items were developed by *my father!*"

"If that's true, why is your father's shop failing while my father's is thriving?"

Dad growls in response and spouts off more curses in Spanish. Miguel throws his hands up before resting them on the top of his head and looking up at the ceiling, like the answers to all our problems are hidden in the pattern of the decorative tin tile.

"You all need to calm down!" Valeria cries from behind the counter, finally stepping in and clearly desperate to put an end to this.

"Valeria, call the station right now so we can get these trespassers out of here," her dad orders.

"What, too scared to deal with me yourself? You're a coward!" Dad spits in response, not cowed by the threat of arrest.

"I don't even know what's going on right now," Miguel mutters under his breath.

I whip my attention back to him. "Admit it. Tell me you did it. Say you stole my recipe in front of everyone, admit your family is nothing but a nest of vipers!"

"No, Ana, I won't do that because I didn't *do* anything! You've been looking for an excuse since the beginning to push me away, and I'm done trying to convince you to stop sabotaging yourself."

"Why sabotage myself when your family does it for me so well?" I spit back.

"You know, I really didn't buy into this bullshit rivalry," he says with a dry laugh. "But maybe I should have bought into it. You're just like them, Amy."

He turns away before I can respond. Miguel disappears through the kitchen door and Valeria goes running after him. I want to shout something back at him, try to get the last word in, but I'm out of things to yell.

As the only two Ybarras in the shop, we're outnumbered by the Moraleses and their supporters. People throw down their plates of doughnuts and start yelling at us to leave, more people threatening to call the police, and shouting all kinds of other things at us.

Then a familiar ear-splitting whistle cuts through the noise.

"NESTOR GUILLERMO YBARRA BORJA, GET OUT OF THIS BAKERY RIGHT NOW!"

Finally, the cavalry arrives in the form of my mother, dressed head to toe in sushi-printed pajamas with her hair in a silk bonnet looking like an avenging angel in the open door of Morales Bakery. Sofía is just behind her, also in pajamas, with her phone out ostensibly recording this encounter with a delighted smile on her face.

The three combatants that remain in the shop freeze at the sound of my mother's commanding voice.

"Mireya, you don't—" Dad tries, but Mom quickly cuts him off.

"Out, now," she says firmly, stepping aside and leaving room for him to exit through the door. He stomps off like a spoiled child sent to time-out, and I follow after him, embarrassed and upset by the entire ordeal. I look over my shoulder one more time.

My eyes land on the table of doughnuts again, and it's like a punch to the gut. Seeing my creation on that table is like looking through a mirror to an alternate world, a reality where my dad is open to change and listens to my ideas. A world where crowds line up to taste my food, where bills don't pile up unpaid, and where I don't have to listen to the hushed sounds of my parents arguing at night. A world where the guy I like doesn't betray me.

But it's not my world. It's the Moraleses'. And they stole it from me.

CHAPTER TWENTY-FIVE

We walk across the road to our shop in charged silence. I see Dad's car parked outside on the street, something he almost never does. I had been so confident that we only needed to check the back parking lot for him, but I'd been wrong.

I've learned tonight that I've been wrong about a lot of things.

"Close up the shop and come home," Mom commands Dad as she unlocks her car. She makes a sharp gesture at Sofía and me, and we climb into the car first.

After we close our doors, Mom steps away and says something to Dad, but she's too quiet and too far away to hear.

"I've never seen anything like that," Sofía says, like she's just left the movie theater after seeing this summer's hottest blockbuster.

"I'm glad watching my life explode in front of a massive audience is so fun for you," I mutter from the back seat.

When Mom finally gets into the car she remains silent, and that feels almost worse than getting yelled at. I sit in nervous anticipation, worried over what will happen when my mom finally does release her wrath upon me and Dad.

I can't say I handled Doughnutgate well, but I think my actions should be excused considering how blindsided I was by the whole thing. The family lore has always felt like a distant thing, a hurt that happened generations ago. As serious as it was to my dad and abuelo, it had never had the same weight for me. But I have learned the hard way that the family lore and hatred of the Moraleses is truly well deserved.

"Go to your room," Mom orders when we pull into the driveway. I jump out first, not ready to look anyone in the eye. Then I sit on the edge of my bed, waiting, knowing that tonight isn't over yet.

Sofía slides back into her bed with Azúcar curled at her feet, and we both wait in silence until the sound of Dad's engine chugs up the driveway. I take a deep breath and get ready for part two of the night.

I don't have to wait long. Just minutes after Dad's engine cuts off, he's blowing through our bedroom door, the rage from earlier not diminished in the slightest.

"I thought you were just sneaking out to practice recipes in the café," Dad says without preamble, and it's clear he's been practicing this confrontation on the car ride home. "Were you letting him into the shop? Ana Maria, what is wrong with you?"

"Papi, I swear—"

"You can't trust those people!" he cries. "They're lying, thieving crooks! They stole your recipe!"

I flinch at this reminder, this new ammo that he can use against the Moraleses when he has never once cared this much about one of my recipes before. He would have laughed off my idea of a Cuban doughnut had I come to him with it, but now it's just another reason to hate the Moraleses.

"Nestor," Mom cuts in, pushing past Dad and into our room. "Please stop screaming, you're going to wake the neighbors."

"Wake the neighbors? Fuck the neighbors! Our daughter is sneaking out with a boy from *that* family."

"Nestor, cálmate." Mom's voice is firm, cutting through my dad's rampage like a machete. "We will discuss this tomorrow. It's late."

Dad seethes in silence for a moment, clearly wanting to yell some more, but he must see some value in what my mom is saying.

"You're grounded," Dad says, his voice level and calm. "That goes for you, too, Sofía."

"I didn't do anything!" Sofía cries out.

"Enough!" My mom's voice cuts through and everyone is silent. "Everyone, to bed, *now*."

Dad stomps out of the room, and my mom shoots each of us a glare before slamming our bedroom door shut.

"I don't know why *I'm* grounded," Sofía complains, more to herself than anything. I get out of bed and put on my pajamas in silence. I turn off the bedroom light before crawling under my covers. Whatever strength I had used to stand up to both the Moraleses and my dad this evening has been completely depleted. There's a hollowness inside me now that I don't have anyone to yell at, a deep pit that aches with something close to grief. Miguel is not the person I thought he was, and I am not the daughter my father thought I was.

Once I'm under my covers with my face pressed hard against my pillow, everything releases at once and I'm sobbing. Heaving, wracking sobs that I try to muffle with my pillow shake out of me as the adrenaline from the confrontation finally runs out.

"Ana Maria?" Sofía whispers, concerned.

I curl into my pillow and cry harder.

Sofía climbs in next to me on my tiny twin bed and wraps her arms around me. I roll into her, grateful for the warmth and compassion she's offering me.

"It's going to be okay," she tells me, in the softest, gentlest voice she has ever used on me. She strokes my hair and presses her cheek to the top of my head. "Everything's going to be fine."

But it won't be, because I broke the number one rule of being an Ybarra. And I don't think my dad can forgive that.

The next morning is hell.

When I wake up, I lie in bed, half hoping that the night before had been some terrible nightmare.

That sharp *snick* of my room-divider curtain catches my attention, and I bolt upright to find Sofía staring down at me with a grimace on her face.

"Okay, so I really only caught maybe a third of what happened last night and I need to know what we're dealing with before I go out there," she demands before flopping down on the foot of my bed and sitting hard on my left ankle. I grunt and give her a half-hearted kick in response but make room for her. I might as well let my sister in on the disaster that was last night.

I tell her about my secret Morales boyfriend who betrayed

me, the scholarship competition he helped me with, and the events leading up to last night's implosion. She listens in rapt attention, clearly thrilled to hear that her buttoned-up older sister has turned into a rebel.

"Your ass is grass," she says. I just moan in response. "I have never seen them like that before. I have to pee so bad, but I'm terrified of leaving this room."

"Why? You're not the one that's in trouble," I mumble as I roll out of bed.

"Like that matters. Dad's on the warpath."

"I'm sorry you're getting caught up in this."

"Hey, I've been out there doing worse things than you—"

"Sofía, you better not be hanging out with Peacoat Kid—"

"Oh my God, *relax*. I mean that you're a freaking Girl Scout literally sneaking out to bake cookies and eat pie with your boyfriend. I'm going to bonfires and jumping off rocks into the water and stuff."

"You've been jumping off *what*?" I ask, thrown off.

"That's not the point. I should be the one asking clarifying questions here—you've been secretly dating a Morales boy?" Sofía returns. "I think that rates lower on the poor decision-making scale than jumping off of rocks."

"He's not like his cousins," I mumble. "And he's technically a Fuentes."

"Whatever." Sofía waves this fact off. "I really have to pee, so can you go out there and talk to them already?"

I wipe my face in frustration, really not looking forward to this confrontation.

"You've got this, champ," Sofía says with a strong swat to the back in support. The loving, soft sister I got last night has been replaced with the usual brash Sofía.

I make the brave leap and open my bedroom door.

Mom and Dad are lying in wait in the dining room, sitting across from each other at the table with cups of cold coffee in front of them.

"Sit down, querida," my mom says when she sees me. Dad won't even look up.

I pull out my chair and sit down, bracing for the worst.

"We are not going to get into the particulars of last night," my mom continues, clearly taking the lead in this conversation. My dad is too emotional to handle this right now, as evidenced by the white-knuckled grip on his mug. "It's clear you've been keeping secrets from us the last few weeks and you know what you were doing is wrong. Correct?"

"Yes," I say meekly, both embarrassed and ashamed. I know I took advantage of their trust in me.

At the time it had felt worth it, but after everything that has happened, I know that I'm wrong. I just hate that everyone had to be a witness to my huge mistake.

"Your father and I have agreed on the terms of your grounding," Mom continues. "We are taking your bike away through the end of the summer. You are only allowed to go to work and back home until school starts. Your dad will drive you to and from all of your shifts. You can't be sneaking around town without us knowing where you are, mija."

"Especially not with one of those Morales—"

"*Especially* with people that you have not introduced to us, okay?" Mom cuts in. "You and your sister have clearly taken advantage of how trusting we've been. I had overbearing parents growing up and I didn't want to do the same thing to you girls, but you've pushed us too far."

"I understand," I whisper, my eyes on the table in front of me.

"And no dating," Dad adds. "None of this dating stuff, and not just through the summer, through school!"

I'm on thin ice, but I can't help but roll my eyes. "I know for a fact you dated in high school! I've seen the homecoming pictures with that one girl with the black lipstick."

"I was not a young lady," he says, in the lamest machismo response ever.

"This is not what we agreed on, Nestor," my mom adds.

"She clearly has bad judgment when it comes to boys, Mireya," Dad says, waving his hand at me, as though it were written on my face: Ana Maria Ybarra, Bad at Picking Who to Kiss.

"Nestor," Mom says in that firm voice that usually puts Dad in his place. Dad settles back into his chair with a grumble, and Mom turns her attention back to me. "Clearly, your father is not happy you are dating a Morales. I, however, am not happy that you are dating someone without introducing him to us."

"We are not dating anymore," I cut in, the memory of Miguel's betrayal still sharp. Even if I had confided in my mom about Miguel, she wouldn't have been able to stop me from being hurt like this.

"The issue here," Mom continues despite my interruption, "is that you broke our trust. You need to *tell* us things, okay? Even if we might not like them, we need to try to understand each other. We are just worried about your well-being. That is what this is about."

"I understand," I say, and I can see my dad trying his best not to yell about the Moraleses some more.

"Good," Dad says, satisfied, as though he were any help in this conversation. "I changed the schedule at the café for the next two weeks. You're opening every morning, and I will be there at twelve to pick you up."

"Fine," I say, and I can see the fire reignite in my dad's eyes at that lackluster response. But Mom shoots him a glare and he settles down.

"Get dressed for work," Dad says, getting up from the table and pointing back at my room.

I hold back the sigh that is clamoring to escape me and leave the dining room. Dad is one wrong move from going completely haywire today, and I really shouldn't push his buttons.

My one consolation is that everything blew up *after* I submitted my application for the scholarship. If this had happened even one day earlier I would be a mess right now, but I can at least take this punishment now and know that it wasn't in vain. For nearly a month we worked hard to produce some truly beautiful cooking videos.

And the truth is, I wouldn't have been able to submit the amazing application I sent in without Miguel's help. I could wish that I never agreed to be his secret friend just to be spared from his eventual betrayal, but then I wouldn't have had his help with the videos. Without Miguel my application wouldn't have been nearly as good, no matter how moving my story or good my recipe.

So where does that leave me?

It leaves me in need of a distraction, I decide. And an opening shift at the shop will be just that.

I get dressed in my usual work uniform—light-wash jeans and a white shirt—and silently follow Dad out to his car. He doesn't even turn on the radio or AC, he just lets us literally stew in silence on the ten-minute drive to the shop. When we pull up to the parking lot behind the shop, he texts Eddie to let him know I've been dropped off and drives off as soon as I'm out the door.

I work the morning shift in tandem with Eddie, helping him take fresh-baked pastries and bread out of the ovens and brewing coffee after coffee for the morning crowd. He knows something is up—I'm sure word of the big fight at Morales Bakery has made the rounds already—but he mercifully keeps things business as usual. Promptly at noon, Mom arrives to pick me up and Dad gets out of the car without saying hello, presumably to work the afternoon shift after me.

It sucks to know that our relationship has been so thoroughly ruined, not necessarily because I lied to him, but because I was morally bankrupt enough to date someone related to the cursed Morales family.

Mom asks about my shift, tells me that Eddie's daughter's birthday party is coming up, and that another packet came in from a university. She chatters on, as though my life didn't completely implode the night before.

And so it goes on, day after day. Rose learns about the entire ordeal before I get a chance to muster up the will to rehash the night with her. She is desperate to come visit and comfort me, but when I make the suggestion to Mom she frowns and reminds me that "grounded means grounded."

Every morning I wake up and Sofía glares at me, upset that she has been grounded because of my antics. She's at least not scared to pee anymore, but I can't say the same for myself. When I'm not eating or going to the bathroom, I'm in my bedroom, curled up with Azúcar and a book in an attempt to escape my reality.

While I work at the shop, Dad decides to make use of the security camera to keep an eye on me.

"Get off your phone," he calls out after a frightening ring from the camera.

I had been replying to comments on my most recent social media post, a video Miguel had put together of me making my Vicky sponge. The overwhelming feedback since I've been posting content he's helped me with has been really positive. The comments are actually about the food and not mean things about how badly it was all shot. Miguel managed to toe the line between authentic and well produced that comes off as effortless, making the editing and shooting style secondary to my cooking.

My follower count has been ticking up, and some people have even replied to my videos with their attempts to recreate my recipes. If I get enough followers I can start looking up ways to get brand sponsorships in hopes of saving up money for Paris more quickly. And I'm reminded once again that none of this would have been possible without Miguel, no matter how good my recipes are.

But Miguel betrayed me. And in a few weeks, once I run out of content he helped me produce, I'll be back to square one with my social media. And what will I do then?

It's past the morning rush, in the dead zone between coffee drinkers and sandwich eaters when the shop is deserted. Out of things to do in back of house, I grab a bottle of Windex and a cloth and start wiping down the front windows. There are a few smears from hands and foreheads, in addition to a splash of coffee from someone who knocked their cup over this morning.

As I'm wiping down the glass, activity across the street catches my attention. I drop the cloth down on the back of the chair next to me and watch the line of people forming outside of Morales Bakery this morning. It's strange to see a line form there on a weekday, but I see a few kids from school outside, all clamoring to get into the worst restaurant in town.

The windows of the bakery have been painted with new illustrations and signage promoting their latest dessert. Arm in arm with the anthropomorphic dessert burrito that haunts my nightmares is a new Morales Bakery mascot: the Cuban Doughnut. It has the classic figure-eight shape of buñuelos and the same creepy eyes and a smile as the dessert burrito. This one is clearly a girl doughnut, judging by the long eyelashes and star anise tucked behind what I assume is the doughnut's ear. They're both painted on the glass with garish smiles, proudly announcing, NEW! CUBAN DOUGHNUTS!

Judging by the line outside, my creation has been an instant hit for Morales Bakery.

Miguel steps out from the door with a notepad and pen in hand, wearing a work apron and hat. He takes orders from people in the line and hands out laminated menus. It's too far to make out any details about him, whether he looks smug and happy or tired and sad. I wonder if the success of these dough-nuts is worth it for him. I wonder if he regrets what he did at all.

CHAPTER TWENTY-SIX

I spend the next week working the opening shift at the shop, watching people walk out of Morales Bakery with my doughnuts in their hands. Meanwhile, business has been slow at Café y Más, with locals curious to try the new Cuban doughnut with their coffee this week. If Dad had let me make additions to the menu, even on a seasonal basis, we could be the ones drawing in new customers like this.

But Dad has made it very clear that he would never allow something like that at our shop, because the only words he's spoken to me in the last two weeks have been to complain about this "stupid new gimmick" the Morales Bakery has created.

"Qué en carajo es un 'Cuban doughnut'?" he complains one afternoon, unprompted, after picking me up from my shift. He takes the longer way home so we can drive past the front of Morales Bakery, just to get another glare in at their Cuban doughnuts sign.

It's the first words he's spoken to me in days, and I'm not sure how to respond. I decide to just let it pass unnoticed, figuring that saying nothing is better than saying anything at all. It still feels like we're one wrong word away from starting another argument.

"Doughnut!" he shouts randomly in the middle of dinner while Mom is asking Sofía how Jac's vacation with his family in the Philippines went. "¡Se llaman *buñuelos!*" We collectively ignore him.

"Eso sabe a rayo," he says the next day. I know for a fact that he hasn't snuck a taste of the doughnuts, and even though it's not *my* recipe he's insisting tastes like shit, it feels like it. "I'm sure of it. They don't know how to do anything right."

Is this how he would have reacted if I had come to him with this recipe first? Or is he acting like this because it's the Moraleses? I have to accept that my creations won't find a home at Café y Más. Especially since I'm not sure how much longer this shop can even keep its doors open considering I haven't had a single customer walk in since I opened this morning.

Rose hasn't been able to drop in like she usually does during my shifts because of the short film project she's been working on. Noah has big dreams about submitting the movie to film festivals around the country and is taking the project very seriously. My texts to her usually don't go through because they've hiked up to a waterfall somewhere without a signal to get the perfect shot and she can only respond once she's back home at night. When I do catch Rose on the phone, she sounds exhausted and on the verge of falling asleep after spending hours hiking and shooting.

Tired as she sounds, it seems like she's having the best summer ever. I don't want to drag her down by crying about the one-two punch of a betrayal/breakup. So for now I just text her pictures of Azúcar sleeping with her tongue sticking out.

This whole mess has at least let me catch up on my reading, and I spend most shifts sitting on my stool and reading a paperback. The local bookstore has a section in the basement with shelves upon shelves of used books, from recent bestsellers to decades-old bodice rippers with scandalous covers. Paperbacks are a dollar each and they're not always in the best condition, but I buy them up like candy whenever I go. Needless to say, not being able to leave my house other than to work has helped me speed through my TBR pile.

Reading has also helped me keep my mind off another anxiety-inducing event: the announcement of the finalists for the scholarship. Keeping my nose in a book keeps me from checking the time on my phone every minute, watching the clock count down until the announcement goes live tonight.

I nearly stumble off my stool when the bell above the door rings and we get our first customer after four hours.

"¡Buenos días!" I call out as I shove my paperback under the counter and look up to greet the person.

The cheesy customer-service smile falls immediately when I see it's James.

James, who I literally ran away from while on a date weeks ago and whom I haven't spoken to since.

"Hey, Amy," he says, in a tone that is honestly way nicer than I deserve.

"Hey," I return, brows pinched as I anticipate how uncomfortable this conversation is going to be. "Listen, I'm really sorry. I shouldn't have just left like that and—"

"Please stop," he says, not unkindly. "I really don't want to rehash what happened that night, it's already embarrassing enough to have experienced it once. Can I get a coffee?"

"Uh, yeah," I say, a little startled by the request. A bit apprehensive of what's going to come next, I begin the process for espresso.

"I wanted to just come by and say no hard feelings, you know?" James says, and I'm thankful my back is turned so I don't have to make eye contact while he says this. "Truth is, I saw you at that party at the beginning of the summer talking to the Moraleses' cousin—before you ran away from him, too, which I've got to say is a pretty weird habit you have when it comes to dudes."

I'm so glad he can't see my guilty face as he says this. He's totally right, I have a pattern.

"I've never seen you like that with someone before, and I think I got a little jealous. I felt like I had to shoot my shot before he took it, you know?"

"We're not together," I assure James, turning around mid–espuma stirring to look at him. "Just so you know."

"Either way, I saw the way you looked at each other that night," James says, brushing my assurances off. "Our date made it very clear that we are better off as friends. And I'm not a glutton for punishment. So, I'm happy to return this to a completely platonic thing with no threats of dates. You thoroughly destroyed my crush on you when you ran out on me to chase another guy."

"Oh no," I groan. "You saw that?"

"Amy, we were at the corner table. I heard you *scream his name.*"

"I'm really not dating him," I assure him, as though that might make it any better.

"I assume that has something to do with the, uh, incident at Morales Bakery?" James asks. "I was taking out some trash when I saw your mom in her pajamas screaming in the middle of the street."

An involuntary shudder wracks through my body at the reminder of the very *public* aspect of that night. The only good part of being grounded right now is that I don't really have to face anyone I know and explain why my entire family was spotted screaming at Morales Bakery. What have people been saying about my family around town? As soon as the question pops in my mind, I brush it away. I really don't want to know.

"Yeah, something like that. Thanks for coming by, James," I say, handing him his coffee and hoping he drops the topic. I grab a bag and throw in some treats from the case for him. "I should have spoken to you sooner, you deserved that at least."

"Yeah, well, it gave me the opportunity to be the bigger man about the whole thing, so now I get to ride that high," he says, snapping the lid on his café con leche before taking a sip. "Ah, I missed these. Honestly, the free coffee is the main reason I decided to repair this friendship."

"Oh really?" I laugh. "Well, on that note take these free pastries, too. Your reward for being the bigger man."

"Ah, sweet," he says, grabbing the bag from me with a smile.

"I'll see you around, Amy." With a friendly nod, James heads out of the shop.

I feel a little lighter after having that conversation with James, like some invisible load I've been carrying has been lifted. I at least have one relationship I haven't totally ruined.

Another silent ride home with my dad that afternoon and then I'm back in my own personal jail cell, sitting in bed and scrolling, waiting for the final eight contestants to be announced on *La Mesa*'s Instagram. If I were living in an alternate timeline where I hadn't managed to screw everything up in one summer, I would be laying on Rose's floor with my laptop open as we await the results. Rose would have something ready to celebrate if I made the top eight or something to take my mind off the loss if I didn't.

Instead, I'm in a pair of old, ratty pajamas with a bowl of stale popcorn, swiping down on my phone screen to refresh it every ten seconds.

If I make the top eight and end up winning, it will make everything that happened this summer *worth it*. I have to make it.

I notice the battery dropping rapidly on my phone and struggle to find the charging cable that lives in the tight wedge between my bed and desk. I spend at least a minute with my hand squeezed in the tight space, grasping for the cable and unable to refresh my phone.

When I finally plug it in and refresh the screen, an update appears.

ANNOUNCING THE FINALISTS OF *LA MESA*'S STUDENT RECIPE SCHOLARSHIP COMPETITION.

My stomach drops and my fingers feel heavy as I click on the link to the article and scroll through opening paragraphs until I get to the section about the finalists.

I scroll through picture after picture of kids my age with their dishes, from a Mexican American guy with a plate full of chiles rellenos to a Dominican American girl with a fresh take on the traditional Dominican breakfast spread.

Picture after picture, and I'm not seeing my name. Dread starts to pool in my stomach and I slow my scrolling, now terrified to get to the bottom of the list.

But there, finally, in the penultimate spot:

ANA MARIA YBARRA: THE CUBAN DOUGHNUT

I'm so surprised to see my name on the screen that I gasp and end up choking on my spit. I cough hard a few times and guzzle the cup of water on my desk before I can recover enough to continue reading through the article. I read it over twice, just to make sure it wasn't a hallucination.

I did it. I'm a finalist. Even if I don't win, I think this feeling alone could buoy me through anything. This is the validation I've always craved from my work, the proof that my dreams and my creations are valid and worth something.

Summer is flying by, and soon the livestream announcing the winners will air and I'll know whether I'll be able to afford going to pastry school after graduation. If I win, I might be able to forge my own path. And eventually, maybe, if I catch them on a good day, my parents will accept my choice.

Even though they don't know what I want to use the money for, I do want to share this accomplishment with my parents.

I haven't won *yet*, but I have made it to the top eight of a very competitive scholarship competition—that has to help get me back in their good graces. I practically run out of my room, eager to tell them the news, but my parents aren't in the living room.

My mom's usual workstation, covered with papers and folders, is empty, and the TV in the living room is still on. Confused, I look around the dining room and kitchen and peer out the front window to make sure their cars are still in the driveway.

Then I hear them.

It's clear they're trying to be quiet and prevent me from catching on, but in a house this small it's hard to hide when you're arguing. My parents are in the bedroom, door closed, yelling at each other about something. I glance at my mom's desk. I think I can imagine what they're arguing about.

I step closer to their door, making sure to keep my steps quiet. At this distance, it's much easier to make out what they're saying.

"Just look at the numbers, it's right there," Mom is saying, her voice pleading.

"I've seen numbers like this before," Dad says. "Before the girls were born things were looking bad, but we made it through."

"Nestor, that was close to twenty years ago! These numbers do not go as far as they did then, we cannot survive the rate at which the café is burning our cash. I'm already pulling into our savings for payroll."

What? I knew things weren't going great at the shop, but I didn't think it was this bad. Like Dad always said, if we survived the recession and Covid, we can survive anything. But he's been wrong before.

My gut twists, thinking of all the times I thought about leaving Port Murphy behind to work at Michelin-starred restaurants in big cities. Even if I were never working at Café y Más in those fantasies, it was still always there. It was there when I would go home for the holidays, where I would walk in to surprise my dad for a weekend and eat a slice of his flan. Never did I imagine that the place where I learned to cook and love food would be gone after I left.

I can't let that happen.

Without thinking, I push open the bedroom door and walk in. My parents are frozen mid-argument, and they're looking at me with a shared expression that's somewhere between horror and embarrassment. I can tell that they hate that I've found them like this, shouting behind closed doors.

"I want to help," I tell them. "Please let me help."

"Ay, mija," my mom says, rubbing her forehead in frustration. "You weren't supposed to hear any of that. This is our problem."

"Listen to your mother," Dad says, "go back to your room." His voice is cold, his displeasure in my choices still at the forefront of his mind.

"No," I say stubbornly. "I have money saved up, almost ten thousand dollars. Let me use it to help the shop."

"Oh my God," my mom says in despair under her breath.

"Ten thousand dollars?" my dad says in surprise. "No, mija, that's your money."

"Your dad's right," Mom adds. "You shouldn't be held responsible for our bad finances."

"It's *my* money," I argue. "Don't I get to decide what I want to do with it?"

"And it's *my* business," Dad returns, proving where I get my stubbornness from. "I get to decide whose money I do and do not take. I am not taking your savings away to fix this."

Silence stretches between us for a moment. Mom looks like she's fighting back tears and I'm not sure why. Dad just looks utterly defeated.

"I need a minute," Mom finally says. "Te quiero," she says, planting a kiss on my forehead before brushing past me.

"Dad, please, I want to help out," I say softly, pleadingly. He sits down at the edge of his bed and brushes a hand over his mouth.

"What did you save that money up for? College?" he asks.

I consider lying, but it seems like now if ever is the moment for truth.

"No," I tell him. "I want to go to pastry school in Paris after I graduate. I don't want to go to college."

"And you don't want to work for me," he finishes. Hearing him say it twists my stomach.

"It's not that I don't wa—"

"You don't have to explain yourself, mija. You're made for more than Port Murphy, and that's okay. That's why your abuelos brought us to this country, so we could do big things. His big thing was opening his own shop. Yours is going to pastry school. Keep the money."

I stare at Dad in surprise, a little slack-jawed and awed to realize that all I had to do to gain his approval was to just tell him what I wanted. In my mind, the only way I would get their approval for my plans would be to come up with a foolproof argument, all my money saved up and every contingency covered. I had envisioned a PowerPoint presentation with Excel sheets, slide after slide of data and facts to convince them that my dream was something I could accomplish.

But instead, I told him here, unplanned and in a rush. And instead of telling me how bad or wrong my dream is, my dad is standing there, telling me to go to pastry school. The thing I've been dreading all summer had, in fact, been as easy as telling my parents I was going to Rose's house for dinner.

"What about your dream, Papi?" I ask him. "You love the shop, you love keeping your dad's recipes alive."

"My dream, my problem. Even if I took your money, your mom is right, the problem is bigger than that. It's getting more expensive to run the shop, business has been slowing down the last couple of years, and I'm getting old. Whatever happens, the shop is *my* responsibility. It's my problem to figure out."

"I don't want to lose the shop," I say, my voice cracking a little.

"Come here," Dad says, lifting an arm up and making room for me on the foot of the bed. I sit down next to him and wrap my arms around him as he squeezes me into his side. "I'm sorry you had to hear me and your mom arguing. I'm sure it's not the first time, either. It's been a rough year for the business. I thought summer would turn things around, but that hasn't been the case. I'm not telling you this so you can make this something to fix," he says sternly. "But just so you understand what's going on right now. Whatever happens, your mom and I will work on it."

"I understand," I mumble into his side.

"And speaking of responsibility," he says, and there's this tiny change in his tone that has me stiffening. I'm not going to like what comes next. "As your parent, it's my responsibility to make sure you're not making bad decisions. And you proved you weren't making the best decisions for yourself a few weeks ago."

I pull away from him quickly and stand up. Heartwarming father-daughter moment over.

"You're not being fair, Dad," I say evenly. I don't want to talk about my heartbreak with such an unsympathetic audience.

"Look what he did to you!" Dad shouts, all his righteous anger back in full swing. "You know his family is the reason our business has been suffering!"

"The business is suffering because the cost of supplies is going up, not some brujería the Moraleses have been casting!" I shout back.

"We don't ask a lot of you girls, but I thought you'd know better than to get close to one of those—"

"¡Me cago en diez!" my mom shouts from the kitchen. "Nestor, do not start this up again." Mom barrels into the room, ready to hash it out with Dad. "We have enough things to worry about. Who our daughter dates is not at the top of that list."

"Cómo que no está 'at the top of that list,' ella está saliendo con—"

"Ana Maria, go to your room, I need to speak to your father,"

Mom says in That Tone that I know has my dad quavering in his boots and regretting his outburst. I shoot Mom a grateful smile and run straight back to my room, scooping up Azúcar from the living room before I go. If ever there were a moment for a comfort cuddle with my cat, now would be it.

CHAPTER TWENTY-SEVEN

Over the course of the next few days my dad warms up a little, and it's clearly because Mom yelled at him. I'm still forced to work opening shift after opening shift, but they decide to return my bike due to "good behavior." I think they felt bad for being caught arguing and wanted to make it up to me somehow. I'm just glad I don't have to sit through any more frosty rides with my dad, given how quickly our warm father-daughter moment turned icy.

Getting some of my freedom back does nothing to help how jittery and antsy I feel. It's so bad I end up abstaining from Cuban coffee, which does ease the heart palpitations but still does nothing for the anxiety. Leading up to the livestream, *La Mesa* posts snippets about the finalists to their social media. And there, right at the top of my favorite food magazine's feed, is a picture of me in Rose's kitchen, a huge smile on my face and a plate of my doughnuts in my hands.

Ana Maria Ybarra is a Cuban American high school senior from the Pacific Northwest with dreams of taking her pastry skills to the next level. She's spent years working at her family bakery, learning how to make all the Cuban classics at her father's side. When she's not whipping up something tasty in the kitchen, she's hanging out with her cat or hunting for used paperbacks in town with her best friend. Learn more about her and her recipe for Cuban doughnuts on our livestream for the scholarship competition. You can follow Ana Maria (@CocinaGuava) to see some more of her amazing creations!

I can't help but scroll through and read all the comments. I get dozens of follows from the post and hundreds of views on my cooking videos. Overall, the response has been extremely positive, and I tell myself this is proof that the hard work and subsequent suffering was worth it in the end, even if I ended up with a broken heart.

Then, finally, it's the big day. From the moment I wake up, I work hard to keep myself distracted. With school due to start in a couple of weeks and the threat of fall looming, I pull out all my sweaters from under the bed and reorganize my wardrobe. I even pull out Sofía's winter clothes when I run out of things to do on my side of the room.

Then it's time to work on my cat's wardrobe. I'm brushing out Azúcar's fur—an activity neither she nor I can tell whether she likes or not, judging by the simultaneous purring and hissing that's happening—when Sofía throws the bedroom door open.

"You have to do something about this," she moans before throwing herself on her bed.

"Elaborate," I say, switching the brush out for one of those tubes of mush that my cat goes feral for. She trills in delight once she sees the packaging and cuddles up to me, nice and sweet. She knows just how to play me.

"I think Dad is losing his mind not having his Mini-Me around," she says.

I snort. "Yeah, right. I'm not even dating said Morales anymore, and he's still treating me like a leper."

"Well, fix it. He tried to get me go to the restaurant supply store yesterday. I can't take the heat anymore, you have to go back to being number one," she moans. Then Sofía sits up straight, her eyes wide and a devilish smile on her face that I dislike immediately. "I should do drugs."

"Oh my God, Sofía!"

"That definitely has to be worse than dating a Morales in Dad's book of *Arbitrary Rules for My Teenage Daughters*. Once I do that, you'll shoot back up to number one," she assures me.

"I think that might actually still be two rungs below dating a Morales," I tell her.

"Let me just call up Peacoat Kid and, what, order some drugs? How do you get drugs?"

"Sofía!" I yell at her again and throw the cat brush for good measure.

"Hey!" she screeches. "That thing has spikes!"

"Just let him ride this temper tantrum out. At least you're not working an endless stream of opening shifts. I'm pretty sure Dad's committing some kind of crime with the amount of hours he has me working so I 'stay out of trouble,'" I say with dramatic air quotes and a hefty eye roll.

261

"Yes, it is a cardinal sin to eat out at a diner with your secret boyfriend, you know we have food at home. Why waste money?"

Azúcar jumps off my bed, having had her fill of her treat, and proceeds to groom herself in the middle of the room with no regard for modesty.

"Girls," Mom calls out, suddenly appearing at our open door and knocking on the frame. "Get dressed."

"Why?" Sofía whines, her body draped across her bed with her head dangling off the side. "I don't want to move."

"Because I'm telling you to," Mom says in a firm tone. "You, too," she adds, jerking her chin at me. "Hurry up."

"Aren't I grounded? Can I skip whatever this is?" I ask, trying to sound sweet but Mom is still frowning. The livestream announcing the winners starts in an hour, and I'm planning to watch it from the comfort of my bed with my headphones in. That way, in case I lose, I can just draw the covers over my head and cry without having to move.

"Get. Dressed." That's enough to get Sofía to sit up. "We leave in ten minutes." Mom backs out of the hallway, leaving my sister and me to speed run getting ready.

"I just finished my shift at the café an hour ago," I complain. "I was really looking forward to not being on my feet for a few hours." Business has picked up a little in the last week, with our regulars returning for their usual coffee and empanadas. But the summer tourists are still lining up across the street, tormenting me as they leave the doors of Morales Bakery with my doughnuts.

Sofía's version of getting ready is putting on a pair of black denim shorts under the graphic tee that's so big on her it sits at mid-thigh. I pick out my favorite summer dress that has pockets so I can sneak a pair of earbuds. My plan is that wherever we end up, I'll fake a sudden bout of food poisoning and sit on the toilet to tune into the livestream.

Mom knocks on our bedroom door again, announcing the cutoff to getting ready. Sofía is sitting up in her bed, her hair thrown into a messy bun that looks surprisingly intentional. I've just tied a scarf over my hair to cover up how messy mine is.

"Get moving!" Mom calls out as she heads to the front door.

"This is weird," Sofía whispers to me as we head out. "Have our parents joined a cult?"

"I doubt it," I tell her, giving Azúcar one final pet before heading out the front door. "Maybe we're doing group therapy."

"Oh no," Sofía says with genuine horror in her voice. "Do you really think so?"

"I really think *they* should go to therapy and keep us out of it," I say.

"I'm hoping it's that Mom found a trampoline on Facebook Marketplace and that she needs all of us to help strap it to the roof of the car," Sofía guesses.

"Sofía, I hate to break it to you, but you are never getting a full-sized trampoline. It's not in the cards."

"Never say never!" she calls out as she jogs up to the car and takes shotgun.

Mom is already in the front seat with the car running and ready to go.

"Where are we going?" Sofía asks.

"You'll see," is Mom's infuriating response.

Our parents refuse to ever use the AC in their cars, even when we get heat waves that reach into the hundreds, so the windows are down and sweat is already starting to pool in all of my crevices.

"How long is this going to take?" I ask, hoping that it really is a quick errand like picking up some chair Mom bought on Facebook Marketplace.

"What's with this inquisition?" Mom complains. "Can't you just enjoy the mystery while it lasts?"

I can practically hear Sofía rolling her eyes in the front seat, and she turns her attention to the radio, which is so old it doesn't have an aux port or Bluetooth. She scans through the local stations before landing on one that seems to be airing spoken-word poetry. Sofía's version of silent revenge for having to leave the house when she didn't feel like it.

Mom is smart enough to not give in to Sofía's antics and doesn't complain about the station. I open my phone and continuously refresh the page that will host the livestream, just in case it starts early.

I'm so focused on my phone that I'm not even looking up to see where we're heading. After a few minutes we come to a stop and I hear the sound of the parking brake being pulled.

"Oh no," Sofía moans. "Is it inventory day? Is this a surprise shift you've foisted upon us?"

"Noooo," Mom says, dragging the word out and turning off the car.

I glance up in surprise to see that we're in the parking lot behind our shop. Frowning, I look around, thinking that there might be a rush catering gig that we suddenly have to work. But why wouldn't Mom just say that?

Shoving my phone in my pocket, I get out of the car and warily approach the back door. The kitchen looks just as I left it, clean and empty. Fresh aprons are folded on the shelf by the door, stacks of deli containers line the back of one workstation, and bins of bulk ingredients are tucked under the worktables. As far as I can see, there's nothing left to do.

I can hear our normal work playlist, a mix of classic salsa artists from Beny Moré to Celia Cruz, but it's playing at a volume much higher than usual.

"Is Papi hosting dance lessons at the shop now or something?" I ask over the driving beat and powerful brass of Celia Cruz's "Toro Mata" blaring from the speakers. I'm not sure it would be entirely legal to host salsa lessons in the dining area of a restaurant after hours, but it's not a bad idea for my dad to start teaching. He is freakishly good at dancing and will take any and every opportunity to grab our mom if she passes by him while salsa is playing. He moves her into a dramatic dip every time and swirls her around like he's on *Dancing with the Stars*. Mom loves the surprise of being pulled into a dance and always laughs as she stumbles to catch up to his steps.

I haven't seen them do that in a while.

"Why don't you go check out front of house?" Mom says, giving me a playful hip check.

"Is this a trap?" I ask, my voice full of suspicion.

"Is it a puppy?" Sofía asks excitedly, as though that is a real possible outcome in this situation. She takes off to the door and I reluctantly follow her. It's well established in our family that I'm a terrible dancer, and if this is a family bonding thing that involves dancing, I'm not going to have a good time. I need to start playing up some food poisoning symptoms. I place a hand over my stomach as I step through the door to front of house.

But it's not dancing that's been waiting for us.

CHAPTER TWENTY-EIGHT

The entire front of the restaurant has been turned into a streamer-and-balloon-filled party room. Streamers twirl down from the ceiling, they're draped across the back wall, they're taped over the front door in a curtain of pink and green. Clusters of white, green, and pink balloons are attached to almost every surface, and all the tables have their own tiny Cuban flag and plates of food for snacking. There are bocadillos, croquetas, plates full of wedges of lime, fresh sliced fruit, pastelitos of every flavor, and a giant cake with my face printed on it.

"Oh my God," I gasp as I take in the room and realize this has been set up for *me*.

Dad is standing next to the cake proudly with a balloon in his hand that says, "Happy Anniversary!" I nearly jump out of my skin when Rose pops out from behind the counter and shoots me with a confetti party popper.

"What . . . is happening?" I ask, stunned. I make my way into the dining area and turn to see a laptop sitting in the spot where the cash register usually is. Emblazoned across the screen are the words "*LA MESA* SCHOLARSHIP COMPETITION COUNTDOWN" with a timer counting down until the livestream starts. A clearly homemade banner has been draped against the back wall that says "You've Got This, Ana Maria!"

"Wait, how did you . . ." Rose is grinning like an idiot, and I realize that she must have seen the finalist results and orchestrated this whole thing. She's been burning the candle at both ends with the short film, but she still took time to make this happen. My nose begins to burn, the early warning sign of tears. I don't have a chance to thank her before my mom comes from behind me.

"Mija, we're so proud of you!" Mom says, pulling me in for a hug. "I wish you would have told us about this competition sooner! And the fact that you are a finalist?! That's amazing!"

Dad rolls up and throws himself into the hug.

"We're so proud of you," he says into my hair.

I look around the dining room and see Eddie is there with our tio Joaquín, who is trying to help his wife entertain my two young cousins, Cristian and Antonio. Noah is sitting at a table with James and some Debate Club kids.

"You guys really didn't have to do this," I say as my parents release me from their clutches. I'm incredibly touched that everyone came out to support me, but now I'm terrified that I'm going to lose this competition in front of an audience.

"Of course we did!" Dad says, happier than I've seen him in weeks. "You're a budding star!"

"I would not say that," I say on a laugh.

"It's nice to finally know what you've been so secretive about this summer," Mom says, as though I hadn't already had a secret revealed this summer. "Rose showed us all those videos and recipes! You're so creative, mi niña."

"You know the fusion stuff isn't my thing," Dad starts, and I brace for whatever he says next. "But you make it look delicious, Ana Maria."

It's enough to make my eyes well with tears, but Rose interrupts before they can fall.

"The stream starts in ten minutes, everyone!" Rose calls out, clearly the party's stage manager. "Take your places!"

Everyone starts moving chairs to surround the small screen on the counter. Rose cuts through and pulls me away from my parents to a table laden with snacks.

"This is amazing," I tell her, gesturing at all the decorations. "How long have you all been planning this?"

Rose looks down at her wrist as though there's a watch there. She looks back up at me with a little grimace.

"As of two hours ago," she admits.

"What!" I exclaim. That would explain the "Happy Anniversary" balloon and napkins with the Minions on them at the table.

"And I'm not exactly the mastermind behind it all."

"Don't tell me it was Sofía," I say, looking over my shoulder at my sister, who is standing in front of the croqueta plate and stuffing her face.

"Nope," Rose says. "It was Miguel."

My eyes snap back to Rose.

"He called me today," she continues. "I had borrowed some lights from him, and I thought it was about that, but it wasn't."

269

So they've stayed in touch after everything imploded? She takes a deep breath, steeling herself. "He asked if we had anything planned for the livestream. He had seen that you made the final round, and I think he wanted to make sure it wouldn't go unnoticed, you know? I know I've been busy and we haven't . . ." She pauses for a moment as she considers what to say. "We haven't been in touch for a few weeks. I've been so busy with this short film project that I forgot about the dates for your competition."

"No, no, don't worry about it," I assure her. "I've kind of been caught up in my own stuff lately, too. But this"—I gesture around—"this is really nice. Although I was hoping I could just sweep the whole thing under the rug so I won't have to be embarrassed when I lose."

"Such a defeatist attitude!" Rose chides. "Anyway, he kind of convinced me to set up a watch party with your parents' help. You might not believe in yourself, but he certainly does."

Those words are like a knife to my chest. After everything, Miguel still believes in me and supports me. How could someone like that also be behind Doughnutgate? I remember how hurt Miguel looked when I accused him that night. My gut churns, and I might have just given myself that upset stomach I had planned to fake.

"Anyway, even if you don't win we should celebrate you! You worked on all these recipes all summer and they are really good. Even the meat ones! My mom said the ladies at work were loving all the treats she was bringing in. Honestly, I think she wishes you would keep doing it; she was the hospital's favorite last month."

"Girls!" my mom hisses. "It's about to start, sit down!"

I grab a can of sparkling water and join everyone in their

circle around the monitor. As soon as the stream starts, everyone in the room cheers and the high energy stays as we watch the chefs from *La Mesa* introduce themselves to the stream. Each of the eight chefs will be working at their own station, preparing one of the final recipes before sitting down together at the end to taste them all together.

Everyone in Café y Más boos when a chef compliments something about another contestant and they all cheer when they compliment me. The chef tasked with making my recipe points out that he had to make most of the components ahead of time for my recipe since it takes a lot of time, but he says the end product is "more than worth it," which I'm immediately going to add to my bio on Instagram. He does show off the process of twisting the doughnuts into the classic figure-eight shape and making the different icings and flavor combinations.

"Wow!" my dad exclaims. "¡Un buñuelo de guayaba!" As though he hasn't been talking shit about this exact same creation for weeks now.

"Papi would have loved that," Tio Joaquín says on a laugh.

"Really?" I ask him in surprise. I always thought my abuelo was a staunch traditionalist like my dad.

"Oh yeah." Tio grins. "Your abuelo loved desserts but hated anise. That's why he never put buñuelos on the menu. They were your abuelas's favorite, though, so he made them just for her on their anniversary every year."

"Wow, I had no idea," I say. It makes me even happier to know that my abuelo might have loved my recipes, even if they aren't entirely traditional. I had always thought my recipes were a dark secret to be kept from my family, something that they would reject on principle. But it turns out there's a place for my creations next to decades of family recipes.

The stream continues, and I'm riveted as I watch one of the chefs work on another contestant's recipe. It's not one recipe so much as an entire meal. Yesenia, the contestant, is Dominican American and is descended from the population of Japanese immigrants that arrived in the Dominican Republic after World War II. Yesenia took a staple of both cuisines—breakfast—and combined it to make a creation that honors both traditions: a Japanese breakfast spread prepared with Dominican ingredients.

I finish one can of sparkling water and then start another. I'm burping from a mixture of nerves and bubbles, and Dad is practically vibrating next to me as we wait for the stream to reach the final announcement.

When the judges sit at their table with the final dishes in front of them, a hush falls over the shop. Rose turns up the volume and we all lean in as the final results begin. The hosts on screen talk about the tough decisions they made picking the winners, but all I hear is the beating of my heart.

Rose reaches across my lap and grasps my hand in hers, giving me a strong squeeze of support. The judges are saying something about how talented all the contestants were this year, and I'm already fast-forwarding to the worst-case scenario in my head. What do I do if I lose? Run out the back door and cry in the parking lot? Grin and bear it in front of everyone?

"Damn straight!" Rose whoops. The sound jolts me back into the present, and I realize I've stopped listening to the livestream. The rest of the shop joins her and my cheeks flush.

"Now onto our winners. Second runner-up is . . ." There's a

drumroll followed by an image of a smiling guy holding up a plate of pupusas. "Nick Davila!"

My heart is pounding so hard against my chest I feel like it must be clearly visible to everyone around me. I rub my hands up and down my thighs, rubbing off the sweat and trying to release some of the nervous energy that has been building in me. It's finally time to find out if everything I did this summer was worth it.

Or I'm going to embarrass myself in front of everyone. My stomach clenches again and I think I might actually need to run away to the bathroom.

"Our first runner-up is . . ." The screen goes from Gloria's smiling face to . . .

Me.

It's a still from one of the Miguel videos I posted recently. I'm in the middle of making tres leches and I'm holding up a whisk to show off the stiff peaks. The room explodes with cheering, and everyone is so loud I can't hear the stream anymore.

I'm so stunned that I don't even resist when Dad pulls me up and hugs me so tight I can hardly breathe.

"You did it, mamita!" Mom cheers next to me.

Dad pulls back from our hug to look down at me with a smile. There are tears in his eyes, and he looks so proud. That burning in my nose starts again and I just let him tuck me in for another hug.

"That's our girl! Five thousand bucks!" Rose cries out.

My heart is still slamming against my chest, but the cold dread that had filled me earlier has been replaced by a steady warmth. Hours of toiling away in the kitchen, working and reworking recipes until they're the best they can be, have finally paid off. It's not the grand prize, but it's something. It's one step closer to Paris.

Looking around the shop, it's amazing to see the group of people that have come to celebrate me today. Rose, who put in all this work despite me being selfish all summer. My parents, smiling and looking so proud even though I broke the number one rule of being an Ybarra.

But as happy as I am to see all these people celebrating my win, I know someone is missing from the room. The person who helped me despite my very mixed signals and overall shitty behavior. I want him to be here, standing in the room next to my family, but he can't. Because I pushed him away, yes, but also because, despite everything, my dad would still try to fight him if he set foot in the shop.

Mom looks at me, and there must be something in my expression that's telegraphing my thoughts because she frowns. I give her a weak smile to try to reassure her, but her lips flatten into a tight line and I know I haven't tricked her.

"I need to go to the bathroom," I tell her, hoping she thinks my face had to do with something other than Miguel. It's not a lie, either. My stomach makes an uncomfortable gurgle, and I know the upset stomach I wished upon myself has manifested in full force. I slip from front of house and go to the bathroom in the back.

CHAPTER TWENTY-NINE

My mom is waiting for me in the kitchen when I come out of the bathroom. From the sounds of it, it seems the dining room has turned into a full-on party and the music is back up at full volume. Mom is leaning against the wall across from the bathroom with her arms crossed.

"Let's go out back," she says, gesturing to the back door with her head. Nervous, I follow her lead without question and head out to the back parking lot.

"What's up?" I ask, sitting up on a pile of milk crates.

"Your dad told me about pastry school," she says.

"Oh."

"So you want to skip college?" she asks.

I've imagined this conversation with my mom a dozen times over. Since I was a kid my mom has always bragged about what a good student I am, how well I performed in school, and all the *potential* I had. When Rose joined the debate team, she urged me to join, too, since she thought I would make a great lawyer one day. When I got the highest score on a biology exam she started talking about medical school and a future where I became a doctor.

When I was younger, I went along with it because it just felt like playing pretend. But as the years have passed, her suggestions have felt more demanding. I'm too smart to waste myself on running a restaurant. I'm too clever to spend the rest of my days folding butter into flour.

"I don't think college is for me," I tell her honestly. Mom spent four years in school, just to spend her life managing a failing restaurant. Her sister also went to college and got a degree in criminal justice, and now she lives in Los Angeles and makes custom jewelry. A degree isn't a guarantee. It's not the end all, be all in life. "I want to be a pastry chef. I want to write a cookbook with recipes I've developed, and I want to work at a Michelin-starred restaurant in a big city somewhere."

Mom sighs and my heart sinks. I never realized until this moment how much I want her to support me in this decision. I want to hear her say that I'm so clever, I'll write the most delicious recipes and inspire scores of people to try them. I want her to tell me that getting a college degree isn't some indicator as to whether a person is worthy or not.

But then she says something different than I expected.

"I wish you had just told me that once we started looking at schools," Mom says, surprising me.

"Really?" I ask.

"Of course!" She heaves a big sigh and leans against the stack of milk crates with me. "Mi niña, you have to talk to us. We can't read your mind, okay?"

"The last time I tried to talk to Papi honestly about something he started arguing and yelling a lot," I point out.

"Your dad is . . ." She struggles to think of the right word. "He's very emotional and not the best at holding things in or thinking through his actions. He's impulsive and sometimes a little thoughtless, but it's always coming from a place of love, okay?"

I nod.

Another tired sigh escapes Mom and she runs her hands through her hair, messing up the perfect blowout that she has been sporting all night. "Ana, I can't help you if you don't talk to me. Instead of looking up all these schools you had no interest in, I could have been helping you with scholarships and planning for pastry school."

I look down, unable to meet Mom's eyes. "I just . . . didn't think you'd let me go. You always seemed so hell-bent on me going to college."

"Listen, I just want what's best for you. Being your mother, and because I'm old, I have an idea of what that looks like. Maybe a degree, a job in a stable career, a loving support system, and living in a city *very* close to me. But just because it's what *I* think would be good for you doesn't mean that it'll make you happy. You need to make sure that you're living for yourself, doing the things that would fulfill you."

"I'm sorry I didn't tell you before," I say softly. "Between Papi not letting me add my recipes to the menu and you talking up college I didn't feel like I had someone in my corner."

Mom wraps an arm around me and pulls me in for a quick and unexpected hug. I can tell by her breathing that she's close to crying and trying to swallow back the tears.

277

"I hate that I made you feel like that," she whispers. "My parents made me feel like that when I started dating your father. I was living with them, and every time I came home from a date my parents had one thing after another to say about it. And when we got engaged?" She throws back her head and laughs. "They hated that. They didn't want me to be with a 'lowly shop owner.' Running a bakery? That wasn't the life they wanted for me. And some of the things they said weren't wrong, but it doesn't matter. I'm happy I made that choice."

"I didn't know my abuelos were so against Papi."

"Oh yeah. I have the wedding album hidden in my closet, but if you look through the pictures you'll notice that my parents did not come."

"Oh my God!" I gasp. "That's cold."

"They didn't come around until you were born," Mom continues. "I lost years with my parents because they hated the choice I made to marry your dad. I vowed I would never do that to my kids. No matter what choice you make, I will be there to support you and love you, okay?"

The burning in my nose is back, and I'm caught between feeling grateful for my mom and sad for the way she was treated by her family for her choices. Suddenly I see all the sacrifices she has made for our family, and I am certain she is one of the strongest women I know.

"Thanks, Mom," I tell her.

She grabs my shoulders and turns me to face her head-on.

"I've seen you these last couple of weeks, mija. I can tell you've been having a rough time, and I think you've learned your lesson about lying to us, right?"

"Yes," I say, nodding enthusiastically.

"Good. I expect you to be honest with me about things from now on." She shakes my shoulders once and locks eyes with me, her eyebrows drawn and face serious. "I want you to be happy. I want you to feel like you can go after everything that makes you happy. *Everything*."

"Okay," I say slowly.

"Remember that I wasn't always an Ybarra. I can be level-headed about certain things." On these last two words she waggles her eyebrows suggestively.

"Oh my God, Mom!" I screech.

"I'm just saying. I talked to Rose today, and she told me some interesting things," she says, pulling back and leaning against the crates again. "I have your back, whatever you choose to do."

"Really? You'd defend me to Dad if I started dating a Morales?"

"Your dad has bigger fish to fry than that right now, I promise you," Mom says. "I'll make sure he expresses the level of displeasure that he would have for any person you brought home. Once he acts out for a week or so I'm sure whomever you like will grow on him. You have a good head on your shoulders, mi niña. All your hard work on this contest is proof of that. Now go celebrate your win!" She gives my shoulder a playful slap and turns to head back into the shop.

CHAPTER THIRTY

The party goes on much longer than any of us expected. We dance and eat and play dominos in the shop for hours. Dad and Eddie win every round of dominos, but Rose keeps insisting on one more round, trying to beat them. The Debate Club kids leave at some point for a party somewhere else, replaced by Sofía's friends.

I end up floating around for most of the night, not quite able to focus on anything as my mind wanders. I started this summer with the lofty goal of winning this competition so I can save up money for culinary school. Back then it seemed impossible, both winning *and* going to school. But now that I've won the runner-up prize, the future is looking a little less blurry.

Between the sounds of the clacking dominos, my mom's loud laugh, and all the music, I'm feeling a little overstimulated. With everyone distracted by one thing or another, I slip out through the kitchen and go out the back door.

The night air is crisp, with a salty breeze coming in from the sound that causes goose bumps to ripple across my arms. A crescent moon hangs in the dark, cloudless sky, barely illuminating the dark parking lot. I gulp in the cool night air and run a hand through my hair, trying to calm my nerves.

I have no reason to still be holding on to this nervous energy. The competition is over. I told my parents about pastry school. It's all done. But I still feel restless, unable to settle or stop moving.

With the competition done, I can look up some other scholarships. I can look up how much room rentals cost in Paris. I can look up neighborhoods in the city, find out which ones have the best food and fun bars.

I've never let myself fully plan out culinary school before. It felt like if I did go through all the research and create this picture of the future for myself, it would hurt even worse if I couldn't make it happen. But with the scholarship money and my parents' blessing (kind of), I feel like I can let myself dream a little bit more.

There's a sudden noise in the alley next to the shop, and I freeze.

Downtown is no stranger to uncommonly large rats, especially in the alleys where we keep our trash bins. But the loud banging sound is followed by the sound of someone cursing under their breath.

On high alert, I quietly reach out for the Cuban mop that's been left out next to the back door. Unlike most mops, it doesn't have the actual mop attached. Instead it's a long wooden stick with a short dowel at the very end, in the shape of a T. When you go to mop with it, you drape a towel (soaked in Mistolin that my dad orders in crates from Miami) over the T part and then push it around.

It's not my favorite mop, but it is my favorite impromptu weapon. Sofía and I used to pretend they were giant swords when we were little, and that's how she lost her front tooth.

I grip the mop in my hands like it's an axe, ready to bonk whoever is lurking with the T end. It's too dark to see much as I creep toward the alley, but I can still hear someone making sounds.

Nothing prepares me for the sight that greets me when I finally turn the corner to peer into the dark.

With the mop poised over my head, ready to drop it down in defense, I scream in surprise at the sight of a tall figure swathed in dark clothes and a dark beanie pulled down tight. I really had been hoping for rats that *sounded* like a person muttering, and I'm not quite sure if I have it in me anymore to bonk a stranger with my mop.

The stranger is just as surprised to see a mop-wielding shadow appear at the mouth of the alley. They move just enough that I see a flash of dark auburn hair in the dim light and a surprised scream escapes them before they cover their mouth with their hand.

My mop drops a fraction of an inch, and I take another hesitant step forward.

"Valeria?" I croak in surprise.

"Damn it," the person who is definitely not twenty rats in a trench coat mutters before ripping off her beanie. "It was supposed to be smoother than this."

"Oh my God," I gasp. "Are you here to kill me? Is this an assassination attempt?" I ask, and part of me genuinely believes that it might be. I broke her cousin's heart and now she's come to take her revenge. Even though I've dropped the mop back to the ground I tighten my grip on it, just in case.

"What?" Valeria asks, sounding bewildered. "No, I'm not here to *kill you*, oh my God. And I thought Rose was the drama queen."

I look around the alley to try and think of another reason why Valeria Morales would be creeping in the alley next to our shop.

"You're going to throw a stink bomb in the shop. Wait, no, your *twin* is going to do that and you're the lookout," I guess.

"Jesus, no, I'm not here to—"

"You are letting loose a dozen rats in our alley so they can ravage our pantry," I continue guessing. "No, that's not nefarious enough. You're on the lookout while Adrian drops a box of nails all over our parking lot—"

"I'm not here to sabotage you!" Valeria snaps, and it's clear I've started to annoy her. "I came here to talk to you."

I eye her suspiciously. I've never spoken to Valeria directly, and she's never tried speaking to me, either. We've managed to always stay in separate orbits in school and, unlike her twin, she's never done anything outright terrible to an Ybarra. She's always seemed more level-headed than her brother and never seems to take stock of much, her head always between the pages of a book or working in a sketchbook.

"Okay," I say, drawing out the word as I drop the mop and set it against the wall. I glance over my shoulder to make sure no one from the party has slipped out to look for me. "What do you need to talk to me about?"

"Miguel."

I don't mean to cringe. It's basically a knee-jerk reaction when I so much as think about Miguel now. I have so many regrets between us, so many things I wish I hadn't done or said. But my regrets don't change the fact that things are just too complicated between us.

Valeria doesn't wait for me to say anything, she just plows on.

"Listen, he's my favorite cousin," she tells me. "I've always been close to him even though he's lived far away our whole lives. There aren't many things we keep from each other, and that includes this whole summer with *you*." There's a note of accusation in her voice. I'm glad she can't see me well in the dim light of the alley because I'm sure I'm beet red with embarrassment right now. "I warned him, in the beginning."

"I heard about the PowerPoint," I mutter.

"But Miguel is a stubborn shit, and no amount of Power-Points or warnings about the feud was going to deter him. He *really* liked you."

Liked. Past tense.

"We don't need to rehash the whole thing. I just came here to explain about the doughnuts." I flinch at the memory of that night, the sharp feelings of betrayal and regret still fresh in my mind. "It set off alarm bells once you started yelling about your recipe. A few weeks ago I was looking for Adrian and found him in the basement where Miguel and his mom are living. He played it off that he was looking for something in the living room down there, but I know my brother. He was up to something. And a few weeks later, Dad announced that he was launching a new menu item and wanted me to work on some promo for it. And then the night of the launch happened.

"To be clear, I've never bought into the whole rivalry like my brother. I'm not all that invested in the bakery or the family lore, and you and your sister have never been heinous to me. But Adrian is different. I confronted him after the party that night, and he admitted to snooping through Miguel's things and finding your notes from the filming sessions. He saw your plans for the dough-nuts and decided it would win him points with Dad if he pretended it was his idea. Dad has always wanted him to take more of an interest in the business, so he was obviously thrilled."

So a Morales *did* steal my recipe. I just blamed the wrong one for the crime. My gut churns with the memory of Miguel's face that night, the hurt and disbelief that should have been a clear sign to me that he was innocent. How could I ever have believed it was him?

"Anyway, I told Miguel as soon as I found out and he was *pissed*. They fought, like, for real. Even broke one of Mom's lamps, and they haven't spoken to each other since," Valeria says, her voice soft now. "He's been miserable, Amy. I'm pretty sure you broke his heart, and I kind of hate you for it. But I thought you deserved to know the truth."

"I hate myself for it, too," I tell her quietly. "I should have just stayed away from him from the very start."

"Is that really what you think?"

"You just said it yourself, I broke his heart. I hate that I put him through that. I knew from the beginning that this couldn't go anywhere, not really."

"Why not?" Valeria crosses her arms over her chest, and even in the dark I can tell she's glaring at me.

I gesture toward the door to Café y Más as if it's the most obvious thing in the world. "Our families, Valeria. My dad has hardly spoken to me since he found out I was dating a Morales. The shit between our families goes too deep for us to ever really get that close without hurting each other or someone else."

Valeria considers that, bobbing her head up and down. "You know, I really thought you were stronger than this."

"What?" I ask in surprise.

"You have always marched to your own drum, Amy. I may not know you that well, but I know that much, at least. When everyone else at recess was playing four square or whatever, you and Rose were out in the field pretending to forage and then making 'food' with whatever you found. And you dress like . . . that. You've never cared what other people think or say."

"But this is family," I argue, choosing to ignore the comment about my clothes.

"Family doesn't always mean they're right," Valeria returns. "Exhibit A, my dumbass twin."

"What are you trying to say, Valeria?" I say with a frustrated sigh. All the buzzing excitement that had filled me only minutes ago has fizzled out and now I'm just . . . numb.

"Look, if you don't feel the same way about Miguel, that's one thing. But if you feel for him what he feels for you? That's something worth fighting for. And I never took you for a coward."

I'm silent for a moment as I let her words sink in. Is that what I've been doing, being a coward? Miguel said that I had been pushing him away from the beginning. And yeah, I've been terrified of him since the beginning because I knew I could fall fast and *hard* for him, and it would end in disaster. Is having a healthy fear of the potential for pain the same as being a coward? Or have I just been incredibly stupid this whole summer?

Because tonight is proof that my parents can get over their hangups. And although the Morales thing might run deeper than other issues, at the end of the day, Miguel is not the person who screwed over my grandfather. He's his own person.

"Is there anything even left to fight for?" I ask Valeria softly, afraid of the answer.

"That's up to you, Amy."

CHAPTER THIRTY-ONE

It doesn't take me long to decide.

"Where is he?" I ask Valeria, powered by the high of my mother's support and my win.

"Oh, so you're doing this now?" she asks in surprise. "No rehearsal?"

"I think if I wait the embarrassment over the whole fiasco will set in and I'll chicken out," I admit. "I have to do it now."

"Well, you're in luck," she says with a cheeky smile. "I know just where he is. I'll even give you a ride."

I shoot Rose a quick text asking her to cover for me while I go try to win Miguel back. She responds immediately.

!!!!!!!!!!!!!!!!!!!!!

Sofía owes me $10.

!!!!!!!!!!!!!!!!!!!!!

On it, boss.

At this point in the evening, all the adults are a couple beers in, and I'm sure Rose can keep them distracted enough to not notice my absence, at least for a little while.

I follow Valeria out of the alley and on to Main Street, where her ancient Honda is parked across from Morales Bakery. The engine catches a couple times before starting and the radio kicks back up, blasting some unrecognizable wailing that seems to pass as music. Valeria lowers the volume with a smile, and before I even have my seat belt on she's peeling out of the parking spot.

If my heart wasn't already on the verge of beating out of my chest due to the anxiety of confronting Miguel, Valeria's driving would certainly have done the job. She takes turns way too fast and drives ten miles over the speed limit. I'm gripping onto the handle on the roof for dear life as I brace for every turn, and I'm not sure whether her terrifying driving is a relief or not because it at least takes my mind off of Miguel.

Valeria glances over at me while we're stopped at a red light.

"Don't stress too much about it," she says, and I don't have the heart to tell her that the reason I look so scared is because of her driving. "Just tell him how you feel. And more important, say you're sorry."

"Say sorry, got it," I say, a slight waver in my voice. "Easy."

Eyes back on the road, Valeria takes off, heading off in a familiar direction.

"Where are we going, exactly?" I ask nervously.

"Devin Nielson's house, she's throwing an end-of-summer party."

"And Miguel is *there*?" I ask in surprise. I remember what he told me on the Fourth of July and how out of place he felt among his cousin's friends.

"Miguel is settling in to life in Port Murphy," Valeria says, clearly proud of her cousin. "Since the . . ." She pauses, considering her word choice. "Since the *incident* he's been keeping busy to keep his mind off things. Rose asked him for some help on this short film project she's been working on, and he's joined the crew. He's actually got his own friend group now, separate from me and Adrian."

"Oh," I say in surprise. It's hard to imagine Miguel existing in Port Murphy outside of the Ybarra-Morales nightmare. It's hard to imagine Miguel making friends and settling in, that the space he had for me has been filled in. The part of myself where I tore Miguel out still feels like a gaping wound, unable to close and heal over.

"Don't make that face," Valeria says, the sweetness gone from her voice.

"No," I say, understanding her ire immediately. She's his best friend, after all. "I'm happy he's settling in. I know how rough it was for him at the beginning of the summer. I just wish—" I cut myself off and groan. "I just wish I could turn back the clock on this summer. Do things differently."

Valeria coasts to a stop on the side of the road, parking halfway into a ditch on Devin Nielson's street. After pulling up the parking brake she turns in her seat to face me.

"I'm not giving you another pep talk," she says sternly. "I only had the one in me."

"That was hardly a pep talk, it was more of a Come to Jesus talk," I correct her.

"Okay, well, whatever it was, you're not getting another one." She takes a deep breath before continuing. "Miguel is inside the house with Noah and the Debate Club guys as of fifteen minutes ago. I've led you to the water," she says before shooing me with her hands. "Now drink."

I climb out of Valeria's car and head toward the house in the dark. It's easy to make my way down the street, the distant thump of music and chatter enough to guide me. Once I reach the driveway, the familiar view of Devin's house comes into sight, and I remember the last time I saw the butter-yellow glow from this very front porch. I had been running away from Miguel, a whole range of emotions cycling through my body at such sickening speed that I felt nauseated with it all.

It's not too dissimilar to how I feel now, although the emotional mix is a little different. Instead of anger and frustration and heartache I'm feeling nervous and ashamed and hopeful. A group of people are leaning on the porch railing on the front, smoke trailing up from the bright orange tips of their cigarettes. I slip past the smokers through the front door, my eyes peering into every room in search of Miguel or the Debate Club guys.

I pass James in the kitchen, where we make quick eye contact and smile. He's talking to a girl I don't recognize, likely from another high school nearby, and he has that flirty smile on that he tried to use on me. The girl seems much more receptive to it than I ever was.

Continuing through the house, I peek out the back doors and head to the living room. Groups of people are congregated around the coffee table, where someone is explaining some very complicated drama using decorative objects as pieces on a strategic map made up of cocktail napkins with words scribbled on them.

Not yet catching sight of any familiar faces, I continue back to the front of the house, nervous that Miguel and his friends have already left. The party seems to be slowing down a little bit, and I overhear someone talking about heading over to someone else's place. Would I have to spend the night jumping from house party to house party until I lose my nerve?

Then I approach the last room downstairs, the spot that was once home to the weenie table. Tonight it seems Devin opted for a simpler food spread and left out half a dozen bags of potato chips and those grocery store cookies that have a thick layer of frosting.

But there's no Miguel in sight. I groan and press my head against the threshold, upset I haven't found him. When I glance back up, my eyes settle on the group of friends streaming out the front door. I hadn't seen them in any of the rooms I had searched but I recognize them immediately. Noah's bowling shirt and Gage's looming height and . . .

There, a head of wavy brown hair, messy yet beautiful. Sloping wide shoulders and a casual gait, and for just a second as his head turns, a flash of a dimple.

His name is out of my mouth before I can stop myself.

"Miguel?" I call out, my voice catching a little bit.

He freezes for a moment mid-step, almost as though he is unsure he hears his name called out at all.

"Miguel?" I try again, voice firmer.

The rest of his friends funnel out the front door, leaving

Miguel standing there, surrounded by the smoky glow of the open front door. Backlit by the warm porch light, I can't make out his features, whether he's frowning with displeasure or smiling in anticipation. But then he takes a small step forward and the light leaking from the dining room fills in his features, illuminating a face I have missed so much it nearly breaks my heart to see it.

"I was hoping that was you," I say nervously.

"Ana Maria?" he says slowly, taking a tentative step toward me.

Suddenly it feels like my tongue is swollen and my breath catches in my throat. I want to say something, anything, in these moments before he remembers the insults I hurled at him and the ruin I made of our relationship. In this moment I could almost imagine it's the start of the summer and I've just seen him for the first time in Port Murphy and the future for us is full of possibility.

The moment stretches, neither of us able to say anything. As soon as one of us starts speaking, the direction of this conversation will be set, for better or worse.

Where was Jordan when you needed him to break through the tension?

"Can we talk outside?" I rasp out finally, my fingers nervously running along the edge of my pockets.

Instead of replying, Miguel just nods and gestures for me to step out the front door.

I walk outside in a rush, holding my breath as I pass him, worrying that if I inhale his familiar scent my brain will go haywire and send this conversation off the rails. I need to focus.

Following the veranda around the side, I stop at the same spot we had settled in the last time we were at Devin's house. But this time, instead of leaning toward each other like there is an invisible string pulling us together, there's a bubble of space that keeps us from getting too close.

"Okay," Miguel says, leaning back against the railing and watching me warily.

"Valeria told me where you were," I tell him, resting my hip against the railing a good five feet away from him.

"Now that text she sent makes sense," he says with a nod.

The silence stretches between us for a moment, and he glances off to the yard where his friends are standing. His eyes return to mine and he watches me expectantly, his face closed off and distant.

"I won runner-up," I blurt, somehow starting this apology with *that* of all things.

"I know," he says, and I blink in surprise.

"You do?"

"I watched the livestream," he says. "Congrats."

"I couldn't have done it without you," I tell him earnestly. "I wish you had been there with me when I found out. You helped me make my dream come true and it hurt so much that I couldn't turn to you in that moment and celebrate. But it's my own fault.

"You were right," I continue, the words rushing out quickly, scared that if I don't get it out fast enough he'll turn away from me. "I pushed you away, over and over again. I gave you mixed signals. I used you. I wasn't honest with you or myself, really. You deserve so much better than that."

"You don't need to do this, Ana Maria. It's okay."

"No, it's not," I insist. "You would never betray me by stealing my recipe, I should never have accused you of that. I *know* you. You are truly one of the best people I know, and yet I still blamed you for something you had nothing to do with. I just—" I cut myself off, struggling to come up with the right way to phrase everything I felt this summer, all the ways I ignored what my gut told me and did something against my better judgment. "I've never felt this way about anyone before and it's terrifying. I think part of me thought it would be better to just . . . cut you out, so I didn't have to face how you made me feel."

"I feel like I should apologize, too," Miguel says to the floor. "I shouldn't have brought my shooting notes into the house. My uncle knows that Adrian stole the idea now, but the doughnuts are selling well and he's unwilling to pull them from the menu." This news hurts, but it doesn't hurt nearly as much as the distant look on Miguel's face. Like I'm a stranger, a person he's never held close and kissed within an inch of her life. "I tried convincing him but he wouldn't budge. If it's any consolation, yours are definitely better."

"Thanks," I say with a wry smile. "But honestly, I don't care about the doughnuts. I don't care about my dad's stupid bias against your family or your cousin's shitbrained ideas." I swallow down the knot forming in my throat before taking a deep breath, ready to dive in. "I care about *you*, Miguel."

"Ana." Miguel sighs and rubs his forehead with his hands in an agitated motion. "I really appreciate this, the apology, but you were right." Dread pools in my gut as I listen to his words.

"At the beginning of the summer you told it to me straight: whatever this is between us, it can't happen. Our families won't let it happen, and if we try it will just cause us both pain."

"No," I say, my voice passionate and determined. "I was wrong. This," I gesture to the space between us, "this can happen. Miguel, I don't care what my dad thinks. I *want* to be with you. This summer has been the happiest I have ever been and that's because of *you*. Working with you, spending time with you, sharing my love of cooking with you. I don't want to lose you because our families can't bring themselves to bury some decades-old hatchet."

"You say that now, but what happens when Adrian does something else stupid to undermine you and your family or your dad decides to send you to live with an aunt because he doesn't want us to be together?"

"I've let fear get between us before and I regret it. I don't want to let it happen again," I say softly.

I think for a moment I've convinced him, but then he breaks eye contact and looks down at his shoes. It's just a small thing, but I can feel him pulling away. I can feel him giving up on this. Is this what he felt every time I pushed him away? It's like my chest is cracking open and the inside of my nose is burning.

"I can't, Ana," he finally says, his voice barely a whisper. "I think it's better if we end things. A clean cut."

This cut is anything but clean. His rejection is ripping me to shreds, but I've put him through enough. I'm not going to let him see how much this crushes me. It will be easier for him to do this if he thinks I can leave this conversation no worse for wear.

"Right," I whisper, my brows drawn as I stare down at the

weathered floor. "I should, um," I glance over my shoulder at the long driveway. "I should head home."

I can't look at him because I know it will break me. So I give him a feeble smile before turning away. I don't run this time, I walk slow and easy like my heart isn't breaking. I choke down the sobs that are threatening to rise and nod and smile at the group of smokers on the stairs. I wait until I'm far from the light of the porch before I let myself go completely.

CHAPTER THIRTY-TWO

If I were to pick anywhere to have an emotional meltdown, it would not be on a dark road in western Washington. As soon as I step off the Nielson property a spitting rain begins to fall. Valeria's car is no longer parked in the ditch, and I'm alone in the middle of the road. Either she had anticipated that things would go well and Miguel would drive me back, or this was all an elaborate plot to strand me far from home.

I swallow down the sobs that fight to break out of my chest, but it's a losing battle. I choke on them as they burst from my mouth on gasping breaths. I could text Rose and ask her to save me from this particular misery, but I need the time to myself. I just need to get away, go somewhere quiet, and cry.

The rain starts to pick up and the cool water seeps into my dress, leaving me damp and shivering. I hope that I do get home soaking wet and catch a cold so I can assume the fetal position in bed for three days straight without having to explain myself.

I could cry for hours on end and my family would just think I'm congested.

A sudden sound pulls me from my thoughts and I glance over my shoulder to look for the source. There, halfway down the block, is Miguel, running full speed in the rain. Even in silhouette I recognize him instantly. I freeze in place as I watch him sprint toward me, his wet hair sticking to his face and his feet slapping against the wet road.

Miguel skids to a stop in front of me looking like a sad, wet dog.

"That was stupid," he says, doubled over and gasping as he tries to catch his breath as he gestures behind himself vaguely with one hand. Back toward Devin's house, where I had just spent the worst five minutes of my life.

"What? My apology?" I ask in despair.

"What?" He stands up and looks at me, confused. "No, what I just did. Ending things like that."

"Oh," I whisper, trying to tamp down the sudden hope that is threatening to rise.

"I thought it would be safe, letting you go and ending things," he explains. "But it's not what I want, not even a little."

He reaches out slowly, watching my face as he takes hold of my right hand and grasps it tightly between his. His grip is warm and the feel of his rough skin against mine, rain slicked and a little shaky, is enough to send shivers running down my spine. I feel like a flower to his sun, reaching and searching for his warmth as I sway toward him.

"After everything with my mom and dad, I told myself I wouldn't make the same mistakes. I wouldn't stay in a bad relationship because it was comfortable or safe or some other excuse. But that means I can't pull away from something good because it would be safer or more comfortable not to. I want to take the chance. I want to take the chance that our families might hurt us, that you might hurt me, because being with you is so much better than not. And I want to fight for it. For *us*."

"You do?" I whisper, stepping in so close to him that our hands are pressed tight against our chests. His thumb gently strokes the back of my hand as he smiles down at me and nods.

"I do," he says, his smile so bright in the haze of the gray evening.

I breathe out in relief and drop my head against his chest. Miguel leans down to press a kiss on the top of my head, and I take full advantage of having him so close. I let go of his hands and let my arms snake around his waist so I can hug him tighter. He does the same, wrapping me up tight in his arms as the rain continues to fall.

"I'm going to fight for you, Miguel Fuentes," I promise him.

"I'm going to fight for you, too, Ana Maria Ybarra," Miguel says into my hair.

The first step in taking care of each other is getting out of the rain. Miguel and I run back down the street toward his car, holding hands and laughing as the rain continues to fall. We make it there safely, and my hand is on the handle when Miguel reaches for my hips and spins me around.

In one deft move he has me pressed up against the passenger door, his hands gripping my hips and his forehead pressing down against mine. My arms reach up and drape over his shoulder, one hand playing with the wet curls at the base of his neck.

"Can I kiss you?" he asks softly. "I really missed kissing you." His nose drifts across my face playfully, drawing circles around my cheeks and making me shudder in anticipation.

"I really missed kissing you, too," I say, angling my face so my lips brush faintly against his as I speak. I feel his lips stretch in a triumphant smile before capturing my mouth in a deeply satisfying kiss.

CHAPTER THIRTY-THREE

I won't pretend that telling my dad that Miguel and I were back together went well. It took weeks, and between it all senior year started and Rose got a decrepit Kia for her birthday. My mom assured me the whole time that she was working on him and that it was getting better day by day.

In the meantime, strict rules were put in place for dating. Miguel is the first boyfriend my parents have dealt with in this two-daughter home, and they suddenly felt it was very important to have ground rules. I know for a fact that these will likely only apply to me and fall to the wayside by the time someone tries to date Sofía.

Miguel and I can hang out until six on school nights and nine on weekends. We cannot ever be caught in my bedroom and must keep all of our socializing to the living spaces or backyard. Rose's house is only acceptable if her mom is home and we can only go on dates to places in Port Murphy.

The Morales house, understandably, is off-limits. Miguel

is still not on speaking terms with his cousin or his uncle, despite Valeria's best attempts to get them to reconcile. We did have brunch with his mom last weekend at Lacey's Diner, where Mrs. Fuentes gleefully told me embarrassing stories about her son as Miguel blushed sweetly.

On the first day of school Valeria walks past the table she normally shares with her twin and his friends and makes her way to the Debate Club table. I'm not exaggerating when I say the cafeteria erupted in shocked whispers at the sight of a Morales and an Ybarra breaking bread together. Valeria is still annoyed with her brother after Doughnutgate and has taken to hanging out with Miguel and his friends and, by extension, me.

Gage and Rose try to recruit Miguel to the Debate Club, but he decides to set his sights on starting a film club with Noah. I join because it means I get to spend a few hours hanging out with Rose and Miguel in a dark, quiet room. While everyone else joins for the lively cinematic discussion that follows the showings, I use the club as an opportunity to develop recipes inspired by the movies. For *The Godfather*, I try my hand at cannoli with lots of orange zest and pistachios. For *Interview with a Vampire*, I make a cake that bleeds when you cut into it.

Now that I'm dating Miguel, my parents are much more vigilant about our comings and goings from the house, and they have an alarm installed on our bedroom window, permanently cutting off any late-night escapes. Sofía was furious when she found out, but she has since figured out how to escape out the bathroom window when she wants to.

One night, a few weeks into the school year, Mom sends a text to Sofía and me, insisting we come home for dinner. I am at

Rose's, helping her practice her audition for the school's production of *Into the Woods* when I get the sudden missive.

Pa' casa! Dinner is ready in 30.

"Weird," I say as I read the text. "I told her I was going to be helping you with this audition tonight."

"Maybe she forgot?" Rose says as she does these weird mouth exercises that make her look like she is practicing to unhinge her jaw.

"Maybe," I shrug. "Could you give me a ride home?"

"Of course!" Rose cries out. The car is still a new thing, and she's always eager to take it out for a ride. She also loves to belt along to music in her car since her mom can't tell her to turn it down.

The ride home is quick, with most of it spent listening to Rose sing her audition song over and over again. I'm not much help beyond confirming that she sounds great and got all the lyrics right.

"Break a leg," I tell Rose before slamming the passenger door shut.

"Tell your mom I'm craving vegan picadillo!" she calls out through the open window as I bound up the steps to the front door. I shoot her a thumbs-up before heading inside.

The living room is empty when I walk in, but as soon as the door closes behind me Azúcar runs out from my room and into the foyer to greet me.

"Hey, stinky," I say as I bend over to give her some scratches behind her ears. She tries to play with my shoelaces as I take off my shoes, and once they're both off and on the shoe rack, Azúcar leaves my feet alone and immediately shoves her face in my shoe. I'm not sure now if she was excited to greet me or my shoes.

"Sofía!" Mom shouts from the kitchen. "Set the table!"

Sofía emerges from our bedroom, headphones around her neck, and I run up to her.

"What is going on?" I whisper, trying not to catch Mom's attention.

"I have no idea," Sofía says, completely monotone and disinterested.

Dad steps out of the bathroom at that moment, steam from his shower curling out of the room behind him. He's wearing jeans and a plain white shirt, and it looks strange to me for a moment before I realize he's not wearing his usual café uniform of khakis and a guayabera.

"Hey, Dad," I say, still perplexed by seeing him in street clothes. Dad is almost always dressed in his work uniform, and I honestly can't remember the last time I saw him in something so casual.

"Hi, mi amor," Dad says, dropping one big arm over my shoulders and planting a kiss on the side of my head. "Your mom made arroz con pollo tonight."

"Help me set the table!" Sofía calls out from the dining room. Rolling my eyes, I pull away from my dad and join Sofía. Together we clear off the dining table, lay out a tablecloth, and place all the plates and flatware down with matching cloth napkins. When we finish up, Mom walks into the room with a huge cazuela full of arroz con pollo and drops it down on the metal trivet at the center of the table.

Arroz con pollo is usually something Mom makes on special

occasions, like when family visits or a birthday. But we only set the table for four and none of us are celebrating anything. I watch my mom with suspicion as she takes off the oven mitts she used to hold the cazuela and looks at the table to make sure nothing is missing.

Dad sets a salad down, and Sofía fills everyone's water cups. This is probably the most functional our family has been since the start of the summer. Even though it seems like things have finally returned to normal among us all, I have a sinking feeling that it's all an illusion. Because I can already see the sweat breaking out on Dad's temples and I've caught the nervous looks Mom has been shooting him.

"All right, let's eat," Mom says with an awkward clap.

Still suspicious, I sit down and begin to serve myself. Our parents start the dinner with their normal evening questions: How was your day? Anything interesting happen at school? Did you do well on that exam you were studying for?

It all feels so stilted and uncomfortable. I finally break, unable to keep up the pretense that this is a normal dinner.

"What is going on?" I interrupt Mom asking Sofía about Jac's parents.

Our parents both freeze like deer caught in the headlights. They glance nervously at each other, and then Dad finally drops his fork and sits back in his chair.

"We wanted to wait until after we ate," he explains.

"For what?" Sofía asks, suddenly catching on to the weird energy.

"We have some news," Mom says, reaching across the table to place a hand on Sofía's arm.

306

"Okay," Sofía says, dragging out the word and glancing at me nervously.

"Ana Maria," Dad says before taking a deep breath, like he's getting ready to fight a bear or run a marathon. "We're so proud of you. Once you set your mind on something, you make it happen for yourself. It's been so incredible to see everything you've accomplished this summer."

"I'm sure you girls know the shop hasn't been doing well the last few years," Mom continues. "We've tried everything to stay afloat, but nothing has worked."

"I don't have it in me to change the shop the way the Moraleses have. I wanted to keep it the way it was when my dad opened it, but times change. People change. And the shop got stuck. And the best way we know to get it unstuck is to—" Dad cuts himself off suddenly and presses a hand to his mouth. I realize suddenly that he's on the verge of *tears*. Sofía kicks me under the table to express her surprise.

"We're going to close the shop," Dad says. He continues to speak after that, business jargon and platitudes, and other things that I simply fail to register. My brain shuts off. I sit there, frozen, as his words repeat over and over in my mind. Café y Más? *Closed?* Gone forever, just like that?

I knew the shop wasn't doing well. I heard the fights. I knew that we'd lost regulars over the last few years to Starbucks or bikini baristas. But I never thought that any of that would lead to this.

"*What?*" I burst out a good minute after Dad dropped the bomb. "Is money the problem? I can give you the winnings from the magazine—"

"No, mija," Dad says sternly. "We're not telling you this so you can try to fix it. We *want* to close the shop. The stress of the last few years has been too much for us. I've tried to keep it running because I felt like it was my duty. But watching you go after your dreams and doing the things you want to do, mijita, that inspired me to do the same. Keeping the shop open has been hurting us."

There's a beat of silence as I try to swallow my tears. It's selfish, wanting the shop to stay open despite how much it's been hurting the family. But that shop is my family's legacy, and closing it feels like losing a family member.

"We've already spoken to Pedro Morales," Mom says. "He's going to buy some of our equipment from us since they are opening up a second location in the spring. And we're putting the space up for sale. We already have some inquiries and hope it will sell soon."

"I'm going to keep the catering part of the business running, mostly working on cakes and smaller gigs around town. Eddie's already lined up a new job with my recommendation, so don't worry about him. And your mother," Dad looks over at Mom with a brilliant smile. "Your mom is going after her own dream."

"I'm going to be managing the bed-and-breakfast downtown," Mom says proudly.

"So what you're saying," Sofía says slowly. "Is that I'm out of a job?"

"Sofía!" I yell, throwing my napkin at her. "That's insensitive!"

But Mom is laughing, and surprisingly, so is Dad. This is the first time they've both looked happy in ages.

"It's a valid concern! Am I getting severance?" Sofía asks.

"The shop doesn't close for another two weeks," Mom says. "And no severance, but you'll get your weekends back. How's that? No more early morning shifts on a Sunday."

Through the rest of dinner Mom and Dad tell us about what these changes will mean for us, Mom's new working hours and Dad's plans to use our home kitchen until he can find a space to rent. Unable to finish my food, I just push grains of rice around on my plate until Mom announces that her telenovela is about to air and Sofía says she needs to finish some homework.

Dad helps me collect the dirty dishes from the table, and we clean up together in silence.

"It's going to be okay," Dad says softly as I rinse our dishes.

"I know," I tell him, trying to sound confident.

"Come here, mija," he says, opening his arms for a hug. I give in quickly and hug him. "I know it's not easy, but this needed to happen. It's giving your mom and me the opportunity to go after things we've always wanted to do. I'm starting something that's all my own, and your mom is finally using her degree. And you, mi amor, gave us the courage to do that."

It's strange to feel both proud and resentful of something. Café y Más is my second home, a place full of so many memories. I never thought I would lose it; in all my fantasies about the future, the shop was always there for me to return to. I understand that it has been a strain on my family, and just because it's something that's always been there doesn't mean it has to stay there.

But it still hurts to lose it. So I hold on tight to my dad, taking in the citrus and tobacco smell of him, knowing that this, too, is something that I might lose one day. So instead of focusing on the things I'm losing, I'm going to try to focus on the things I have.

CHAPTER THIRTY-FOUR

Two weeks pass in an instant. We put up flyers inviting the whole town to come celebrate the last day for Café y Más. The poster advertises live music, dancing, and free food. In school, teachers tell me they are sad to be losing their favorite coffee spot, and Rose does her best to help me keep my mind off of it.

The night of the closing party, Sofía, Rose, and I head to the shop directly after school to help set up. My uncle and some of his friends are setting up instruments for live music, so we clear the dining area of chairs and tables to make room for a dance floor. Rose borrows some party lights from the theater department, and Sofía and Jac help set up the sound system.

In the end, I think we're all surprised by the turnout. All the business owners on Main Street and their families have shown up, along with our longtime regulars and their friends. The shop ends up being absolutely packed, with people hanging out on the sidewalk outside eating Cuban sandwiches and drinking cheap wine from plastic cups.

People come up to my parents to express their condolences, like this is a restaurant funeral, and other people pull me or my sister aside to tell us a funny story about our abuelo back when he ran the shop.

But all the sound and music come to a screeching halt when Pedro Morales walks into the shop, trailed by his family.

Port Murphy knows what it means to see a Morales cross the threshold of an Ybarra establishment. I can hear whispering in the crowd as Pedro casually strides up to my dad and offers him his hand.

Not wanting to look like an asshole, Dad puffs up his chest and takes Pedro's hand in what looks like a too-firm grip. They shake once and let go.

"I'm sorry to hear you're closing the shop," Pedro says. "Café y Más was an important fixture on Main Street, and this town won't be the same without it."

"Thank you," Dad says stiffly, as though waiting for Pedro to pie him in the face or something.

"I have a gift for you," Pedro says, handing Dad a piece of paper. I sidle up closer to get a better look and am surprised to find that it's the menu for Morales Café. My dad flips it over, as though seeing the back side of the menu would help him make more sense of the gift. It doesn't. We both look back up at Pedro skeptically.

"Read the back, Mr. Ybarra," Miguel cuts in from behind his uncle.

Still skeptical, Dad flips the menu around and begins to read. He brings it close to his face, taking the text out of my line of sight. It takes him only a few seconds before he drops the menu down and gazes at Pedro with . . . respect?

311

The two men, once sworn enemies, embrace, and the entire shop gasps in surprise. Unable to hold my curiosity back any longer, I yank the menu from my dad's hand and scan the text. The back features an illustration of the Morales Bakery storefront and an about section with the story about the shop's origins.

The section tells the story of the Morales family fleeing Cuba and arriving in Port Murphy, where they opened up a Cuban café for a community that had never heard of Cuban food before. The little backstory made no mention of the work my family put in to help build the bakery up to what it is today.

Until now.

The about section has been revised.

"In 1982, old friends from Cuba joined the Morales family in Port Murphy," I read aloud to the audience. "Felipe Ybarra helped Andres Morales develop many of the recipes that are still on the menu today. The Ybarras went on to open their own restaurant in Port Murphy, Café y Más, which spread the joy of Cuban food to Pacific Northwest for many years. Today, the Ybarras' legacy at Morales Bakery continues, with Felipe's granddaughter, Ana Maria Ybarra, developing our new recipe, the Cuban doughnuts."

My eyes are wide as I look up from the menu.

Valeria steps forward and gifts my parents an illustration of the Café y Más storefront. Miguel follows up with a gift of his own, a framed series of pictures of the storefront over the years. How he got his hands on these, I have no idea, but the last picture is a recent one. It's taken from the street outside in the early morning, just before the sun has risen. Inside, you can just make out me behind the counter with my dad, both smiling.

My dad hugs Miguel and whispers something into his ear that I can't hear over the music. I'm not sure if it's a threat or a secret. Knowing my dad, it's probably a threat. But Miguel pulls back from the hug with a smile, so I can't be sure.

Someone taps on my shoulder, and I hastily wipe away the tears that have started to well in my eyes. To my surprise, Pedro is standing behind me, looking a little contrite with an envelope in his hands.

"I want to apologize for what my son did to you," he says earnestly. "And I'm sorry it took me this long to make it up to you. My daughter knocked some sense into me."

"I've learned that Valeria can be pretty scary when she wants to be," I say, remembering the stalking black shadow in the alley behind the shop.

"My father was an ambitious man, but he was not always a good man. And I hate to see that my son inherited that quality and that I supported him in those actions." His hands twist on the envelope he's holding, and he looks like he's struggling to get this apology out, not because he doesn't want to do it, but because he's embarrassed. "I should have done this as soon as I found out you were the one behind the doughnut recipe," he says, handing me the envelope.

A little confused and unsure of how to respond, I gingerly take the envelope from his hands and look down at it.

"What is this?" I ask.

"An apology and an offer, if you're interested," Pedro says with an encouraging smile.

The back of the envelope is sealed with only a strip of tape that is easy enough to break through. When I open it, I find a sheaf of papers stapled together and a loose check. The check, made out to me, is for a sum that has me double checking the zeros.

"What is this?" I ask nervously, flipping the check back and forth to try to see if there's some fishing line connected to it that will result in some kind of prank.

"It's sixty percent of the profits from all Cuban doughnut sales, from the first day we started selling them to last Sunday," he says. "You came up with an amazing idea, and you deserve to be compensated for it."

"Keep talking," a curious voice says behind me, and I'm surprised to find that my mom has been listening to our conversation.

"I want to offer your daughter sixty percent of all doughnut-related profits, which includes the stickers and shirts Valeria designed that we are selling. There is also a contract in there for you to look over. It lays out your right to a share of the dough-nuts profits for as long as we sell them."

"Wow, I . . . Thank you, Mr. Morales," I say with a smile.

"Of course," he replies. "It won't fix what happened with your grandfather, but I hope this helps to mend the rift between our families, especially now that you're dating my nephew," he adds with a cheeky smile. I blush immediately. "Best of luck to you, Ana Maria."

Pedro leaves us and I turn to face my mother, the look of surprise still not wiped from my face.

"What do you think?" I ask her.

"It seems like a fair deal," she says as she flips between pages.

"I'll set up a meeting with the family lawyer, but this seems like a great opportunity for you, mija. And it will help cover your costs when you move to Paris." Her eyes began to water a little and she pulls me in for a tight hug. "I'm so proud of you," she whispers into my ear. "You're going to do so many great things," she says with a kind of confidence I envy.

Once everyone is over the shock of the Morales-Ybarra truce, the party picks back up. People are dancing, Jac has pulled the dominos table out, and Eddie is singing a Pearl Jam song.

But I'm not ready to party with everyone else just yet. Too much is happening, and I'm feeling all over the place. Excitement over this potential deal with the Moraleses. Then grief when I remember where I am, at the thing that I am losing today. I'm not ready to let go of this shop. I slip out back to the kitchen, and it's already starting to look unfamiliar to me. Some of the equipment has already been sold, the bins are empty, and it no longer looks like the kitchen where I learned to cook. The plancha where Sofía burned her hand when she was thirteen is gone, the espresso machine where I pulled thousands of shots of Cuban coffee is packed up and sold, and there are no pastries ready to be baked for the morning rush.

And I'm never getting any of that back.

The sight of the nearly empty kitchen and the music spilling over from front of house is too overwhelming. I head out the back door and try to settle myself. I know that closing the shop is the right choice for the family. But it hurts so much.

My nose burns and I'm moments away from ugly sobbing in

this parking lot. I don't want to cry, I want to be able to accept the changes life brings with a smile on my face and hope for the future. But I can't do that because the overwhelming emotion I'm feeling right now is fear.

The back door pops open, letting out a rush of sound from the shop. Salsa music, laughing, and the clacking of heels dancing on tile. Miguel walks out and spots me on the stack of milk crates. He lets the door shut quietly behind him and watches me for a moment.

"I just needed some air," I say, trying to sound casual, but even I can hear the waver in my voice. There's no point hiding my emotions from Miguel anyway; he can always see right through me, even in the dark.

Miguel takes a step toward me and opens his arms in invitation. I don't hesitate, I fall into his firm embrace. This move has become so familiar to us, so easy. We slot together perfectly, my face against his chest and his head resting against the top of mine. My arms wind in around his waist and his arms cage around my shoulders protectively. He feels safe and familiar, and the feeling is enough to ground me a little bit.

"I feel like this is all my fault," I whisper into his chest. "I'm losing this huge part of who I am, an actual physical piece of my childhood, the place that made me who I am. I could have saved this place." My voice cracks, and I suck in a deep, steadying breath before continuing.

Miguel rubs gentle circles on my back, staying silent and letting me take the time I need to get everything out.

"But is it horrible that I feel kind of relieved, too?" I admit, so quiet my voice is barely a whisper. The secret tastes bitter on my tongue, and I wish I could take it back.

Miguel pulls back, his hands falling to reach for mine. He looks down at our clasped hands, his brows furrowed as he seems to consider something.

"No, not horrible at all. I mean, I was happy when my mom told me she was going to divorce my dad," Miguel says without looking up from our hands, his voice just as quiet and careful as my own. "I thought to myself, *finally*, I'd been waiting for this day for years. But on the heels of that came the fallout of that decision: my dad cutting her off, us moving out of my childhood home and into my uncle's basement, and starting my life from scratch at the start of my senior year.

"I was miserable those first few days, stuck between this feeling of joy for my mom finally leaving this terrible relationship but also, selfishly, upset that my life had been turned upside down. I hadn't left the house in days, and Valeria somehow managed to convince me to go to some party. As soon as I set foot in that house, I was ready to leave. I didn't know anyone, there was a table full of weird cheeses, and it was so different from life back home. But then I saw you. I swear I saw just a glimpse of you out of the corner of my eye. I was convinced I was hallucinating. But I decided to say your name anyway. And it *was* you. Suddenly, a future in Port Murphy didn't seem so bleak anymore. I felt hopeful for the first time in months."

"What's the lesson here?" I ask bleakly. "Everything good comes with a cost? If I want to go to culinary school and go after my dreams, my family's legacy has to crumble to dust?"

"No!" Miguel says quickly, pulling back to look at me. "That's not what I'm saying. What I mean is that it's valid to mourn the loss of this, while still, I don't know, gaining something from that loss? Sometimes letting something go is the only way forward."

I think of my family the last few years, struggling to keep the business afloat. Mom cutting costs at home and in the shop, Dad working far too many hours and rarely coming home, and Sofía and me stuck in the middle of it all. Things certainly won't be easier now just because we've let the shop go, I'm sure we'll be wiping with single-ply toilet paper for a bit longer, but for the first time in a long time I think the Ybarra family is finally feeling hope for the future.

"I just hate that moving forward means losing this," I say, making a sweeping gesture toward Café y Más.

"Your family's legacy is more than just this building, Ana. It's not gone or over just because this chapter is closed."

"Ugh," I groan, pressing my face into his shirt. "You're going to make me cry."

"I thought you already were crying?"

"No! I was close and now I actually am crying," I complain.

"It was hard to tell in the dark," he says, rubbing my back as I sob into his chest.

The back door creaks again, letting out another rush of sound.

"Papi is going to eviscerate you both if you're making out back here!" Sofía shouts, sounding almost gleeful at the prospect.

"We are not making out!" I yell at my sister as I pull away from Miguel. "I'm crying! My childhood is ending!"

The back door pops open again, and this time a slew of people slip out into the parking lot.

"Ana Maria! Your dad has the mic and he's singing a duet with Pedro!" Rose shrieks as she barrels out of the door. It's still a little weird to hear Rose calling me by my real name. At the beginning of this school year, I asked everyone to stop calling me Amy. I was ready to let go of the person people wanted me to be and ready to be the person I'm planning on becoming. Maybe letting go of Café y Más is the next step toward that.

"Everyone in there has definitely had too much rum," Rose continues with a giggle.

"It was a very touching scene," Valeria says. "Miguel, your mom and Ana's mom are dancing together. I think we can say the hatchet has officially been buried." Valeria boosts herself up and sits on the stack of milk crates by the door where Rose joins her.

"I don't know, my money is still on Adrian pulling some stupid prank before the end of the night," Sofía says.

"Don't worry, our dad put the fear of God into him," Valeria assures us. Adrian skipped out on tonight's festivities due to football practice, but we all know it's a convenient excuse. He's still mad about being punished for stealing my doughnuts.

"Are you good?" Miguel whispers, his mouth close to my ear so no one else can hear.

I look up at him, lit only by the dim orange streetlamps, and smile. I could use a tissue, I'm still a little sad, but despite all of that, I am good. I'm surrounded by people I love, and my dreams feel closer than they've ever been. It hurts a little bit right now, but it's just growing pains. It will pass, and on the other side is a future full of possibilities.

"I'm good. And soon," I say, a big smile on my face, "I'm going to be great."

GUAVA CREAM CHEESE THUMBPRINT COOKIES

At the end of my first book, *Isla to Island*, I included a recipe for arroz con pollo a la chorrera. Arroz con pollo plays an important role in the story and it happens to be one of my favorite family recipes, so I decided I would share it with readers. Since the book published, I've had so many readers reach out to tell me that they've tried the recipe and loved it. So when my next book ended up being about a Cuban American girl and her family's bakery, I knew I needed to include another recipe.

At first I wanted to go all out and develop Ana Maria's award-winning Cuban doughnuts. I quickly realized that between work, life, and my new time-consuming sewing hobby, I wasn't going to be able to develop the recipe. It also called for some ingredients that some readers might find difficult to source, like malanga and yuca. So I pivoted.

I decided to ask myself, what was Ana Maria's first original recipe? It would probably be something she could make with ingredients found around the house. It wouldn't be too complex, but it would have a certain amount of flair. I decided to center the recipe around one of the most common Cuban desserts/snacks: cheese and guava paste.

It is miles away better than *my* first original recipe, which was a raisin bread made with no yeast and too many eggs. I served it proudly to my mom and abuelos, and they ate it with smiles and dozens of compliments despite the fact that it was objectively gross.

Ana Maria is a much better baker than I am, I promise.

Makes about 24 cookies

INGREDIENTS

4 oz. softened full-fat cream cheese

4 oz. softened unsalted butter

130 g (¾ cup) white granulated sugar

1 egg

1 teaspoon vanilla extract

1 teaspoon packed lime zest (about 1 lime)

1 teaspoon lime juice

200 g (1 ½ cups) all-purpose flour

1 teaspoon baking powder

½ teaspoon salt

4 oz. guava paste (or jam/marmalade)

INSTRUCTIONS

1. In a stand mixer with a paddle attachment, or by hand with a whisk, beat the cream cheese, butter, and sugar until light and fluffy.

2. Add egg, vanilla extract, lime zest, and lime juice into the cream cheese mixture and whisk until fully combined.

3. In a medium bowl whisk together flour, baking powder, and salt.

4. Add the flour mixture to the wet ingredients, a little bit at a time, while mixing at low speed. If mixing by hand, switch from the whisk to a spatula. Mix until all the dry ingredients are just combined. Avoid overmixing.

5. Cover the dough and let rest in the fridge for at least one hour.

6. Once the dough has rested, heat the oven to 375°F and line a baking sheet with parchment paper.

7. Lightly dust your work surface with flour. Portion out your dough into 1 ½ tablespoon-sized balls, either with a spoon or cookie scoop. The dough will be very sticky! Plop the ball of dough on your floured work surface and roll into a ball with the palm of your hand. Keep your hands and surface lightly dusted with flour to avoid sticking; you want to avoid adding too much extra flour into the dough. Place the cookies on the parchment-lined baking sheet.

8. Using the back of a teaspoon or your thumb, press an indent into the middle of each cookie. Once finished, put in the freezer to chill for ten minutes.

9. While the cookies are chilling, place guava paste in a microwave-safe container and slowly warm up 10 seconds at a time, mixing between intervals, until completely melted. Once melted, add 1 ½ tablespoons of water until the paste is the consistency of jam. If you are using marmalade or jam, this step isn't necessary.

10. Take the cookies out of the freezer and add ½ teaspoon of guava paste into each of the indents you made earlier.

11. Bake the cookies for 14 to 16 minutes until the cookies are slightly golden around the edges. Remove and allow the cookies to rest on a cooling rack for at least 30 minutes. These are best on the day of, but they will keep in a covered container for up to five days.

TIPS

- If you want to try these "Sofía Style," place the dough ball on a Maria cookie before pressing the indent to the top.
- You can decorate the cookies with a sprinkle of powdered sugar or a drizzle of icing. But they're just as good without!

ACKNOWLEDGMENTS

A book! With words!! What a concept. (This is a joke that only makes sense if you read my first book.) These words would not have been possible without the great support system I am so lucky to have.

To the people who helped me bring this book to life: my fiancé (!!!), I'm so lucky to be loved by you; to Ashley Burdin, without whom I'm not sure I'd know how to write a book; to Ali Hinchcliff, who really is the best hypewoman in the game; to Marietta Zacker, who is always game for my ideas; and to Alex Borbolla, I'm so grateful to have an editor who *gets* me and my stories.

To the *fantastic* team at Bloomsbury. I was devastated when I left my job there in 2018 to move to Seattle with Reed because I was leaving not only a job I loved, but a group of coworkers who inspired and empowered me every day. I'm so lucky to be working with y'all again.

I was so excited to *not* be illustrating my book cover this time; it's very stressful!! I'm so grateful to Flor Fuertes for providing the cover art. From Ana Maria and Miguel to the loving detail you added to the bakery, it all meant so much. I loved seeing you bring my characters to life.

To my D&D group, who have given me the opportunity to play for hours on end every month: Katy Rose Pool, Tara Sim, Jamie, Meg, and Alys. There is no joy like telling a story together with friends.

To my writing group, who over the years have created the most supportive and caring community: Akshaya Raman, Amanda Foody, Amanda Haas, Axie Oh, Charlie Lynn Herman, Claribel Ortega, Janella Angeles, Kat Cho, Maddy Colis, Mara Fitzgerald, Meg RK, and Melody Simpson.

To all the friends who support me (and by support, I mean answer my random text messages about topics ranging from cat care to how to survive being an author): Allison Saft, Ashley Poston, Molly Owen, Nina Moreno, Susan Dennard, and Zoraida Córdova.

And of course, to my family: to my mom, who never failed to get me more books to read as a kid. And to my dad, who never fails to give me another good story because he's always up to something unintentionally hilarious. To my brothers, you're great and all, but I always wish I had a sister. I guess I'll make do.

And lastly, to you. Thanks for picking this book up, I hope you enjoyed your time in Port Murphy.